# RECKLESS

## BENSON SECURITY 1

JANET ELIZABETH HENDERSON

First published in 2016 by Janet Elizabeth Henderson

© Janet Kortlever 2016

This edition 2019

This edition ISBN: 9780473461362



Author's Website: http://www.janetelizabethhenderson.com

Text design by Vellum

Cover design by Janet Elizabeth Henderson

Editing by Liz Dempsey

# CHAPTER 1

## TWO WEEKS EARLIER, IN THE HIGHLANDS, SCOTLAND

Dimitri held his gun tightly at his side as he trudged through the snow behind the psychopath who'd hired him. The sound of gunfire rent the night as the residents of the castle fought back. Reynard Durand, his boss on this job, was an idiot. But a dangerous idiot, the kind who was fluent in violence and lacking in empathy.

Durand's plan had been simple: go to Scotland, kidnap Claire Donaldson, hand her over to his boss and climb further up the ladder of Abramovich's skin trade business. To achieve this aim, Durand attacked a bachelorette party. He thought he would waltz in, intimidate the women and waltz out again with Claire under his arm. Idiot. If he'd been watching them for the past week, as Dimitri had been, he would have known that nothing was simple when it came to the women of Invertary.

He might also have known that Claire had an identical twin.

Yeah, Durand was that dumb. He'd managed to nab the wrong woman and Dimitri was scrambling for a plan to get her out of this mess. A plan that didn't involve blowing his cover.

It was the soap opera finale of fuck ups.

To prove his point, Megan Donaldson chose that moment to trip and head-butt Durand in his back. Dimitri grabbed her arm and yanked her upright before Durand could lash out. His body tensed, ready to strike if the idiot laid a hand on the woman.

"Watch it," Durand snapped. "Keep hold of her. We need to speed up. I have a couple of snowmobiles stashed at the west exit."

"What about the others?" Dimitri's left hand wrapped around Megan's upper arm. Her silver sweater was way too thin for the icy conditions, but he knew if he shrugged off his jacket and gave it to her, it would set off alarm bells for Durand. Instead he pulled her closer to his body and hoped she took some of his heat.

"They're on their own," Durand snapped. "I don't get paid enough to save their asses."

Dipshit. You *never* left a man behind. It was a fundamental code of the armed forces. But then Durand had never been in the military. Another strike against the man.

Dimitri made a show of motioning Megan to move forward and telling her to hurry. It earned him a glare, which even in the middle of this fucked up operation, made him want to grin. He held her tight to keep her upright. Far too aware of her gentle curves. The ones he'd been drooling over since he'd first set eyes on her.

He needed to come up with a way to get her out of this situation, before it became a whole lot worse. A way that didn't make Durand suspicious of Dimitri's allegiance. His mind frantically searched for options. And then it hit him. What if he didn't get her out of this mess quite yet? What if he let Durand take them straight to his boss? It would be the fastest way for Dimitri to get access to the information he'd gone undercover to get.

He glanced at Megan. Would she help him? Would she be willing to play hostage until he had what he needed? And would she do it knowing that he didn't have a plan to get her out of this at the end of it? Sure, he'd come up with something. He always did. But it was still a huge risk for her to take. A risk he was desperate enough to ask her to take—if he could just get a chance to talk to her alone.

As he reasoned through his plan, he felt Megan's grip cover his gun hand. Before he could process what was happening, she jerked his hand up, flicked off the safety and pressed his trigger finger down. The gun went off. Durand fell face first into the snow.

"What the—" Dimitri started.

He was too stunned to react, which left him vulnerable. That's why he wasn't prepared when she turned and kneed him in the balls. Hard. A white light appeared before his eyes and he forgot how to breathe. A low howl escaped his frozen vocal cords as he bent double, holding his poor decimated balls. Through the pain, he vaguely registered that Durand was out cold. Megan grabbed Durand's automatic weapon and pointed it straight at Dimitri's head.

"Drop the gun," the blonde bombshell ordered.

Dimitri hesitated. Too long. The sadist kicked him again. Dimitri made a gurgling sound deep in his throat as the gun fell from his grip. A second later he was writhing in the snow, hands cupped to his crotch.

He looked up to find Megan standing over him. She was an Amazonian warrior. Her blonde hair a bright halo around her head, her cheeks flushed pink and a manic gleam in her blue eyes. She pointed his handgun at his head and smiled.

Even in agony. Even bested by a Barbie doll. Even though she'd just blown his operation. Even then, part of his brain was applauding her actions and wondering how fast he could get her into bed.

That's if his poor, mashed equipment ever worked again.

# CHAPTER 2

"Earth to Buffy, come in Buffy."

Dimitri Raast grinned when Megan scowled at him. The blonde beauty was easy to wind up. It had become his main hobby since he'd met her in Scotland two weeks earlier. She sat opposite him at the conference room table in the Regency townhouse that was now the new London office of Benson Security. Her long white-blonde hair was in a high ponytail and the striped T-shirt she wore slid off one creamy shoulder. She could have been a model, instead she'd set her sights on becoming a security specialist. Or as she liked to call it, a gun-for-hire. Yeah, her background in baking and doing hair wouldn't get her far in her new profession. In fact, Dimitri knew for sure that the boss wouldn't have let her anywhere near his business if they didn't need her for this operation.

If *Dimitri* didn't need her.

Her blue eyes narrowed at him. "You do know that calling me Buffy isn't an insult, right? Buffy was a superhero. She saved the world countless times. She had a fantastic wardrobe and got to bonk sexy vampires."

"And she was an airhead." He bit back a laugh. Megan Donaldson was too much. Really.

"Have you even watched the show? Do yourself a favour and look it up on Netflix. Get back to me once you know what you're talking about."

"Would you prefer I call you Blondie?" He folded his arms and watched as her gaze lingered on his biceps. Oh yeah, she felt the burn between them too.

"Blondie was another cutting edge woman. A music pioneer. That isn't an insult either."

"Barbie?"

"Now you're pissing me off."

Dimitri laughed. Which probably wasn't smart, as he'd learned the hard way that Megan was unpredictable when she was pissed off. Unpredictable, wicked and violent, with a penchant for hitting men where it hurt most—and grinning while she did it. He shifted in his seat at the thought, trying to free up more space in his jeans. He wasn't sure if the sudden tightness was due to fear that his crown jewels weren't safe around the woman, or because her being crazy and violent seemed to press all the right buttons for him.

Most of the women Dimitri had gotten hot and heavy with over the years were on the Suzy Homemaker end of the spectrum—naive, pretty, predictable and safe. In other words, reliable wife material. Not that he'd been looking for a wife, but if a man was going to fall into that pit, he'd rather it was with someone he knew would make a good family and home life. Yet, none of those women got him worked up the way crazy Megan Donaldson did. Turns out, at the ripe old age of thirty, he'd discovered his type actually lay more towards the wicked and twisted end of the spectrum. Who knew?

The door to the conference room opened and Joe Barone and Ryan Granger swaggered in. Like Megan, the guys had come down from Benson Security's main office in the Highlands. Unlike Megan, they were both ex-military and knew what they were doing.

"Coffee?" Joe said by way of hello.

Dimitri pointed to the table in the corner of the room where Julia, the office manager, had set up a coffee pot and a plate of Danish pastries. He assumed Joe's grunt of reply was a thank you. The big Italian-American filled his mug, glugged it down and refilled it before taking his place at the table.

"Rough night, old man?" Ryan filled his own mug and snagged a plate of pastries. "Can't keep the pace, eh?"

Joe stared at the younger Englishman. "Unlike you, I was up most of the night working the case."

Ryan shrugged. "Is that supposed to make me feel bad? Yeah, you were working hard, but I'll take a night of hitting London's clubs with a lingerie model over being conscientious any day of the week."

A growl rumbled from Joe's chest. Ryan just laughed. The door slammed open and all heads turned to watch Rachel Ford-Talbot make her entrance. She scanned the room with a look of disgust. Her iPhone was in one perfectly manicured hand, her designer handbag was hanging from the crook of her arm and her equally expensive suit was teamed with her usual red-soled pumps. Dimitri was pretty sure someone who gave a shit about fashion would be able to name each of the designers Rachel wore—he wasn't one of them.

"This," she gestured with a red tipped talon, "is the A-team?"

Ryan pointed a croissant at her. "The A-team is still in Scotland, love. You got saddled with the B-team."

"Kill me now," Rachel muttered as she headed towards the coffee.

"That can be arranged." Megan's tone was pure cat.

Rachel arched an eyebrow at her. "Tell me again why

you're on the team?" She stirred her coffee. "Without your twin to do your thinking for you, and that awful Goth friend of yours to fight your battles, just what use will you be?"

Megan made her own little growl. It was more kitten than monster, which didn't help the menace vibe she was aiming for. "My *Goth friend* should have kicked your scrawny backside harder when you were in Invertary."

Rachel smiled—it made Dimitri shudder. Now *there* was a woman who knew how to do mean. "Thanks for noticing my backside. It's my new Pilates regime. I can recommend a divine personal trainer. She'll help you lose that extra chub you carry in no time at all."

Dimitri thought Megan's head might actually explode. He tensed, ready to jump out of his seat and do some damage control. Or duck. Whatever came first.

Megan faced off against Rachel. "Just because I don't think anorexia is a lifestyle choice doesn't make me fat. You should try eating sometime, it might improve your disposition."

Rachel faked a pout. "Well done. I'm so proud. You used words with more than one syllable."

Megan sprang to her feet as their new boss entered the room. His hand clamped on her shoulder.

"This meeting is about to start." Callum McKay released his hold. "Fight on your own time."

"I'm not sure Rachel can confine being a bitch to her off hours." Megan plopped back into her seat.

"I said enough." Callum's soft Scottish burr rounded out the accents in the room.

"Aye, aye, captain." Rachel smirked at him. "We wouldn't want to undermine your tenuous hold on authority. After all, we know how much a man's ego is tied to his position." Her gaze scanned down his body, lingering on his fly. "It would be *such* a shame to damage your fragile, teeny-tiny ego."

Callum stared Rachel down until the two of them were locked in a contest of wills.

"Should we place bets on who cracks first?" Ryan whispered. "My money's on Callum."

The lights suddenly dimmed and a photo appeared on the wall. Everyone's eyes shot to the picture.

"Sorry," the large potted palm said. "I thought it was time for the slide show."

The lights came back up and the image disappeared.

"Julia?" Megan said, as everyone eyed the plant at the other end of the table from Callum. Sure enough, the office manager was sitting behind it, a laptop balanced on her knees. "Have you been there the whole time?"

There was some shuffling. "Um, yes," Julia said softly.

"I thought we were going to have breakfast together this morning," Megan said. "I waited for you."

Dimitri knew the two women were sharing one of the tiny flats on the top floor of the building. With Megan's extrovert personality and Julia's social phobia, he could only imagine how well that was going.

"Sorry," the plant said. "I had a lot of work to do, so I came in early."

"This is ridiculous," Callum barked. "I refuse to talk to foliage. Get out from behind the plant."

"I can't. I'm plugged in here. The equipment doesn't work out there." Julia's voice was barely a whisper, making them strain to hear her.

"You can make it work out here," Callum snapped. "You're so bloody efficient you're making my head spin. Get to the table."

The plant shook. "I haven't had time to wire up the table area. I will for the next meeting. Right now, if you want a PowerPoint, I have to stay here."

The tremor in Julia's voice was pronounced. Callum was

on fragile ground. Julia had been adopted by half the team. She was practically the office pet.

"Leave her alone," Joe said. "Let her do her job."

"She's hiding behind a plant." Callum pointed at the plant. "How can she do her job from there?"

"Have you had any problems with her work since we arrived in London?" Megan asked, although they all knew the answer. Julia could run the country if she tried. Okay, so she'd do it from inside a closet, but she'd still do a great job. "The answer is no. She's way ahead of schedule with the office renovations. We all have everything we need to work. She's doing her job great. So what if she's a little shy? Leave her alone."

"A little shy?" Rachel barked a laugh. It sounded like nails on a chalkboard. "We've been working together for over a week and I've yet to see her face. That isn't normal. If I was in charge," she directed that comment to Callum, "I'd fire her."

"Aye," Callum told the witch. "But you're not in charge, are you?"

"Yet." Rachel gave him a look designed to make his balls shrivel. "You're not exactly making a great impression as a boss. You can't even get your secretary out from behind a plant."

"Office manager," Joe, Megan and the plant said at the same time.

Ryan laughed until he had to wipe his eyes.

Callum turned his attention back to the potted plant. "Slide show, Julia. And next meeting that damned plant will be gone from the room. Are we clear?"

"Yes, sir," Julia whispered.

"In fact, I want *all* of the plants removed from the building. It's like a bloody jungle in here."

In reply the lights dimmed again. A photo of a man filled the wall.

"This is Rudi Abramovich." Callum pointed at the photo. "This man has Dimitri's sister and we're going to get her back."

Dimitri felt his blood turn to ice. This is why he'd joined Benson Security after the fiasco in Scotland. He needed the team's backing to find his sister. He'd done everything he could on his own, made it as far as he was able, now he needed help.

Dimitri had never felt hate until he'd come across Rudi Abramovich. He hadn't realised the emotion burned like acid. He looked at the man who'd ruined his sister's life. The crime boss could have stepped off the cover of GQ magazine. He was in his early forties and wore it well. His wavy brown hair was professionally styled. His grey suit and open-necked white shirt were tailored to fit his shoulders and make it clear he knew how to use gym equipment. His eyes were contact lens blue, his lips were full like a girl's and his jaw was sharp like a cartoon character.

"Who knew evil came in such a pretty package?" Megan said.

Her approval of the guy's rip-off, George Clooney get-up punched Dimitri in the gut. "There's nothing attractive about him."

Megan blinked before she softened. "Of course not. He's evil. And has obviously had some plastic surgery. Nobody looks that good naturally." She leaned across the table to pat his hand. "He's evil *and* fake."

Dimitri nodded. That was more like it. He lounged back into his chair, twirled a pencil and hoped he hid exactly how much the sight of Rudi affected him.

"As I was saying," Callum gritted out, unhappy at the

chitchat during his meeting. "This guy has Dimitri's sister and our mission is to get her back."

"Don't you mean get her back *if* she's still alive?" Rachel asked the question as though she was enquiring about the weather.

The pencil in Dimitri's grasp snapped in two. So much for keeping his cool. The tension in the room ratcheted up. All eyes were on Dimitri as he carefully placed the two halves of the pencil on the table in front of him. Every muscle in his body felt tight as he fought to control his rage. Slowly, very slowly, he looked up at Rachel.

"What?" Rachel tossed her glossy auburn hair over her shoulder. "I'm not saying anything that everyone isn't already thinking. Your sister has been missing for a year. We haven't heard even a whisper about her whereabouts. She's most likely dead. I know it. You know it. We all know it."

"That's enough," Callum snapped.

Rachel opened her mouth but Callum's palm slapped the table, so she huffed and closed her mouth.

Slowly, Callum turned to Dimitri. "Bring us up to speed. We've all come into this operation at different stages. Start at the beginning so we're on the same page."

As if by magic, the image on the wall changed and his sister appeared. Dimitri felt his chest clench as pain, sharp as a knife, speared through him. She had long black hair, a pretty smile and hazelnut eyes that were identical to his.

"My sister." Dimitri worked to keep his voice devoid of emotion. He cleared his throat and sat up a little straighter. "Katrina Raast. Twenty-five."

"She's only two years older than I am," Megan whispered.

Dimitri totally understood Megan's shock. At twenty-five he'd been on his second tour of Afghanistan. He'd seen a lot of things that had changed him, hardened him. But Katrina had been sheltered. Her world consisted of college classes and fun with her friends. So yeah, she was young. Way too young to be out there on her own, dealing with an evil bastard like Abramovich.

"When she finished her Master's degree at Brown, she decided to take some time out to travel before going back for her PhD. She's smart." He smiled, but the action hurt. "She got a job as an au pair in Germany for six months, to raise money for travel. In February last year her job wound up and she decided to backpack through Europe for the rest of the year."

"Was she alone?" Megan asked.

Dimitri shook his head. "She'd made friends with two other au pairs who were placed by the same programme, both of them American."

Two more images of young women flashed on the wall. Their smiles seemed to mock the people watching.

"Did they go missing too?" Megan said.

"No. They'd split up for a day in Greece. The other two wanted to visit museums, but Katrina wanted to visit the refugee camp." He felt a tiny smile break through his pain. "She majored in development policy and international politics. She wanted to see the problems first hand. She wanted to change the world."

The look in Megan's eyes was the same as the one she'd had in Scotland the first time he'd told Benson Security about his sister. It was the look he'd seen before she held his hand and offered him comfort. A kindness that had almost broken him. Dimitri tore his eyes from her to look back at the image, which had changed to a candid shot of his sister posing in front of the Acropolis in Athens. Her arms were wide and she was grinning.

"She didn't make it back to the hotel as they'd arranged." Dimitri focused his comments on Callum. At least there was no emotion in his boss's eyes to derail him. "The guide she'd hired to take her to the refugee camp disappeared off the face of the planet. When the agency she booked him through was questioned, they had no records of Katrina's booking or the guide."

"Abramovich's organisation was using it to target tourists," Callum said.

"That and several other tourist agencies on the same street. The police found discrepancies in all of them."

"More missing women?" Ryan asked.

Dimitri nodded. "At least eight over the past three years. All tourists. All travelling alone. All women in their twenties."

"And nobody noticed they were missing? Surely family or friends would lodge a complaint." Megan's outrage was a reminder of how sheltered and naive she was. "What about your parents? They must be going nuts."

"They died in a plane crash on a holiday to Alaska six years ago." He kept his tone even and focused on the table in front of him rather than on the sympathy, or pity, he knew he'd see in Megan's eyes.

"People go missing all the time." Joe rescued Dimitri from further questions. "Tourists run out on their bill and leave without checking out. How do you know if someone is really missing or has just moved on to the next stop on their tour? Only five of the women had anyone looking for them. The complaints weren't investigated properly. No one connected the women."

To everyone's surprise, it was Julia who spoke. "I don't understand. How is that possible?"

Dimitri sat up straighter in his seat. "It's more than possible in a country where there's a high turnover of tourists. Where the borders are weak and refugees are flooding in. A country where the economy is a mess and all public sectors are underfunded and run by people who are scraping by. The police are overwhelmed, overworked and lack the resources they need to follow everything up properly. Cases like this fall through the cracks." He looked back at his sister's smiling face. "People fall through the cracks."

"Did they do *anything* to find her?" Megan said.

"They did what they could initially. The time and effort they put in dropped off dramatically after the first couple of months. I realised then that there had to be a private investigation, but I was on assignment and couldn't get away. As soon as I was able I resigned my commission with the US Rangers, headed to Greece and started digging. A couple of months in I noticed one name kept coming up—Rudi Abramovich. I did more digging and discovered he'd built an empire on trafficking women. He targets tourists, homeless and poor women who won't be missed. His speciality is educated, western women. If you want a particular type of woman, he's the man to go to. He kidnaps to order."

His stomach turned at the thought and he was comforted to see the same looks of revulsion on his teammates' faces.

"You're sure he took your sister?" Rachel sounded sceptical.

Dimitri took a moment to gain control of his anger before he answered. The woman didn't seem to realise how her words cut through the people around her. Or she just didn't care. "I found the tour guide who was supposed to take her to the refugee camp."

There was a heavy silence as Dimitri's memory replayed the screams the man had made when he'd beaten the information out of him.

"He was working for Rudi?" Joe said.

He noticed no one asked what happened to the guy.

"He was working for a middleman. I worked my way up the chain until I knew for certain Rudi had her." He turned to Rachel. "So, yeah, I'm sure he's behind my sister's abduction."

"Did you get any idea where she's been taken?" Callum said.

"No." Dimitri ran a hand over his hair which was growing out from its military buzz cut. He suddenly felt exhausted. No, not exhausted, worn out. "That's where I ran aground. Then I heard about the job Reynard Durand was putting together and manoeuvred to get on his team. Word was the guy had a straight line to Rudi and I wanted to get on that line."

"Instead you ended up in Scotland." Megan glared at him. "Trying to kidnap *my* sister."

Yeah, that had been the job.

"Hey." He held up his hands, hoping the gesture would make him appear non-threatening. Megan didn't seem to buy it. "Don't blame me for the plan to kidnap your sister. That was all Rudi and the idiot he hired."

"The idiot who then went on to hire you," she pointed out.

The woman would not let this issue go. Every time he turned around she was needling him about it. "I. Was. Under. Cover."

"Which brings us to the second aim of this mission." Callum glared at Dimitri and Megan, making it clear their argument was over. "Rudi wants Claire Donaldson."

"Claire Dayton," Megan interrupted. "She married that freaky man mountain. I don't know why, but then Claire has always had a thing for lunatics."

Callum raised his voice, "As I was saying, Rudi wants Claire and will go to any length to get her. That means this mission has two aims. We need to retrieve Katrina and eliminate the threat to Claire."

"And by eliminate you mean—" Megan made a slicing motion at her throat.

Everyone stared at her.

"Why is she here?" Rachel pointed at Megan. "She knows nothing about security. She has no training, or experience. She's a liability." She turned to Callum. "Does your boss know she's here?"

Callum looked like he'd had his fill of Rachel. "Lake isn't my boss. Benson Security is owned by three partners now—Lake Benson, myself and Harry Boyle. Who, if you care to remember, *is* your direct boss."

The woman rolled her eyes. "Harry is more like my younger brother than a boss."

"And now Harry, Lake and I own Benson Security and you work for us." Callum leaned forward. "If you don't like the new situation, I'd be happy to accept your resignation."

"Like that's going to happen." She tossed her expensive haircut. "Someone needs to stick around to pick up the pieces once you screw up." Her eyes narrowed. "And when you do, I'll be waiting in the wings to take charge."

"Or, I could fire you," Callum said softly.

"You can try." Rachel tapped her talons on the table in front of her before turning to Joe. "Why on earth does this Rudi person want Claire Donaldson?"

"Dayton," Megan said again and was ignored.

"Claire is married to Grunt," Joe said. "Grunt and I helped Rudi's wife escape him and get back to America. We think Rudi wants to take Grunt's wife from him as payback."

Rachel held up a hand to stop Joe. "What on earth kind of name is Grunt? Is that one of those Highland things? You'll have to forgive me if I'm not up to date on the goings on in Invertary. Unlike some people, I actually like to spend my time in civilisation."

Dimitri was pretty sure he could actually hear Callum grinding his teeth.

"What?" The woman smirked at Callum. "Am I disrupting this extremely professional briefing?"

"Professional or not, after the meeting I want you in my office, Rachel."

"Of course, *boss.*" Rachel's tone made it clear she'd do exactly what she felt like after the meeting.

A threatening rumble sounded from Callum just as loud music blared throughout the room. It took Dimitri a few seconds to realise it was Bette Midler singing *Wind Beneath My Wings*. He fought a grin as he watched Megan cover her mouth with her hand to stifle her laughter, at the same time as Ryan turned his into a cough.

"Julia!" Callum roared.

The music stopped dead.

"Sorry," Julia said. "I told you there were gremlins in the system. I will make a note of each one and personally ensure they're dealt with. There are more pastries in the kitchen, if anyone is interested. Along with another pot of coffee."

"I'll get them." Ryan's chair scraped the floor as he rushed to get at the food.

"I'll help." Joe followed their teammate. "If we let you get them they'll be gone before you get back."

"I can't help it if I have a better metabolism than you." Ryan grinned. "It's age. I bet you could eat what you liked when you were my age." Joe swatted the back of Ryan's head.

"Bring me a Diet Coke," Megan called after the men.

"Honestly." Rachel's voice had all the subtlety of a PA announcement. "It's like being back in kindergarten. There is nothing professional about this new business. Harry should never have joined forces with Benson Security. It will damage his reputation."

Callum growled again, but this time Julia was smart enough to keep her finger off the media controls. The guy stared at the ceiling. Dimitri bet he was praying for help. He recognised the action because he'd used the same one quite a bit since he'd met Megan.

Megan clasped her hands and leaned onto the table. "Tell me," she said to Rachel. "Are you even aware just how bitchy you are?"

Rachel gasped, her hand flew to her chest. "I'm bitchy?"

"I'll take that as a yes. You really don't give a crap, do you?"

"Darling." Rachel smirked. "I care about things that *matter.*"

Before Megan could waste any more breath on the woman, the guys came back with supplies. Joe carried a coffee pot and two cans of Diet Coke. He put the pot onto the counter, tossed a can at Megan then headed for the huge plant. He crouched down in front of it and smiled as he offered Julia a drink.

"I like your conflict management style, babe," he told her.

A timid hand appeared and took the offered drink. Joe sat back in his chair, his legs stretched out in front of him. He reminded Dimitri of a leopard he'd seen on a stint in Africa. He looked relaxed but he could pounce without a hint of warning if the need arose.

"As I was saying, before you and Callum got into a pissing contest," Joe said to both of them, earning almost identical death glares which made him grin. "Grunt is a nickname because the monosyllabic bastard barely talks. His wife calls him Samuel. She's the only one who does. Well, she's the only one who's been allowed to live after calling him Samuel. Anyway, Grunt and I were in the marines together. When we got out, we partnered up to work private security. One of our first jobs was to escort a woman back to the States from Romania. Her father wanted to help her escape her abusive husband. He told us she was married to a business man, someone who owned a chain of coffee shops. We didn't do more than a surface check and the information was solid. Speaking of coffee…"

Joe waved his empty mug at Ryan who was over at the snack table, working his way through a platter of pastries. With a sigh, Ryan lifted the coffee pot and sauntered over to Joe.

"What did your last slave die of?"

"Heart attack," Joe said solemnly. "Too many baked goods."

Ryan gave him a one fingered salute before he headed back to the pastries. Joe's amusement faded as he looked back at them.

"We thought the job was a straight bodyguard deal—protect the woman while she got the hell out of there. We were wrong. When we met with her, all hell broke loose. She was being followed by a whole load of Rudi's men. I grabbed the wife while Grunt stayed behind to deal with the assholes that jumped us. That's probably how they got Grunt's ugly mug on camera. Knowing Rudi's rep, he'll think it's quid pro quo to take Grunt's wife away from him. Poetic payback, so to speak—a wife for a wife."

"Did you get Rudi's wife to safety?" Ryan sat back down beside Joe—with a plate piled high with snacks.

Joe nodded. "But it was a total cluster f—"

Julia cleared her throat loudly, cutting him off. Joe grinned at the plant.

Clearly, Callum's patience had reached its limits. The guy stood, folded his arms over one of the many Henleys he owned and wore like a uniform. He was six foot of honed instincts and sharp muscle. If you didn't know the guy was walking around on two prosthetic legs, you would never have guessed.

"We all up to date now?" It was clear his question was purely an exercise in sarcasm so there were no replies. "Great, then maybe we can get down to business. As Dimitri said, with Durand out of the picture his investigation's hit a brick wall. That's where we come in. Lake is working his London contacts to see what info he can dig up as to Rudi's whereabouts. Abramovich moves around a lot. For Dimitri to set up a meet with him, we need to pin down a location fast."

"The plan," Dimitri said, "is to get a personal meeting with Rudi, disable him and access his files for Katrina's location."

"Disable him in a way that will make sure he keeps away from Claire," Megan added.

"But no killing." Callum stared her down. "We're security professionals, not hitmen."

She waved the words away with a flick of her hand, making Dimitri worry about exactly what was going on in her fluffy little head. He made a mental note to grill her about it later. It was important that the whole team were on the same page when it came to Rudi. They couldn't afford anyone to go off plan—especially not when his sister's life was at risk.

"Even if Abramovich is in one place long enough to arrange a meeting with," Rachel waved her phone in Dimitri's direction, "what makes you think you can get close enough to him to access his records? He doesn't know you from Adam."

He swallowed his irritation at her condescending tone. "Because, I have something he wants. Rudi Abramovich wants Grunt's wife, Claire. He's desperate to get her. And Claire is an identical twin. So…"

All eyes turned to Megan who gave them a royal wave.

Rachel's glee was almost palpable. "You're going to give him Megan and pass her off as Claire." Her grin was face-splittingly wide. "This is so much better than I could have imagined it would be. Well done, Megan. You do have a purpose on the team. One totally befitting your station in life —you're bait."

# CHAPTER 3

Rachel's laughter was still ringing in Megan's ears hours later as Dimitri navigated their car through central London's traffic. They were on their way to meet up with one of Lake's contacts. Someone who had a lead on how to get to Rudi.

"I don't like being called bait." Even though that was exactly what she was.

"You're not bait. You're my partner. We're in this together. You saving your sister. Me saving mine. Partners." To his credit, Dimitri even managed to keep a straight face while he said it.

They were stuck in the endless traffic around Piccadilly Circus. "Why is this called a circus anyway? I don't get it. It isn't a square, or a roundabout, so I can understand that the town planners wouldn't want to call it that. But circus, that makes no sense at all." She turned in her seat to face Dimitri. "Do you think there was an actual circus based here at some point?" She couldn't see it. The grand Victorian buildings, with their white stone facades and weird little turrets and domes, didn't look like the sort of place you'd house animals.

"Can we focus on the job?" Dimitri swerved around a

double decker bus and into Shaftesbury Avenue, the home of London theatre.

"I came down here to see a play once, when I was in secondary school," Megan said. "Shakespeare. I can't remember which one. I was more interested in getting the attention of Hamish McIntosh at the time." She remembered the kiss they'd managed to sneak in, in the theatre foyer when the teachers weren't looking. Good times. Now Hamish was a farmer up near Aberdeen and Megan was bait.

She spotted a large banner over a theatre. "Helen Mirren and Libby Collins are doing a play." With a grin she turned to Dimitri. "When this is all over we need to go. They're two of my all-time favourite actresses. Helen Mirren especially."

"Who?"

"Seriously? How can you not know who Helen Mirren is? She's like acting royalty." She gaped at him. "You're one of *those* guys, aren't you? I should have realised."

He drummed his fingers on the steering wheel, irritated with traffic, and probably with her. "What guys?"

Poor ignorant man, he needed her help. "Guys fall into two categories. *Die Hard* and *Star Wars*."

"You're making this shit up."

"The *Star Wars* guys watch everything sci-fi, think they're intellectuals and can quote comic books. The *Die Hard* guys think movies ended with John McClane."

A sceptical look was all she got for her efforts to educate the guy. "That's it? Comic-Con geeks and John McClane wannabes?"

She waved a hand. "I'm over simplifying. The point is, you're a *Die Hard* guy. Prove me wrong. Name a movie you've seen that was made after *Die Hard*."

Honestly, she could almost smell rubber burning while he thought about it. At last, he grinned in triumph.

"*Die Hard 4*," he said.

"I rest my case." Posters advertising *Les Miserables* caught her attention. She'd never been to one of the big West End musicals. "When this is over, I'm going to help you with your cultural ignorance. We'll go to all the West End shows." The urge to bounce in her seat like an excited two year old was difficult to resist. "I might even take you to a movie that doesn't have Bruce Willis in it."

His smile was dazzling. "Do your worst, Buffy. I look forward to it."

Traffic started to move again and their focus returned to the reason they were fighting their way through London's city centre. Megan thought about his earlier declaration. It didn't make a whole lot of sense.

"How exactly are we partners? You plan to trade me for your sister." She held up her hands when he growled at her. Touchy man. "Don't get me wrong. I'm all for it. I'd just like to know where the partner part comes in."

"I don't plan to trade you for my sister." He shot her an irritated look. "You're just the key to getting close to Rudi and his records. As to partners, we're here, aren't we? Talking to contacts together. Doing the legwork together. That makes us partners." He swung a left and headed for the part of Soho that housed its infamous red light district. The streets were narrow, the buildings tall. A mish mash of sixties office blocks and modified red stone tenements.

"I'm only here because you're terrified to leave me alone in case I do something you deem stupid and ruin your plans."

"That too." He steered the car into a purpose-built parking garage that was squeezed between two older buildings.

They found a free space on the third floor, parked their generic SUV and headed down the stairs and out into Brewer Street. As Dimitri gallantly held the door open for her to exit, he leaned into her.

"For the record." His voice was a low, sexy growl against her ear that made it hard to concentrate on his words. "Stop saying I plan to hand you over to that piece of dirt. It is not, nor ever has been, in the plans to trade you for Katrina. You think I want to hand another woman over to him? You're simply my ticket into Rudi's office, where we'll get the information we need and then *both* of us will leave together. You got me?"

Megan blinked at him for a few seconds. "You are seriously sexy when you're earnest."

"Get a move on." Dimitri shoved her out of the door, making her laugh.

They walked side by side through the throngs of tourists and Londoners that filled the narrow street.

"I don't remember this stuff from when I came here with the school," Megan muttered.

They passed shops with windows stuffed full of adult toys, neon signs flashing copulating couples, and bookshops with blacked out windows. In amongst the seedier businesses were designer cafes, uptown boutiques and pricey galleries.

"Are you sure this is the right place?" she said as she stared at Starbucks. "It doesn't look like a red light area to me."

Dimitri turned into a narrow alley. "What were you expecting? Half-naked women on street corners and live sex shows in shop windows?"

"Well, yeah."

He shook his head at her ignorance.

Halfway down the alley there was a traditional English pub taking up the whole bottom floor of an old tenement block. The exterior was painted burgundy, with dark wood and hanging baskets filled with pansies. A blackboard told them the soup of the day was potato and leek. A sign on the door said soliciting would not be tolerated. The sign sat beside a vending machine that was filled with condoms. Interesting place.

Megan followed Dimitri into the shady interior. The outdoor colour theme continued inside, with heavily varnished dark wooden tables, a paisley-patterned carpet in browns and burgundy and matching burgundy and cream walls. Framed photos filled the walls, showing the area in times past—the odd famous face amongst them.

Dimitri wended his way around the tables, which were beginning to fill with the after-work crowd, past the long dark bar, to a booth in the corner.

"You must be Dimitri." A middle-aged woman in a form fitting purple dress that screamed Hollywood heyday stood and held out her hand.

Dimitri took it. "Thanks for agreeing to meet with me."

"Anything for Lake." Her smile was sultry as she said Lake Benson's name, making Megan wonder what the history was between the two of them.

With her husky voice and immaculately made up face, Carla was the last person Megan expected to meet when Lake said he had a contact in London who would know about Rudi's whereabouts. This woman could have been a retired catwalk model. She was elegant, sexy and comfortable in her skin. She waved at the booth.

"Please, take a seat." She sat back down. "Lake didn't mention that he was sending me a sexy toy boy," she said to Dimitri before turning to Megan. "And you, darling, you are just divine. Look at those cheekbones. And that hair. Oh, I'd kill for your hair."

Megan smiled at the compliment, although the woman had nothing to worry about. Her long hair was dyed Marilyn Monroe blonde and styled in gentle waves to her shoulders.

Megan slid into the booth and Dimitri followed her. She

wasn't sure if it was a protective move, or if he was blocking her escape.

"Lake said you might have something for me." Dimitri ran his arm along the back of their seat.

He looked perfectly relaxed. A man at ease in his natural habitat, but Megan knew he was aware of every single thing going on in the room beside him.

"Straight to the point. I like it." Carla smiled seductively before leaning towards them. "I'll do likewise." She glanced casually around before she spoke. "Word is Rudi's coming back to town. He'll be in his London house by the end of the week."

Dimitri was no longer pretending to be relaxed. Now he looked like the predator she knew him to be. Ready to pounce. To strike. To decimate. Was it wrong that she thought he looked kind of sexy? Yeah. Probably.

"How good is this info?" Dimitri asked.

"Top notch." Carla sat back in her seat and stirred her drink with the straw. "They're getting the house ready for him as we speak. Apparently his mother is turning seventy next week and her son plans to take her to *Madame Butterfly* after dinner at Gordon Ramsay's."

"He has a mother?" Megan blurted. Because—shocking.

Carla smiled at her, clearly amused. "Are you in the business, love?"

Megan looked at Dimitri, but his mind was obviously elsewhere seeing as his jaw was clenched tight enough to break. "You mean, security for hire?"

"No, I mean sex for hire."

"Oh!" Megan lowered her voice. "No. Are you?"

She nodded. "I run a brothel two streets over. And before you ask, we don't deal with Abramovich or his organisation. All of my girls are there by choice." She eyed Megan speculatively. "We're always looking for new talent. With your looks and that gorgeous accent you'd be an instant hit."

"Really?"

"The men would be lining up round the block for you. You'd make a mint."

Megan put her elbow on the table. "How much are we talking?"

"Megan!" Dimitri came out of his vengeance-induced trance.

"What? I'm just asking." She looked back at Carla. "Give me a ballpark figure."

Carla started to chuckle. "I like her," she said to Dimitri. "She's got spirit."

"Yeah, that's one word for it."

Megan elbowed him in his side. He didn't even flinch, so she turned her attention back to Carla.

"Would I have to do any really kinky stuff? The thought of dealing with someone who has a foot fetish makes my skin crawl." It wasn't like she planned to take her up on the offer, but it didn't stop her from being curious.

A large hand covered her mouth. "Don't answer her. Don't encourage her. Don't humour her," were the droll commands.

Megan bit his palm. He jerked his hand away as she frowned up at him. "There's no harm in being informed."

Dimitri ignored her. "I need a contact for Rudi. Someone who has access to him and can help me get close enough for a personal meeting with the man."

"That's a hard ask, darling. Rudi Abramovich makes that guy in North Korea look friendly. The man has paranoid down to a fine art." Carla tapped a perfectly manicured fingernail on her bottom lip. "There is someone. Does the security for the house when Rudi is in town." She opened her tiny purple handbag, brought out the latest iPhone and tapped at the screen. "I'm sending you his number. He's in charge of the team at the house, so he should have Rudi's ear, or at least someone close to Rudi." She gave a delicate shrug. "Worth a try."

Dimitri nodded his thanks, which irritated Megan.

"Thank you, Carla," she said pointedly to the oaf taking up most of the bench seat. "Why don't you pretend you're a proper human being for a minute and use some manners?"

Her answer was a scowl. Which, she was beginning to believe, was his thinking face.

Dimitri climbed out of the booth and motioned for her to follow. And like a good little soldier she did.

"Later," he said to Carla and headed for the door.

Megan hesitated before turning back to the woman. Carla had a business card in her hand, which she held out to Megan. She took it, because it would be impolite not to, and put it in the pocket of her jeans.

"Take some time and consider my offer," Carla said.

"I don't really think I'm cut out for the sex industry," Megan said, not wanting to string the woman along.

"Then call me if you want to chat. I think I'd enjoy that." Her eyes sparkled with amusement.

"That I can do." Megan grinned. "But really, just between you and me, how much do you think I could earn a week?"

"Megan," Dimitri barked from the door, making Carla laugh hard.

With a glare in his direction, she waved at the woman and headed towards him.

"You're driving me crazy," she told him as he held the door open for her.

"Likewise, Buffy."

Dimitri called the new contact while Megan browsed through one of the more sedate adult shops in the street. This one was on the women's lingerie end of the spectrum, although they still carried designer bondage gear and a whole array of flavoured gels. Megan bought a blindfold, which was pretty much a bedazzled eye mask. When Dimitri cocked an eyebrow at her purchase she kept her lips closed and let his imagination fill in the gaps. He didn't need to know it was a gift for Claire who liked to nap during the day now that she was pregnant, but hated when it was too light.

"We're meeting Rudi's guy at seven."

The look in his eye said it all. The man was primed for vengeance. A year, that's how long he'd been looking for his sister. A year of chasing down the slightest lead. A year of coming up against brick wall after brick wall. And now, with the help of Benson Security, he was making headway at last. Megan bet he could practically taste the end.

"We're going to find her." It was a false promise, born from desperate hope more than anything else. As soon as it fell from her lips, Megan wished it back. Dimitri didn't need placating, he needed action.

"Yeah," he said.

Megan put her hand on his arm and held tight. At last he looked in her eyes. "No. I mean, we'll move heaven and earth until we find her. We'll do whatever it takes." It was no less than she would do if it was Claire who was missing.

It was no less than she *was* doing now to save Claire from a similar fate. For a moment, they held each other's gaze, a silent understanding between them.

With a deep breath, Dimitri took a step back and glanced at his diver's watch. "We've got over an hour. Might as well eat something." And then he strode off, expecting her to follow. And like a freaking lemming, she did.

# CHAPTER 4

Dimitri led them to Chinatown, on the other side of Shaftesbury Avenue from the red light district. The pedestrianised street was lined with restaurants, but Megan picked *Soon Fatt*, purely because she thought the name was hilarious. Dimitri didn't question her decision, even though there were better looking restaurants on the street. He was learning there were some fights that just weren't worth the effort.

The interior was standard Chinese restaurant—white tablecloths, red paper lanterns and gold dragon motifs. They ordered a menu for two, the one with crispy duck, plus a few added extras.

"So what's the plan?"

Megan confiscated all of the spring rolls as soon as they arrived at the table, then stabbed his hand with a chopstick when he reached for one.

"The plan is to use this guy, John Martin, goes by Johnny Rotten, to—"

She stopped with a spring roll halfway to her mouth. "Johnny Rotten? Seriously? Like the punk singer?"

"I kid you not, but I don't think he's named after the punk

guy." To be honest, it wasn't the worst nickname he'd come across. "The plan is to convince Johnny to okay a visit with his boss and arrange it for us."

"I don't get it." Megan waved her chopsticks around for emphasis. "We have a team of hackers at our disposal, can't they just find Rudi's email address and give it to you? Wouldn't that be the easiest way to set up a meeting with Rudi?"

"If only it was that simple." He snatched one of the spring rolls before she could stop him. Her glare was adorable. "He lives offline. Everything is done through his assistants."

He swore he could actually see her brain working. "So none of the trails lead to him. Smart. I suppose it's the same deal with his cell phone number."

He didn't answer. He didn't need to. Rudi Abramovich had his personal contact information locked up tight. Either he approached you, or you got to him through his team. It was time consuming, difficult and seriously cautious. And it worked. He was still free while other men in the same business were long behind bars.

The waitress arrived with a large silver platter loaded with food and Megan bounced on her seat at the sight of it. She'd gravitated towards everything on the menu that was deep fried and when he'd asked her about it, she'd shrugged and told him she was Scottish. Before she could nab the sweet and sour chicken, again crispy fried, he loaded her plate with some of the steamed vegetables he'd ordered. The look of horror on her face was priceless.

"What did you do that for?"

"You need something that isn't junk food."

"I eat healthy food. Just not here. What's the point of eating steamed broccoli when there's fried rice on the table?" Her outrage almost made him laugh—he fought it back.

"Humour me. Cover the damn things in sweet and sour sauce if you like, but eat them. Your arteries will thank you."

She pointed a chopstick at him. "Just for that comment, I'm ordering more spring rolls." She covered the vegetables with sauce until they were practically swimming in it.

Dimitri shook his head. "You eat like a teenager."

"Scottish," she said again, like that was supposed to mean something.

He must have looked blank because she gave a long-suffering sigh. "We're the nation that eats deep fried Mars Bars and Irn Bru sausages. The same country that claims haggis as its national dish, but eats more curries than anywhere outside of India. Our supermarkets have three aisles dedicated to biscuits and cookies and one for fruit and veg. This," she pointed at the table, "is amateur night for a Scot." Then she chomped on a piece of deep fried chicken.

Dimitri shuddered before loading up on noodles and veg. "As I was saying, I'm hoping this guy is our access to Rudi. If he isn't, we'll need to come up with another plan."

"Won't it tip your hand going to Johnny first? I mean, if he doesn't help us then Rudi knows your plan. He might send someone to take me from you. It would cut out the middle man. If I was him, that's what I would do."

"If the meeting starts to look like it's going to go belly up I'll think of something."

She stilled. "This is just like in Scotland. You're going to make this up as you go along, aren't you?"

"No. I'm going to come up with a plan when it's needed. A plan based on a lifetime of experience and training."

"Yeah. Right." She pointed her chopsticks at him. The woman used the utensils like a weapon. "That's the attitude that left me rescuing myself in Scotland."

"Here we go again." He put his elbows on the table and clasped his hands. "You just cannot let this go, can you? I would have gotten you out of there. I was waiting for the right time."

"Who are you kidding? You were going to march me all the way to Rudi's base in Romania and trade me for the whereabouts of your sister."

"That was before I really knew you. And I wouldn't have traded you. I'd have used you, like I'm doing now. Big difference."

"Yep. I can hardly tell the two plans apart."

"Eat your food." Then just to annoy her, he moved the rest of the fried rice across the table and out of her reach.

They ate in silence for a few minutes. Dimitri tried to focus on his food while mentally preparing for the meeting he'd scheduled. It was hard with Megan sitting so close to him. Everything about the woman was a distraction, from her bright blue eyes, to her luscious pink lips, through to her perfectly curved hips. He couldn't be in the same room as her without wanting to touch, tease, taste. Even her crazy attitude and bad temper were temptation to him.

Twelve long months he'd eaten, breathed and slept the hunt for Katrina. Megan was the first thing that had been strong enough to break through his obsession. Being around her was like a time out from the stress and anxiety that constantly plagued him. And the more he was in her presence, the more he wanted to hold on to her. But he couldn't. He had to focus. She had to focus. There was too much at stake to get distracted. Especially when they were this close to getting to Rudi.

He cleared his throat and cast around for a safer topic. "The workout room is finished. We start training tomorrow morning."

She patted her lips with the white linen napkin, making his mind flood with all the other things he could do with those lips. "What training?"

He sat back in his chair, needing the space between them. "Self-defence."

"Oh, in that case, no thanks. I'm covered." She tucked her hair behind her ear.

"You're covered?"

"Yep. I know how to take care of myself."

Oh, this he had to hear. "Okay, Buffy, I'll bite. What makes you think you'd be any good in a fight?"

"You mean, apart from the fact I managed to knock you unconscious. Not to mention the time I rendered you incapable of speech with a kick to the groin. You'd think those events would have clued you in to the fact that I have skills."

"You don't have skills. You have luck. And it was your sister—not you—who knocked me out. As for the knee to my balls, you took me by surprise. I thought we were on the same side at the time."

Megan barked out a laugh. "The same side? You turned up in *my* home town with a bunch of thugs intent on kidnapping *my* sister to hand her over to a maniac. We were never on the same side."

"I. Was. Under. Cover."

"Blah, blah, blah. Like being undercover is an excuse for ineptitude. You almost got me killed."

"You were never anywhere near getting hurt. We agreed on a plan. All you had to do was pretend to be Claire and I would make sure you were freed at some point."

Megan threw up her hands. "Listen to yourself. That isn't a plan. That's just optimism. You said," she deepened her voice and affected an American accent, "play along and I'll think of something." She dropped the accent. "Think of something? Yeah. That was reassuring. Good job I was able to save myself."

"Yeah, by kicking me in the balls and shooting Durand in the ass."

"You say that like it's a bad thing. I took on two armed, trained men and won. I realise it was a blow to your ego, but you need to get over it. I think this conversation makes it clear why I don't need self-defence training. I can defend myself just fine. I took Lake's class in Invertary, my brother made sure we knew what to do growing up and I did two years of judo when I was a kid. I'm. Covered. So how about we spend any training time you have booked going over something I don't know, like how to use a machine gun."

Dimitri felt his jaw clench tight. "There is no way I'm letting you anywhere near an automatic weapon."

Megan leaned across the table, closing the distance between them. "You are not the boss of me."

"For this job I am."

"We're partners. Equal partners."

"Like hell."

"Yes. It will be hell."

He made a strangled noise and threw up his hands as someone cleared their throat. The red haze in front of Dimitri's eyes cleared enough for him to notice they had the attention of everyone in the restaurant and their waitress was standing beside their table. Fantastic. Talk about how *not* to keep a low profile.

"Can I get you anything else?" The woman's eyes were wide as she looked at them.

"Just the bill." Dimitri tried to smile at her, but his face wouldn't work with him. "In fact, don't bother. We'll pick it up on the way out." He looked at Megan, who was still fuming. "Let's go."

She grabbed her navy blue padded jacket from the back of her chair, thanked the waitress and strode to the front door, her head held high and her gorgeous ass swaying. Dimitri paid the bill, leaving a hefty tip and chased after the annoying woman.

By the time he'd made it outside, Megan was halfway up the street. He jogged after her, dodging the many people who were reading the menus posted outside the restaurants. The infuriating woman had to know he was chasing her and yet she strode on, in the opposite direction to where their car was parked. With her head held high, her fists clenched and her back ramrod straight, it didn't take a genius to figure out she was still mad at him.

"Wait up." He grabbed her arm and spun her around.

Her fist came out, but he was prepared for her violent streak. He caught her hands and held them behind her back.

"Let. Go. Of. Me."

Her eyes flashed pure fire. Her cheeks were flushed and her chest heaved. She was stunning.

"Promise you won't hit."

"Promise you won't annoy me."

"See, I can't do that, Buff. Annoying you has become my main hobby."

Her eyes narrowed. "Find another one."

"Why would I do that when this one is so entertaining?"

She struggled in his arms, making him hold her tighter. "You have three seconds to release me or you're going to regret it."

"Hey," a guy passing said. "You okay there?" He looked between the two of them, obviously worried. Dimitri became aware they were standing in the middle of a crowded street and they'd attracted quite an audience.

"Fine," they snapped at the same time and the guy backed off, shaking his head.

Megan glared up at him. With her heeled boots, she was just a few inches shorter than he was. He could feel her warm breath on his jaw. It would be so easy to lean down, close the gap between them and taste those luscious lips.

"Three seconds," she reminded him.

"Or what?" He couldn't remember the last time he felt this alive, this delighted. Playing with Megan was a rush to his system.

"Oh to hell with it." She angled her head and bit his throat. Hard.

Dimitri released her and slapped a hand over the bite. There was a smattering of laughter and applause from the onlookers. Megan folded her arms and cocked her head at him, as though considering. It had to be the most disconcerting look he'd ever been subjected to and it made part of him want to run. In that moment, he really didn't care what that said about him.

"That's going to leave a mark." He prodded the bite gently. No blood, but it would definitely bruise. "I'll get you back for this."

She smirked. "You mean you'll try to get me back for it." She stepped into his space. "You might as well face it." She patted his T-shirt through his open jacket, her palms a brand on his chest. Long dark lashes batted over blue eyes. "You are no match for me."

He opened his mouth to correct her ludicrous assumption when her hand curved around his neck and she yanked his face towards her. It took a split second for his body to tense, ready to defend itself, but by then it was too late. Her lips were on his and nothing else mattered except the delicious pressure of Megan's kiss. In that moment, he would have willingly laid himself at her feet and let her trample him.

He was vaguely aware of the wolf whistles and cheers, then he heard nothing, felt nothing, except Megan. His left arm wrapped tight around her, his right hand clasped the back of her head as he angled her mouth to suit him. It wasn't a kiss like any he'd ever experienced. This was a duel. A battle of wills. A fight for dominance. And he couldn't have said who was winning. All he knew was he wanted more. He wanted all of her.

"Get a room," someone shouted.

Megan's lips moved away from his and he followed them. A sharp tug to his hair halted him and he realised Megan's fingers had clutched him tight. She leaned back. She was breathless. Her normally pink lips were swollen and red. Her blue eyes had turned dark with passion. For a second she just looked at him, their breaths mingling, their heartbeats racing together. Then she released him and stepped back, leaving him cold. His fingers itched to reach for her. He shoved his hands in the pockets of his jeans to stop himself. Megan looked as stunned as he felt.

An old Chinese woman came up to them. Her smile was wide, her eyes sparkling with mischief. She took Megan's hand, placed something in the palm and curved Megan's fingers around it.

"For luck," she said. "You have long life together."

Megan's eyes went wide. "Oh, we're not together."

She tried to hand back the gift.

"No, no." The woman refused to take it as she backed away. "You young love. You have many happy years. I know this." And then with a chuckle she was gone.

Megan seemed bewildered. She opened her palm and looked at the charm. A symbol written on a polished stone. She looked back up at him.

"We're not together."

Dimitri knew he shouldn't feel insulted. They were partners. Nothing more. The job had to come first. His sister's rescue had to come first. There was no time for anything else. For anyone else. Yet, part of him still felt annoyed.

"Damn straight we're not together."

A flare of anger. Her shoulders went back. "Thanks for

the kiss." She walked past him, then cast a glance over her shoulder. "It was nice."

"Nice?" He rushed to catch up with her. At least this time she was heading in the right direction.

She shrugged like it was nothing. Like it had no impact at all. Like they hadn't just rocked their worlds. "Sometimes you have to try these things. See what they're like. Now we know."

*What the hell?* "Know what?"

"That it wouldn't work between us." She sighed. "It's okay, Dimitri. You can't help it."

He bristled. He was about ten seconds away from shaking the infuriating woman.

"Help what? What the hell are you talking about?"

"The lack of passion, of course. It's not your fault that the kiss was just okay. There's nothing wrong with your technique. We just don't have any chemistry." She gave him a sunny smile. "I'm sure your past lovers thought you were perfectly adequate."

With that she turned on her heel and stalked away, leaving him gaping after her.

# CHAPTER 5

Julia knew there were people who were introverted but weren't shy. Steve Martin was one of them. The actor liked to be alone, but he had no problem talking to people when he had to. Unfortunately, Julia was nothing like Steve Martin. Nope, she was introverted, terminally shy and ever since her last job where her boss had been a bully, she'd become even more terrified of interacting with people than ever before. She was well aware of her issues and grateful that Lake Benson had employed her in spite of them. She was working hard to get past her fears and be the type of employee Lake would be proud of. And her current meeting was proof of how far she'd come—she was alone, in her office, going over the renovation plans with two men.

So what if both men were in their seventies and looked like garden gnomes. It still counted.

"Julia, love." Bill Granger was Ryan's grandfather and a complete darling. His relationship to one of the team was the reason Julia had hired him and his brother to do the carpentry work in the building. That and the fact they were just too adorable to say no to. "You need a panic room."

"It isn't on my list, Bill." She pointed at the two huge whiteboards that filled the walls behind her desk. One had a detailed plan of the renovations. The other had a list of jobs the security team were doing and which member was responsible for which part of it. Seeing as the business wasn't officially open yet, there was only one job on the board—finding Katrina Raast.

"The wives made us watch that Jodie Foster film last night." Bob was the younger brother of the pair, by two whole years. A fact he delighted in.

"Date night." Bill shuddered. "I don't understand why we need a date night, but it's their new thing."

"What I don't understand," Bob said, "is how date night is any different to every other night. Normally we watch TV and have dinner. What did we do last night? Watch TV and ate dinner. You're a woman. Do you understand the difference?"

"Uh…" Julia was at a loss.

"See?" Bob pointed at his brother. "This isn't normal. The wives are winding us up."

Bill nodded. "At least the movie was useful. It made us think about this place. You take risks here. You need somewhere safe. You need a panic room."

The two men nodded. In their matching beige overalls they looked like older versions of the cabbage patch dolls Julia had as a kid.

"I know you want to build a panic room," Julia said. "But it isn't on the schedule. Right now, we need to get the office kitchen finished. That's more important."

"It is to Ryan," Bill said with a grin. "That boy thinks with his stomach."

She couldn't argue with that. After she'd seen the amount of food Ryan could put away in one sitting she'd doubled the office budget for snacks.

"He's a growing lad, your grandson." Bob returned the grin. "And a greedy bugger."

"Which is one of the reasons the kitchen is next on my list." She rearranged the paperwork on her desk, even though it didn't need rearranging. Everything was precisely where it should be. "But I will put your idea for a panic room on the agenda for my next meeting with Callum. Will that make you happy?"

"Absolutely. Thanks Julia," the men chorused, making her smile.

"Now, did you two sign the confidentiality agreements I gave you?"

They rooted around in the many pockets of their overalls until Bob exclaimed he had them. He handed over a folded mess of crumpled papers. "There might be jam on there," he warned.

Julia took them using her thumb and forefinger, then looked around for somewhere to open them that wouldn't cause a mess. "I'll look them over later." She put them on top of a plastic folder. The kitchen was the best place to check the forms. And to wipe off any jam she found.

The men told her they were going back to work and left. Bill winked at her and Bob blew her a kiss, leaving Julia staring at the empty doorway with a bewildered smile on her face. She was just about to get up and close the door after them, when she heard Bob say, "You looking for Julia, Joe? She's in her office."

For a split second, Julia was paralysed by blind panic. Then she ducked under her desk. It was an instinctive reaction. A really stupid one. Because as soon as she was under the desk she knew two things—one, that Joe knew she was in her office and would therefore know she was under the desk, and two, now she was there she couldn't come out.

"Julia?" His lazy baritone with its curling American vowels made her mouth go dry.

She saw his feet appear as he strode through the doorway. He stopped on the other side of her U-shaped desk, which she'd positioned unconventionally. Instead of fitting the U part into the corner, she'd put her chair there and fit the desk around her, making a kind of desk fort.

"Julia." There was clear confusion in his voice. "Are you under the desk?"

Honestly, if her face burned any brighter her whole head would combust. She cleared her throat, but her voice still came out as the timid squeak she hated. "Yes. I'm…fixing cables." *Lame!* "What can I do for you Joe?" Unreasonably terrified that Joe would crouch down to check her excuse, or worse, offer to help her, Julia started randomly unplugging everything in front of her. She heard her computer beep then die. Great. She really hoped she hadn't just lost the work she'd been doing.

"Can you come out for a minute? I've got some hard copy files on Abramovich that I need to go over with you." Joe sounded amused. Julia wasn't sure if that was a good thing or a bad thing.

"I'm sorry, I can't do that right now. It's essential that I get this wiring sorted. Just put everything on the desk and I'll send you an email about it later." She held her breath, waiting for his response.

The man moved. The desk creaked and from the angle of his shoes, she thought he might be perched on the edge of her desk.

"I can wait until you're done."

Julia didn't use swear words, but she thought this might be a good time to start.

"I realise your time is valuable." She aimed for a bland, professional tone that in no way made the man realise that her heart stuttered any time he was in the room. "I may be down here some time. There's no need to wait. Please, leave the files."

The desk creaked some more. Julia tried hard to use her non-existent x-ray vision to see what he was doing. It didn't work.

"I have to say, Miss Julia, you look mighty fine in that skirt." It was a teasing drawl that took a second to register.

Then it did. Julia's head twisted to look behind her. Sure enough her backside was sticking out from under the desk.

"Joe!" She scrambled to get her whole body under the damn thing. With a desk this size it should have been easy, but it wasn't. As soon as she got out from under it, she was calling the Granger boys back in and demanding they remove the side drawers. That way, if this ever happened again, she'd fit under the desk on the first try.

She resisted the urge to thump some sense into herself by banging her head on the floor. She'd actually caught herself planning to hide under her desk in the future.

"Julia, baby, we talked about this."

Joe's voice was soft, compassionate even. It made her bite her bottom lip to stop from sobbing. Stupid, stupid behaviour. She knew it and she still couldn't seem to stop it. Dealing with two eccentric old men was one thing—dealing with Joe Barone was something else entirely. Something she wasn't ready to do. Something she might never be ready to do.

"You can't keep hiding from the people you work with," Joe said gently.

Julia wanted to protest that she didn't hide from all of them. Just the really scary ones. The ones that were too demanding, or too loud, or too masculine. Okay, that was pretty much everyone who worked for Benson Security. She wondered again if she should just quit this job while she was still partly sane and go to work for a nursing home. Or better yet a petting zoo. She could deal with animals. Animals didn't intimidate her to the point of making her hide.

Joe let out a heavy sigh. The desk creaked again as he stood. "Okay, we'll let it go this time, but there's gonna come a day, Jules, where I'm not going to let you run and hide. You hear me?"

"I'm neither running, nor hiding. I'm fixing cables." She told herself it wasn't really a lie because now she really did have to fix cables.

"I'm leaving the files on your desk." He walked to the door. "And Julia, I think I'm a little bit in love with the skirt you have on."

With that the man sauntered away. Julia sat on the carpet with a thud. She placed her hands to her burning cheeks and closed her eyes. Normal. All she wanted to be was normal. Because a normal girl wouldn't have hidden from a man like Joe Barone. No, a normal girl would have smiled and flirted. A normal girl would have known how to tease a kiss from a man with lips like heaven.

Unfortunately, Julia would never be a normal girl.

# CHAPTER 6

They were meeting Johnny Rotten in a dark alley. Of course they were meeting a guy called Johnny Rotten in a dark alley. Megan rolled her eyes. Obviously Johnny went to the TV movie school of how to be a bad guy.

"You stay here." Dimitri pointed at a dumpster. Yeah. A dumpster. She half expected some guy with a camera to shout cut and make them start again.

"You don't mean in the dumpster, right?" Because—eew!

"No. Beside it. In the dark." He didn't even try to disguise that he was losing patience. "Don't move, don't make a sound, don't interrupt."

Blah, blah, blah, let the big boys play. She was so tired of hearing the same old tune. It was time to change the radio station.

"Right," Dimitri said. "I'm going to drive round and come in from the other end."

"Why can't I just wait in the car? It's cold and it stinks here."

"Because…" He stretched the word out. "You're supposed to be my hostage. I can't just let you hang out in the car."

"I can pretend to be drugged."

"No. Too dangerous. He might spot you, know who you are and that Rudi wants you. Then what would stop him deciding to eliminate me and take you to Rudi himself?"

She stamped her feet to get her blood circulating before the chill removed her toes. "Why didn't you just take me back to the office?"

"You're my backup." There was a silent 'idiot' attached to that sentence, she just knew it.

"The backup that hides in dumpsters?"

"The backup that phones for help if it looks like things are going south."

Megan blushed, grateful he couldn't see it in the dark. "So, I need my phone?"

He put his hands on his hips and looked skyward for a moment. "Where is it?"

"Car." She gave him what she hoped was an apologetic smile.

He stomped off, cursing under his breath and came back a few minutes later with the phone. "Sorted now?"

Megan nodded. It probably wasn't the best time to tell him she really needed to use the bathroom. She could hold it. How long did it take to have a covert meeting in an alley anyway?

She gave him a thumbs up and watched him march back to the car. Leaving her alone in a stinky, dark alley. Alone and *not* thinking about how good Dimitri's lips felt against hers. Nope. She wasn't thinking about that at all. She was a professional—nearly. She had a job to do. She backed into the shadows and tried to become invisible. Ninja Megan. She could do it. It was all about the power of the mind. She closed her eyes and took a few calming breaths.

That's when her stomach rumbled. Her hand smacked flat

on it as she bit her lip. Maybe all that fried food wasn't such a great idea after all. Not that she would ever admit that to Dimitri. She was still mad at the man. Sure she'd been the first to say they weren't in a relationship, but he didn't have to agree so enthusiastically. He'd sounded affronted. As though she was the last person on earth he'd consider dating. It was insulting. Her stomach made a strange bubbling sound as she saw Dimitri's SUV pull up at the other end of the alley. He got out and stood under the yellow glow of the street lamp. Waiting. Alert. Moody.

Megan's stomach rumbled again. Loudly. This wasn't good. So much for not making a sound. Her own body was working against her. She crouched down in an attempt to dull the noise, and hoped it worked. She closed her eyes, tried to calm her stomach and think thoughts that made her invisible.

That's when she farted.

It wasn't silent.

Megan dropped her head to her knees. If the bad guys didn't get her, she'd die of humiliation.

And then her stomach rumbled again.

DIMITRI GLANCED AT HIS WATCH. Johnny was three minutes late. Three minutes wasn't much. It wasn't time to worry, just yet. He scanned the area continually, looking for the slightest thing out of place. He worked to keep his mind on the job and not on Megan's kiss. He could still taste her. A hot, sensual delight he wanted to taste again. But he wouldn't. Apart from the fact it would be a seriously bad idea, apparently he was just fucking adequate. He wanted to storm over to her and show her exactly how far from adequate he was, which made him mad. Here he was, on the most important job of his life and he was thinking with his dick. He needed to shut this crap down and fast. Before he got them both killed.

It was quiet, for this neck of the woods. They were off the tourist track, near an industrial park that was closed for the evening. There were no pubs nearby, no restaurants, no homes. Just closed businesses and dark alleys.

He checked his watch again. Five minutes. He was starting to get antsy. He should have brought some proper backup. What the hell he was doing coming here with Megan, he didn't know. It was a dumb move and proof he couldn't think straight when she was around. But he couldn't blame it all on her—he was used to handling situations like this by himself. Being part of a team again took some getting used to. He glanced up the alley, but all he could see was blackness. He was going to give the guy five more minutes, then he'd call it a bust.

A car drove past. It didn't slow. It didn't stop. Not Johnny. And then he heard a foot shuffle behind him.

Dimitri spun fast, reaching for the gun in the small of his back.

"Don't bother." A raspy male voice. "Keep your hands where I can see them."

A man appeared out of the dark alley, dressed top to toe in black. He held a Beretta 9mm in his right hand. And Megan's hair in his left.

Dimitri's world stopped in a heartbeat and he had to fight to get it moving again.

"Sorry," Megan mouthed at him.

The barrel of the gun brushed over her cheek. Dimitri fought back rage at the sight. He had to be rational. For Megan's sake. He was stupid. So fucking stupid for walking her into this.

"I found something that belongs to you." Johnny's accent was pure East London. He had at least a foot of height on

Megan and about a hundred pounds—not all of it muscle. He didn't carry himself like he'd been trained, but his movements showed he was no stranger to violence. He was completely at ease holding Megan and the gun.

"What do you want?" Dimitri kept his eyes on the gun.

"Now, see, that's the question I had for you."

Dimitri could see why Rudi hired the guy. He was cold, calculating and suspicious. A blunt instrument that took pleasure in inflicting pain—something obvious from the way he pulled Megan's hair tight enough to keep her on her toes.

"I told you on the phone. I worked in Scotland with Durand and I have something Abramovich wants. I want to set up a meet."

"Rudi has never heard of you."

Yeah, Dimitri could see where that would set off alarm bells. "Ask Durand. He hired me."

"No can do. Durand is still sorting out business in Scotland. He's out of touch."

Dimitri saw Megan stiffen. He silently willed her not to panic. Grunt was with her sister. Claire would be fine, no matter what Durand planned.

"What you got that Rudi wants?"

Dimitri buried his relief that Johnny didn't know the value of the woman he held in his hands. "That's between me and Rudi."

"I don't think so. I think you're going to tell me everything I want to know, or your girl here is going to suffer until you do."

He heard Megan squeak as Johnny tugged her hair higher. Her hands shot out to hold his wrist, as she strained to get as far up on her toes as she could, to take the pressure off her head. A strange bubbling sound came from the pair. Dimitri dismissed it as he took a step closer to the threat.

"Don't move." The gun swung to fix on Dimitri.

Better. Much better than having it pointed at Megan's head. Megan writhed in Johnny's grip, but she didn't make a noise. She didn't scream. She didn't panic. Part of Dimitri was aware just how damn proud he was of her. He held out his hands. "How about we play nice? You set up a meeting with Rudi and I'll tell him how helpful you were. I'll even cut you in on my reward."

The guy's eyes gleamed with wicked intelligence. "So, it's something he's lost. Or something he wants bad enough to put a bounty on it."

There was another louder rumbling. This time, Dimitri was pretty sure it came from Megan.

The gun turned back to Megan. Dimitri took another step forward without thinking.

"One more step and I shoot." He pointed at Megan's knee. "I'll start here and work my way up. First, we're going to play a little game. For every answer you give me, your girl here gets a minute more time without being hurt. We clear?"

"Don't hurt her." Dimitri clenched his fists as the man pulled Megan tight against his body. Her face was pale. She looked ill. She had to be terrified.

"Oh no," Megan moaned quietly. "This isn't good." Her arms dropped to curl around her stomach.

Johnny smiled—it was nasty. "Listen to the woman. She knows what she's talking about."

Another rumble. It was Megan's stomach, he realised. She gave him a wide eyed panicked look before mouthing sorry again. And then the woman farted. Loudly.

"What the fuck?" Johnny's hold on her loosened as he angled away from her. "What the fuck did you eat? Holy shit, woman!"

"That's it, I've had enough of this crap," Megan snapped. "I need to get to a toilet."

She elbowed Johnny, hard, in his side. He jerked backwards. Dimitri took a step forward but Megan was too fast. She stamped on Johnny's instep. Aimed an elbow at his face, but it hit his throat, making the guy choke. She brought her arm down hard to punch Johnny's groin. He wobbled, made a strangled noise and crumpled to the ground. Megan didn't miss a beat—she stamped on his wrist to release the gun, then kicked him in the jaw. He was out cold by the time Dimitri was by her side.

And, whoa, the smell!

He stepped back again before forcing himself to retrieve the gun. He flicked the safety on, tucked it in the waistband of his jeans, pulled some flexi cuffs out of his jacket and secured Johnny.

Megan's stomach rumbled and she curled in on herself. She looked grey. He moved to hold her, but she held up her hand to stop him.

"That proof enough that I don't need self-defence training?" The words came out strained.

"Are you okay?" Dimitri was livid with his need to get near her. To touch her. To make sure she was fine. "Did he hurt you?"

"Only my scalp." She groaned and bent over some more. Dimitri wrapped an arm around her. He couldn't stop himself. She was in pain and he hated it.

"What the hell is wrong, Megan, you're freaking me out here."

He could have sworn she was blushing. "Dinner. That's what's wrong. I think I have food poisoning. I need a toilet. Fast." She pointed to the end of the alley and the road. "I'm going to lean on the wall over there. You won't want to come near me. I don't think either of us could handle it. Please call Julia so she can take me back to the flat."

"I can take you."

"No! Call Julia."

She pushed away from him and she staggered off, muttering something about humiliation, leaving Dimitri to stare after her. He wasn't sure what stunned him the most, the fact she'd disarmed her attacker in ten seconds flat, or the fact she'd said please. He pulled out his cell phone, keeping watch on Megan and the unconscious guy at his feet.

"I need a pick up," he said when Joe answered. "I've got one guy down and a woman who needs a toilet, stat." There was silence for a second before Joe asked for his location.

# CHAPTER 7

"I don't like this, but seeing as it's the closest anyone's managed to get to Rudi Abramovich, I'm prepared to let it run its course." Tessa Sharp was another one of Lake Benson's contacts. She was also a Commander with the Special Crime Investigation division in London's Metropolitan police force.

She watched two of her officers remove Johnny Rotten from one of the holding cells in the basement of Benson Security's office building. Dimitri and Joe had already questioned the guy and confiscated his phone. The one with a number for Rudi Abramovich.

"It was pure luck," Callum told the woman. "We knew he had access to Rudi, not that he had a number for him."

The woman wasn't in uniform, but her tailored black suit was designed to be intimidating. The team had already filled her in on the details of their operation, making it very clear that their priority was to secure the safety of Claire Donaldson and Katrina Raast.

"Pure luck that took a year of following leads and pushing doors." Dimitri felt the need to remind his boss.

Callum inclined his head in agreement.

Tessa eyed Dimitri thoughtfully for a minute. He had no doubt she was running scenarios in her head. "I'll let you meet with Rudi."

She didn't seem to care when he bristled at her affording him permission he in no way needed and never requested.

"We've been after his business records for years," Tessa said. "The bastard spreads his operation over too many countries, which means multiple split jurisdictions. It's been hell trying to cut through the bureaucracy to set up a joint operation. Even after this long, we're nowhere near the agreements we need to investigate Abramovich fully. This," she signalled to the men in the room, "cuts through that."

"We need to go through the information first before we hand it over." Callum was immovable on that point. They all were.

It was clear from the set of her mouth that Commander Sharp was about to argue the point.

"No." Dimitri stood and stared at the woman. "No discussion. No negotiation. We'll hand over everything we get, but not until we know where my sister is being held."

Tessa's eyes darkened. "She isn't the only woman who's suffering out there."

"She's the only one I'm related to."

"You don't call the shots here." Her tone was calm, in charge. "I can shut this operation down like that." She snapped her fingers.

"Then you won't get the information you need, because right now myself and Megan are the only two people with any chance of getting close enough to Rudi to get those records."

She inclined her head, conceding the point. Her eyes narrowed. "Okay, you can pinpoint your sister's whereabouts. But the operation to retrieve her has to be done under the radar. I don't want anyone tipping Rudi off that we're onto him. Not before plans are in place to bring down everyone involved in his organisation in one fell swoop."

"How long will that take?" Joe said, from where he was leaning against the doorframe.

"A couple of months, maybe more."

Dimitri shook his head as Joe cursed.

"Too long," Dimitri said. "We can't leave Rudi operating for that long. Claire Donaldson is at risk every minute the guy is walking around free. We're giving you his records so you can lock him up and keep him away from Claire. That's non-negotiable."

"If we lock him up, someone else within the organisation will step in to take his place. We need to take the whole thing down at once or it won't work. That sort of operation, on that scale, takes time to arrange."

"Unacceptable." Dimitri put his hands on his hips to stop from hitting something. "Megan is putting her life at risk to get this information and save her sister and you want to tell her that she'll have to wait? That Claire will still be at risk for months yet? That's assuming Rudi doesn't get wind of your investigation and run. He could hide for years on the money he has stashed. And each minute he's free is a minute Claire is at risk."

"You think I don't understand that?" Tessa took a step towards him. "Twenty years. That's how long I've been working the sex crimes division. I know exactly what kind of risk Abramovich poses to women. I know exactly what he's done to the women he's sold. You think I want to leave any of those women in his hold for one minute longer? No, I don't, but I need to ensure their long-term safety once they're out of his grasp. To do that, the Abramovich organisation needs to be completely wiped out." She glared up at him. "You're thinking about Katrina and Claire. I understand they're your priority. My priority is the hundreds of nameless women whom no one is hunting for." She turned to Callum, a blaze of fury. "You can keep the information long enough to find Katrina's location. Everything else will have to wait. Rudi will be arrested at the same time as the rest of the organisation is hit. I won't risk those other women to protect Claire Donaldson. Right now she's safe in the Highlands. Those other women don't have that luxury."

There was silence. Callum caught Joe's eye, then Dimitri's.

"She's right," his boss said. "You know she's right."

"Megan is going to lose her mind over this," Dimitri warned.

"Then I suggest you don't tell her until you've retrieved Rudi's files," Tessa said.

"We can protect Claire until Rudi is put away." Joe didn't look any more pleased with the situation than Dimitri felt.

"Could be months," Dimitri reminded him.

"We can do it. I'll talk to Harry, see if he can cover the costs." The third partner in Benson Security had made millions developing a security programme for the government. He was also Claire's cousin.

"I don't like this," Dimitri said.

Joe nodded. "What choice do we have? Like the commander said, we can't protect Claire at the expense of those women."

No, they couldn't. "Do we tell Megan?" He looked at Callum.

The man pinched the bridge of his nose. "Not until the meet with Rudi is over. We can't risk what she might do. She's a loose cannon as it is."

To her credit, Tessa didn't gloat over winning the argument. "Trust me, gentlemen, I want Rudi off the streets as much as you do, probably more. Now tell me what I can do to help."

Dimitri tuned out Callum's answer. "I'm going to call Rudi," he told Joe.

"What you going to tell him about having Johnny's phone?"

"The truth. That the guy was an ass and I've got him locked up tight until I sort out this thing with Rudi."

Joe nodded. He cocked his head towards Tessa and Callum. "You okay with this?"

"Like you said, we don't have much choice so I guess I have to be."

"Megan…" Joe didn't need to say anything else.

"Yeah," Dimitri agreed.

Megan was seriously going to blow when she found out there was a change in plans. Dimitri just hoped they could all deal with the fallout.

# CHAPTER 8

Megan walked into the conference room the following morning to find that each place at the table had a gasmask in front of it.

"Just in case." Ryan beamed at her.

"Funny. Oh so funny." Megan was beyond mortification. Who knew it was possible? But all it had taken was some dodgy Chinese food, an explosive stomach and a ride across London in a car with her flatmate.

"You're our secret weapon." Ryan was loving every minute of this. "If we ever need to clear a building we'll just take you to Chinatown first, then send you in. Ten minutes and the enemy will be out cold."

"Or they'll surrender." Joe grinned at her.

"Everybody's a comedian."

Ryan and Joe laughed loudly before occupying each other with toilet jokes.

Megan pulled up a seat beside Dimitri. It was on the tip of her tongue to apologise for screwing up the meeting. Instead what came out was, "I blame you. I'm sure it was the broccoli."

She'd expected some ribbing, maybe a lecture about being unprofessional. Instead his eyes softened when he looked up at her. He brushed her cheek with his knuckles. A gentle, caring touch that disarmed her.

"You okay?" His voice was soft, for her ears only.

"Yeah." She swallowed hard at the huskiness in her voice.

"You did good last night, Buffy."

The words went straight to that secret place inside of her that protected the core of insecurity she was terrified the world would see. "I made noise. That's how he caught me."

"You couldn't help it."

Megan was vaguely aware of Joe and Ryan winding each other up in the background, but all of her attention was on Dimitri.

His warm hand rested on the curve of her throat as his thumb brushed the edge of her jaw. "He would have found you anyway. He came in from a direction that made you easier to spot. It wasn't your fault. It was mine. I shouldn't have put you in that position."

"Rubbish. We're partners. Remember?"

Something flickered in his eyes and he looked away from her. His hand dropped back to the table. "Yeah, we're partners." His voice was louder. "You did great disabling him. Professional. I was impressed."

Alarms went off in Megan's head at this sudden coldness. Then she realised what she'd seen in his eyes was guilt. Stupid man, probably blamed himself for her getting caught.

"Lake's classes," she confessed. "He drummed those moves into us."

"No, not just the classes. You have an instinct for this business. And you're freaking lucky."

There was no denying it, she was definitely lucky.

Whatever he was going to say next was lost as the door opened and a burst of colour rushed in. The woman was wearing a bright pink T-shirt with *Hello Kitty* on it, lime green jeans and her bobbed hair was dyed pastel blue with purple streaks. She blinked unnatural lavender coloured eyes at everyone. Megan knew at one glance that she'd found a stand-in for Claire. Julia was lovely, but Megan missed the like-minded mischief her twin was capable of. This woman looked like she was more than able to make trouble with Megan.

"Did I miss anything exciting?" the woman said with a cheeky grin.

"This is our tech liaison." Callum came in behind the woman, spotted the gasmasks and glared at Ryan. "She's going to go over our comms system with Megan after the meeting."

"Hi." Megan waved at the woman. "I'm Donaldson, Megan Donaldson. You must be Q."

The woman grinned. "I wish. Just call me Elle."

"L? Is that a code name?"

"No. It's my name."

Megan ignored Dimitri's groan. "Do I get a poison dart pen and camera shoe?" She really hoped she did. So far being a gun-for-hire did not live up to the hype.

"Very *Man From Uncle*," Elle said. "I like. Unfortunately, you don't get any cool tech. We're totally standard ops here." She pointed at her laptop. "There's some wizardry on the programming, hacking side, but you won't get any gizmos from this department."

"Bummer," Megan said. "This gig isn't as much fun as I thought it would be."

"I know," Elle said with a pout.

Callum slammed his mug down on the table. Somebody really needed to teach the guy how to call a meeting to order without getting all grumpy. "We about ready to start?"

"Wait." A thought popped into Megan's head. She pointed at Elle. "If she's the tech liaison, what's the point of Rachel?"

"I've been wondering that for years," Elle mumbled.

"Rachel is division manager," Callum said as though that would put an end to the discussion. He had a lot to learn. "Before we get into it—Joe, what's the status on Durand? Our captive mentioned to Megan and Dimitri that he was still in Scotland."

Megan instantly dropped the issue of Rachel's purpose as worry for her twin took over. She'd been so occupied with stomach problems the night before that she'd had to trust Dimitri to get the word out about Claire. Obviously he had. She wanted to pat his head and tell him good boy. But she didn't.

"Grunt says there's no sign of him," Joe said, "but he's on the lookout. Lake too. They've got guys on Claire twenty-four seven. They managed to track him to a clinic outside Edinburgh where he demanded someone re-stitch the wound in his ass, where Megan shot him. Apparently he burst it open making a run for it."

Was it wrong that Megan felt all sorts of glee at that news? She didn't think so.

Joe looked at her. "He's gunning for you. He knows you aren't Claire and he's looking for payback."

Megan stiffened. "Did he tell Rudi that Claire is a twin?"

"As far as we can tell, Durand hasn't been in contact with Rudi since the Scotland screw up," Joe said.

Megan didn't know what to make of that and from the looks on the faces of her teammates, neither did they.

"Keep an eye on things," Callum told Joe. "Let us know the instant you hear something." Joe nodded as Callum pointed at Dimitri. "Fill everyone in on the status of your contact with Rudi."

"I called him last night on Johnny's phone. He was pissed

about losing his head of security for the house, but I promised to return him after the deal went through." Dimitri looked around the table. "I think Johnny's days working security will be over pretty fast if we hand him over."

"Good for Johnny that he's getting a holiday courtesy of Her Majesty then," Ryan said.

"Safer," Dimitri agreed, and Megan knew even Johnny Rotten would rather be locked up in prison than wearing cement shoes at the bottom of the Thames. "Anyway," Dimitri said. "Rudi's checking me out. Thanks to Elle, he'll only find what we want him to find. An ex-army guy turned private contractor, looking for a fast buck and crazy enough to kidnap Claire to get it."

Megan held up her hand. "Wait. Why is that a cover story? That's what you've done."

"Elle buried the parts we didn't want him to find. Parts like I'm working for Benson Security now. Parts like I have a sister called Katrina Raast. Elle gave me another last name, a different birthplace. Made sure the connection to Katrina was buried deep."

"Oh, okay." She felt a bit embarrassed at asking the question.

Dimitri gave her a heart-warming smile before turning his attention back to the group. "We have a tentative meet for Friday morning. At his house."

"That's two days from now." Megan thought she'd have more time to prepare. Now it was happening it seemed awfully fast. She looked at Dimitri, she'd only known the man two weeks and yet she was going into a situation where she had to trust him with her life. He stared back at her and it was as though he could read her mind.

"I won't let anything happen to you," he promised.

For once Megan didn't remind him she could take care of herself. "Is that enough time to set up cover?"

"We're all over it," Joe said. "We've been watching the house and grounds for days. Cover is under control."

The door opened and Julia appeared. She clasped her iPad to her chest like a shield and spoke to her feet.

"Rudi's wife is on the phone. She wants to talk to Joe." Her cheeks flushed red as she started to back out of the door.

"Take the call here," Callum ordered. "Put it on speaker."

Julia took the phone from the top of the cabinet against the wall and placed it in the middle of the table. She pressed the flashing button and nodded at Joe who gave her a dazzling smile.

Callum pointed at Julia and mouthed "stay". Her frown of disapproval at being ordered around like a dog disappeared quickly and she scurried to sit in her usual spot behind the huge plant.

"Hope? It's me Joe. We're in conference right now. I've got you on speaker with the team. Is that okay?" His voice was gentle, coaxing.

"Yes, yes, that's fine." The woman's American accent was mid-western.

"What can we do for you, Hope?" Joe leaned towards the phone.

"Um, I um remembered some stuff. I don't know how helpful it is, but I thought, you know, you said to call if I ever..."

"No. That's good. You did the right thing," Joe crooned. "What did you remember, honey?"

The room was deadly silent as they waited for her reply. People seemed scared to breathe, let alone move, in case they spooked the anxious woman.

"It was after a party in the house in Romania. I was pretty drunk. I spent a lot of my time drunk..." Her voice faded out, heavy with shame.

After everything she'd lived through, the last thing the

woman should feel was shame. Megan caught Joe's eye and saw he agreed.

"We understand," he said. "You did what you could to make it through. No one here is judging you, Hope."

There was a pause. She cleared her throat and they heard her take a shaky breath. "We were in our suite after the party and I had conked out on the bed. For some reason I woke in the middle of the night. I was thirsty and battling another hangover. I wanted water and some aspirin. I staggered out of the bedroom aiming for the kitchen area off our lounge. Rudi was at his desk. He was shocked to see me. I saw him unplug a tiny USB drive from the computer and put it on his finger. It was such an odd thing to do that it stuck with me."

Joe's smile was slow and wide as he looked over at Julia's hiding spot. "Give us that shot of Rudi again, babe. You know the one I mean."

Megan heard her tap at her iPad and the lights dimmed. Rudi appeared on the wall.

"What do you mean 'put it on his finger', Hope?" It was clear from his excitement that Joe already knew the answer.

Every eye in the room was on Rudi Abramovich's hands. More specifically, on the oversized gold insignia ring on his wedding finger.

"It was his ring. The one he always wore." Hope's voice echoed through the room. "I know it doesn't make much sense. But I saw it, Joe, I promise you. Somehow that ring connects to the computer."

The computer expert looked up from her laptop, straight at Joe. "You think it's a hidden flash drive."

Joe nodded. "I'm sure of it. It makes sense. Every source we've tapped said that Rudi doesn't have a dedicated computer that he takes with him wherever he goes. The information has to be moving around with him somehow. If he's carrying it in a hidden storage device, that would explain a lot."

Elle must have noted Megan's frown because she elaborated. "A flash drive is essentially a tiny storage device, or a thumb drive. The smallest one I've seen was tinier than a penny. It could definitely be hidden in a ring and it would have more than enough space for Rudi's business files."

"I may be blonde, but I know what a flash drive is, Elle," Megan said to the blue-haired tech. "I'm just wondering why the guy keeps his files in a ring. Doesn't anyone else think that is seriously dumb? What if he forgot to take it off when he showered? Or lost it down the garbage disposal?" She looked at Joe. "Are you sure you aren't just stretching here?"

Joe faced the speaker phone. "Hope, honey, tell us exactly what you saw."

They heard her suck in a breath. "When I staggered into the room, he snatched the ring from a USB port in the computer. I remember thinking it was weird that his ring was stuck to the computer. When he pulled it off, there was something sticking out of the ring. He pressed the centre of the ring, the insignia part, and the thing sticking out disappeared. He quickly slipped it on his finger and then he…he became angry about me being in the room…he…"

Yeah, they all knew what he did. She didn't have to say it. Every person sitting at that table had read through years' worth of medical reports, filed from a variety of different hospitals, listing broken bones, split lips and swollen eyes. Everyone knew exactly what Rudi did when he wasn't pleased with his wife.

"It's okay," Joe said. "We don't need to hear the rest. You did good, Hope. This is good information."

"You did great," Elle agreed. "We already knew Rudi kept a backup of his records in a secure information site that's off the grid in Switzerland. Now we know where his localised files are kept too. It makes everything so much easier." Elle was typing and talking at the same time. Her fingers flew across the keyboard.

"I didn't know about the Swiss thing," Megan said.

"Read the reports, Buffy, don't just look at the pictures."

Dimitri grinned when she gave him a death glare in response.

"Okay," Elle said, "then *most* of us knew his record archive was kept offline. Hence unhackable unless you're on-site. And let me tell you getting into the Swiss facility would be a bitch. That's why we were hoping he kept a copy on his personal computer. Now we know exactly where to look. This is good." Her eyes went wide. "Tell me, Hope, does Rudi call the ring his Precious by any chance?"

"Um…" Hope said.

"Never mind." Elle waved a hand as she muttered something about one ring to rule them all.

"This is insane," Megan said. "The guy keeps his business files in a ring. Seriously? Who the hell works like that?"

"Paranoid assholes who peddle in flesh," Joe said.

Megan's lips pursed. "Well, we need to get that ring."

"No? You think?" Ryan said, which made Megan lob her gasmask at his head.

"There's more," Hope said, bringing their attention back to the phone.

Everyone stilled.

"Go ahead, Hope," Joe said. "We're listening. Anything you can tell us will help."

The woman cleared her throat. "As I said, we were in the Romanian house that night. There'd been a party of some sort. I'd been told to dress up and impress. Rudi flew in fashion from Milan for the event and a makeup artist to make sure I looked my best. It was all about how I looked. He became very angry when he thought I wasn't perfect." She paused. "I got a bad feeling as soon as we went downstairs. The ballroom was crowded and I recognised some faces as being high up in European politics, not the kind of men who usually attended Rudi's parties—although it wasn't through his lack of trying to reel them in.

"Halfway through the evening a group of women I'd never seen before turned up. They were all decked out in couture, but looked like they weren't used to wearing clothes like that. They each had the same look in their eyes. Glassy. I realise now that they were drugged."

Megan felt Dimitri tense beside her and without thinking she placed her hand on his thigh. He relaxed slightly under her touch.

"The women didn't mingle," Hope was saying. "In fact there were a couple of guys, hired muscle, watching over them, guarding them. Rudi's personal henchman, Durand, was there close to the women. I hated that man almost as much as I hated my husband. Whenever Rudi wasn't looking he'd...touch me."

There was a pause. Megan met Dimitri's eyes. They'd known Durand was part of the organisation. They'd known Abramovich trusted the man. What they hadn't known was just how wrapped up in the whole thing he'd been. Now they knew and the answer wasn't comforting. Durand was in Abramovich's business neck-deep.

"Rudi liked Durand," Hope said. "He never believed me when I told him Durand took liberties." They heard her swallow hard. "I guess I should count myself lucky. I heard rumours, things he did to other women. H-he hurt them."

There was a heavy silence. Dimitri's thigh was stone under Megan's touch.

"You were telling us about that evening," Joe prompted. His gentle tone was at odds with the rage that had turned his face into a vicious mask.

Megan glanced around the room and noticed all of the men wore the same look. It was clear Durand's days were numbered. And that thought warmed Megan's heart no end. She hadn't been around the man for more than an hour, but it had been enough. He emanated evil. His eyes were shark flat and he got off on pain. Yeah, she could just imagine what he would do to any women he managed to get his hands on.

"As the evening went on," Hope said into the tense silence, "the VIP guests began to mingle with the women. They seemed to be choosing a companion from amongst them. Some of the men disappeared with the woman they'd singled out." They could hear the woman fidgeting with something as her voice began to shake. "I'd had too much to drink. I thought at the time they were call girls, brought in for the party."

"But now you don't think so," Joe gently prompted.

"No," Hope whispered.

"Tell us why, Hope." Joe stared at Dimitri as he spoke.

Megan had a very bad feeling about this. Very bad. She turned to Dimitri. The man had morphed into stone. He was staring at nothing and his muscles were tightly coiled as though ready to strike.

"It was the photos you sent me," Hope whispered. "I recognised two of the women."

Dimitri stopped breathing. Megan began to panic and tightened her grip on his thigh.

"Who did you recognise?" Joe said.

There was a pause before Hope's words hit Dimitri with more accuracy than a sniper's bullet.

"Amanda Freer and Katrina Raast."

# CHAPTER 9

Megan felt the tension build in Dimitri's body just before it exploded. He shot to his feet sending his chair flying behind him. His palms hit the table with a loud smack as he leaned towards the phone.

"Where is she? What happened to Katrina?" he shouted.

"Dimitri, calm down or leave the room." Callum's words cracked like a whip, cutting through Dimitri's rage.

Megan watched as Dimitri forced himself to take a deep breath.

"Hope, you still there?" Joe's tone was coaxing.

"Y-yes."

"Honey, you have to cut Dimitri some slack. Katrina Raast is his sister."

There was a gasp. "I'm so sorry, I'm so, so sorry." The woman was rushing towards hysteria.

Joe clenched the back of his neck, keeping an eye on Dimitri.

"It's not your fault, Hope. None of this is your fault," Joe soothed.

Dimitri's fingernails bit into the polished surface of the table.

"If I hadn't been drunk that night." Hope's words tumbled out in a rush, as though she was speaking to herself and had forgotten she was on the phone. "I shouldn't have drunk anything. If I'd been sober I would have known something was wrong. I would have been able to do something to help. Oh no, oh no, those women." The last words were a wail.

"You couldn't have done anything." Joe's voice was strong. Firm. "Dimitri knows that. He isn't blaming you. You did what you could to make it through your time there. Things weren't easy for you either. If you'd spoken out or interfered, Rudi would have killed you. Hell, he nearly did anyway."

"No, no. No you're wrong. I shouldn't have been drunk. I should have paid attention. I should have…"

"You should have nothing." Dimitri cut through her rant. His words were squeezed through clenched teeth as though he fought to get them out. "Joe is right. There was nothing you could have done. You were in the same position as all the other women. Your life was in Rudi's hands. I don't blame you, Hope. I blame the bastard who took my sister. I *don't* blame you."

Megan placed a hand on Dimitri's back, offering comfort, but he tensed then stepped out of her reach.

"See?" Joe ran a hand through his overgrown hair, making it stand on end. "No one blames you. Don't even think about feeling guilty. This is all on Abramovich. All of it."

There was a single, agonising sob from the other end of the line. Joe cast a panicked glance at Callum. Callum's lips were in a tight thin line. He nodded once at Joe before stepping towards the table.

"This is Callum McKay," he said in a calm, confident voice that instantly made Megan relax. She hoped it had the same effect on the woman at the other end of the line. "Joe told you I'm in charge around here, didn't he?"

There was silence, interspersed by tiny muffled sobs.

"Hope." It was a snapped command. "Listen to me now."

"Yes." Her voice trembled, but she seemed to calm.

"Good. Now here's the thing. You couldn't have done anything to save those women a year ago, but the information you're giving us now will help us to find them and stop other women from being harmed. Do you hear me? Do you understand what I'm saying?"

"Yes." It was hesitant, but it wasn't hysterical.

"Then believe me when I say that what you can tell us is invaluable. Focus on that. Not on the past. We can't do anything to change the past, but we can change the future—with your help. And we need your help, Hope. Are you willing to give that to us right now?"

"Yes, yes, I want to help. What can I do?" She sniffed, but the panic had fled her voice.

Joe visibly relaxed. He nodded at Callum then took over the conversation again. Callum stepped back to his spot at the whiteboard.

"That's good, honey," Joe said. "Real good. We need you to tell us everything you remember about the night you saw the women. Especially anything you remember relating to Katrina. Can you do that for us?"

"I was so drunk, Joe. I'm not sure what help I'll be."

"Anything at all is good. No matter how insignificant it may seem. Just try to relax and focus on that night. Can you remember which man chose Katrina?"

Dimitri shut his eyes. His hands turned to fists on the table. His knuckles were white. Megan's hand twitched to touch him again. The silence in the room was thick, making it difficult to breathe.

"She had on a yellow dress." Hope sounded hesitant, as

though she was feeling her way through the memory. "I remember thinking that I recognised the dress—I'd seen it on a runway in Paris. She stood closer to the door than the other women and seemed to sway on her feet. At least, I think she was the one swaying. It could have been me." She took a deep breath. "I remember Rudi being mad at me for being so drunk. He took my champagne glass out of my hand and ordered me to my room. I headed for the door nearest the women. As I made my way across the room, a man approached Katrina and took her arm. He said something to her. I was too far away to hear what it was, but she didn't react. He handed her off to his bodyguards and they took her from the room. The man watched her until she disappeared. I remember she staggered and I thought she was as drunk as I felt."

"Can you name the man?" Joe said. "Had you seen him before then?"

"He wasn't a politician, he was a businessman, based in Dubai, I think. I'm pretty sure he was French. Yes, he definitely spoke French. I remember meeting him at lunch one day, at the club, and thinking that the French accent wasn't sexy on some men."

Callum nodded at Elle who began typing furiously at her laptop.

"Think hard," Joe said. "Can you give us a name? A business? Tell us what he looked like? Anything at all, no matter how small or insignificant."

"He was fit. Obviously worked out. Middle aged, I think. There was grey at his temples." She paused then let out a gush of air. "I can't remember a name. I'm sorry, that's all I can remember about him. There was nothing remarkable. Nothing that stood out."

"Okay." Joe ran a hand over his face. "Can you remember

what happened after Katrina was taken from the room. What did the man do then?"

"Yes, I remember this, because I stumbled and Durand caught me before I fell. He held me a little too long and I looked over to see if my husband noticed. Rudi had his head together with the Frenchman, whispering. Then they shook hands and Rudi patted him on the back. He was grinning widely, the way he did when things went well for him. After the man strode away, I thought I saw Rudi put something in his pocket. At that point he noticed me and ordered his men to escort me to our suite. I didn't see the Frenchman after that."

Callum looked over to Elle, who shook her head. There wasn't enough information for her to search.

"That's it, Joe," Hope said. "That's all I remember right now. I'm sorry it isn't more."

"Don't be, honey. You did good," Joe said, but his eyes were on Dimitri's tension-filled body. "We really appreciate it. If you remember anything else, call us, no matter what time it is. Okay?"

"Yes." The woman sounded tired. Worn out.

"And Hope?" Callum stepped towards the phone. "Call a friend to stay with you. You are not to feel guilty about any of the decisions you made while with Abramovich. Make sure your friend keeps you occupied. Get your mind off this for a while. Understood?" It was a series of orders barked out by a commander to his subordinate.

"Understood." There was a smile in her voice.

"Okay then." Callum reached across the table and pressed the button to end the call.

The room was silent. Nobody moved. Nobody spoke. All eyes were on Dimitri. Slowly, he opened his eyes, uncurled from his position and flexed his hands. He reached behind him for his fallen chair. Megan thought he intended to straighten it. She jerked in her seat when he threw it at the wall, smashing it to pieces. Then without a word, he strode from the room.

"Poor sod," Ryan said as they watched Dimitri leave.

"Joe," Callum said. "Go after him. Keep an eye on him."

"I'll do it." Megan stood. The guys looked sceptical. "Chill, guys. I can be sensitive."

She ignored the looks of patent disbelief and went in search of Dimitri.

She found him in one of the unfinished offices on the second floor. The room was dark and he'd slid down the wall to sit on the floor beside the window. She paused as she watched him. His hands were clasped behind his head and his eyes were closed. Every muscle in his body radiated tension. There may as well have been a neon sign above his head with the words "back off" on it.

Megan had never been one to pay attention to signs. Without a word she crossed the room and slid down the wall to sit beside him. She brought her knees up to her chest and cuddled them to her body. Dimitri didn't acknowledge her presence in any way, and that was fine. Megan was content to sit beside him and offer her silent support while he worked out his inner turmoil alone. She stared out into the cloud-covered sky as she listened to the rain fight with the traffic noise on the street below. It was strangely peaceful. A temporary cocoon against the horrors that pressed in on them.

"I wish she could have given us a name." Dimitri sounded hoarse, as though he'd been crying when she knew he hadn't.

There was nothing she could say. They all wished they'd been given a lead to follow. Instead, all they'd been given was the horrid confirmation that Katrina had indeed been sold into slavery. Megan's stomach roiled just thinking those words.

"She never even had a boyfriend." Dimitri's eyes were on the dull sky. "Not someone serious anyway. She joined that purity for marriage group. She told me she was saving herself for her wedding night. And I told her, there are some topics a brother didn't want to discuss with his sister. Right at the top of the list is her sex life." His fingers dug into the back of his neck. "She started a blog about it. She said it was important to get different voices out there, for people to know that all sorts of choices were normal."

He fell silent. He didn't need to say anything else. The dreadfulness of it wasn't lost on Megan. His sister's first sexual experience hadn't been on her wedding night. It hadn't even been at the hands of someone who loved her. It was just one of the many things stolen from her, along with her freedom.

"She won't be the same." It was a tight declaration, filled with agony that made Megan want to pour herself out in an attempt to soothe him. "Even if we manage to get her back. She won't be the same. You can't live through something like this and not change. She was always so freaking hopeful, naive even. That will be gone now."

Megan leaned her head against his shoulder and stayed silent. There was nothing she could even think to say that would lessen his burden. There were no reassuring words, no promises, that would help. All she could do was use her presence to let him know she shared his pain.

After a long moment, Dimitri shifted. He wrapped an arm around her and pulled her tight to his side. Together they watched the rain fall down on London.

# CHAPTER 10

Megan didn't know how long she'd spent sitting with Dimitri, but by the time Joe came to get him for a meeting with Callum, night had fallen. Something subtle had shifted between them in the hours they'd sat in silence. Megan was very aware of the dull throb of pain Dimitri carried around with him every minute of every day. It was a pain that spoke to the heart of her and connected them in ways she couldn't understand. It also made her long for her own sister.

Once the men had disappeared into Callum's office, Megan headed up to her flat. She grabbed a bagel from their tiny kitchen and made herself a mug of steaming hot tea. The corridor outside her flat led out onto a metal fire escape, the top of which was a mesh platform. It was a poor man's balcony, affording her a view over the rooftops towards Big Ben. Not that she could see the famous clock through the buildings, but it was enough to know it was there.

She sat on the kitchen chair she'd dragged outside while the kettle boiled and dialled her sister. The rain had stopped hours ago, but the sky was still heavy and the air sharp. She shivered in her yoga pants and padded jacket.

"Twin Two!" Claire's voice in her ear made Megan simultaneously grin and tear up.

"Don't tell me you're using Joe's stupid nicknames now."

"I kind of like them." Megan could hear the grin in her sister's voice. "It makes me think of Dr Seuss. You know, Thing One and Thing Two."

"I know." Megan had been trying to get Claire to upgrade her pop culture references to something an adult would use, but the kindy teacher could not be taught. "How are you? How's my niece?"

"You idiot. It's too early to tell the sex of the baby." Claire's voice softened with wonder.

"Son!" came the shout from the background.

"I hope the caveman you married gets twin girls." Megan knew her grin was evil.

Unfortunately, Claire couldn't see it. "Oh that would be so cool," was her enthusiastic response.

"Yes, it would." Megan knew she would make an awesome aunt. Plus they knew how to be twins. Think of all the advice they could pass along to younger girls. It would be invaluable to them.

"What's up?" Claire said. "I can hear it in your voice."

Megan closed her eyes and rested her head back against the cool stone wall. Damn, but she missed her twin. They might not have the psychic connection they'd dreamed of having as kids, but no one knew her—no one understood her —like Claire.

"We're meeting Rudi on Friday, I kissed Dimitri and I don't think Benson Security is going to keep me on when this job is over." Her worries came out in a gush and she felt much better. She looked out over the rows of roofs identical to the one behind her. A conclave of Regency homes turned into offices and flats.

"Wow."

"That's it? That's all you have to say? I need more." She bit into the bagel.

"Okay, we'll deal with the mundane first and work our way up to juicy. Rudi first. My advice is don't get yourself killed."

"Helpful." It was interesting what her twin thought was mundane.

"I try. As for keeping you on, of course they will. You're a natural at this security stuff. Look how you handled the situation at the castle. You're an asset to any team."

"I appreciate your support, but we both know I'm a liability." Something she would only admit to her sister. She took a deep breath and filled her sister in on the events from the night before—sparing no detail of her gastronomic disaster. There was silence, then deep, very male laughter. "Claire! Do you have me on speaker phone?"

"Sorry," came the contrite reply. "I'm knitting a baby blanket and wanted to work while I talked."

Great, now her brother-in-law knew what a screw up she was. She heard more laughing, Claire ordering Grunt to leave the room and a door slamming shut.

"Sorry about that," Claire said. "Next time give me a heads up that we're talking about something that needs privacy."

"I don't suppose it matters." Megan sipped her tea. "Joe will fill Grunt in next time they talk anyway."

There was a giggle. "Did you really fart on the bad guy?"

Megan groaned. "It was humiliating. I didn't think it was possible to feel mortified, furious and terrified all at the same time. All I could think about was getting the gun out of my face and getting home to my toilet. I'm never going to live this down, am I?"

"Probably not. But look, you also proved you are capable. You disarmed the guy. Don't sell yourself short. You can do this job. You just need time to settle in."

This was why she missed her sister so badly. No one on the planet had her back like Claire did. "I don't know. There are literally millions of ex-service men and women out there. All of them way more suited to being a gun-for-hire than I am. I might as well face the fact that once my usefulness is over, I'll be back on the plane home." A car honked in the street beside her and she became aware of the constant white noise of London. "I really don't want to lose this job, Claire. For the first time in my life I feel like I fit. Like I've found what I'm supposed to be doing."

Although they were identical in appearance, Megan was very different to Claire in other ways. Claire had everything she'd ever wanted out of life. She had the career of her dreams as a local kindergarten teacher. She had a Neanderthal who adored her and kissed the ground she walked on and she had a baby on the way. Home, family, that's what Claire had dreamed of her whole life. And Megan would be the first to make sure her sister's perfect life was never damaged. Claire deserved to have everything she dreamed of. But Megan was different, she'd never known what she wanted out of life. She'd tried lots of different careers and none of them fit. There was always a restlessness inside her, driving her to find something, and until she signed up to be part of Benson Security she'd never felt at peace. Now she did. She was where she was meant to be. And she was worried she was the only person who saw it.

"Maybe I should go get some experience?" A few years wasn't so long to wait to become a proper part of the team. She could do a few years. "I could join the army, or the police."

"You'd hate the uniforms. Polyester." Claire made a shuddering sound. "Not to mention the early mornings. And the taking orders. You're rubbish at taking orders..."

"Okay. I get it. You can stop now."

"Look, just prove to be indispensable and everything will be fine. You can do it. I believe in you." And she did. Megan heard it in every single word that came out of her sister's mouth.

"I miss you, sis." She blinked back tears.

"Me too!" Claire's hormones got the better of her and she started to sob.

There was a shuffling noise, then Grunt came on the line. "Don't make her cry," was the order, before the phone was handed back to Claire.

"He's very protective," Claire explained unnecessarily.

"Yep, in a totally insane, I-own-you sort of way."

As usual, Claire thought the criticism was funny.

"As for the important part of your confession." Claire lowered her voice. "So you kissed Dimitri. What was it like?"

"Claire!" came the roar from her husband.

"Oh baby," Claire said away from the phone. "You don't need to get jealous. You know the only man I see is you."

"I think I'm going to puke," Megan said.

"I'm back. He's gone to make me some hot chocolate. Now, spill. How was it?" The sound of Claire settling in for some gossip, and her delight in sharing it, made Megan ache for home. This was the longest she'd ever been away from her twin and it still didn't feel natural.

"It was hot," Megan confessed. "We were arguing. He was doing that arrogant 'I know everything' thing he does. And I got so mad with him that all I wanted to do was show him he wasn't in control of everything."

"So you kissed him?"

"It seemed like a really good idea at the time." To be honest, it still seemed like a really good idea. "The man can kiss. He does this thing with his tongue..."

"No!" Grunt roared. "Claire doesn't need to know about

other men's tongues. Why can't the two of you talk about something normal? Like football?"

"Claire! Speaker again?!"

"Sorry. Knitting." There was a click and she was back off speaker phone. "We're private again."

"Are you going to go off and knit again?" Seriously, if she was in Invertary she'd smack her twin upside her head. Pregnant or not.

"I'll resist the lure of the wool," Claire promised, sounding like one of the retired women from the town's knitting club.

Megan shook her head. Her twin was a mystery sometimes. "I can't kiss him again," she said, more to herself than to her sister. "It complicated things. He's hurting over his sister and he needs to focus on the mission. We both need to focus on the mission. It was a dumb thing to do." Because now she'd had a taste of him, she wasn't sure she could resist another one.

"Or," her evil half said, "you could just burn up the sheets and get it out of your system."

"You are not a good influence on me." Megan smiled at the joke. Neither one of them had ever been known for their good behaviour.

"That's why you love me," Claire sang and Megan laughed away some of the tension that had been building throughout the day.

"If you kiss a woman and she tells you it's nice," Dimitri said to Joe as they sat in Callum's office. "It's a bad thing, right?"

"Who'd you kiss?" Joe had his ankles crossed and his feet propped on the edge of Callum's desk.

"Who do you think?" With a question like that, Dimitri was seriously rethinking asking Joe for advice.

"Twin Two." Joe grinned. "You're nuts, you realise that. The woman is certifiable."

Callum smacked his pen down on his desk. "This is exactly why I didn't want to be part of this business. I saw Lake and his guys sitting around in Scotland, gossiping like a bunch of women and knew it was contagious. What's next? Installing a day spa in the basement?"

Joe laughed at the man. "Haven't you ever talked about women?"

"Never." Callum frowned at them.

Joe pointed at him. "Maybe that's why you're still single. Maybe if you'd shared some tips with the guys you'd have been able to keep hold of a woman."

Callum looked outraged. "You two are single. Why the hell would I take advice from you?"

"Hey." Joe held up his hands. "I'm in my early thirties, you're hitting forty. That's midlife. I've got plenty of time to settle down. You wait much longer and you'll be past it."

For a minute it looked like Callum might punch something, possibly Joe.

"About the kiss." Dimitri needed input. The woman was in his head every minute of every day and he was losing his mind over it. Nothing she did made sense. Nothing.

"Nice means you're crap," Callum snapped. "End of discussion. Now how about we plan this meeting with Abramovich? Or do you two need to go pull on your big girl panties to help you focus?"

Dimitri glared at the man, while Joe shot him a far more obvious hand gesture.

"Now," Callum said as he stood and pointed at the blown up aerial photo of Rudi's house. "I think we need to position a sniper here, and here."

"Who you thinking?" Joe said.

"Me and Ryan. The kid's got the best record for long

range shots and you can run faster than I can." Callum wasn't embarrassed by his change in skill set since his legs were replaced with prosthetics. The man knew how to assess his strengths and weaknesses and play to them. And no one who looked at the guy would think he was anything less than deadly.

"I need to be close," Joe said. "In case I have to get in fast. Parking in that street will be a problem. There are no public spots and as soon as a car sits there for any length of time, security from one of the houses checks them out. We need to look into parking in one of the drives close by."

Callum made a note on the paper in front of him. "I'll make some calls."

"Can we get Elle to tap into their security feed, give us eyes inside the gates?" Dimitri said.

Callum made another note. Joe ran a hand through his overgrown hair. "We really need more guys. A job like this, you need bodies covering the exits."

"We're working on it," Callum said. "Most of the guys Lake has in Scotland are out on jobs. We're interviewing to fill up this office."

"Yeah, but they won't be here in time for this op," Joe said.

There was silence. The team was set as is. Dimitri glanced at Joe as Callum studied the aerial photo some more.

"She said I'm perfectly adequate," Dimitri said. "That isn't good, right?"

Joe burst out laughing, while Callum groaned.

"What?" Dimitri demanded. "If your technique was called perfectly adequate, it'd be stuck in your head too."

"Bloody hell." Callum folded his arms over yet another grey-coloured Henley. "Get your mind on the job. Stop screwing around with Megan. It's distracting you. Do I really need to tell you how important this is? If you want to do something useful with the woman, train her. She needs firearms training for a start."

"Guns?" Joe looked at Callum like he was mad. "You *want* to put a firearm in her hand?"

"I don't want to," Callum snapped. "But if she's holding one I'd rather she shot the enemy than me. Right now I wouldn't trust her with a Taser. No, scrap that, I wouldn't trust her with a water pistol." He glared at Dimitri. "Now stop acting like a teenage girl and get your head in the game."

"You're right." Dimitri shook his arms, working the tension out of his body. "Okay. I'm ready. No more Megan talk."

"About bloody time." Callum turned back to the map.

Joe nudged Dimitri and when he turned the guy passed him a piece of paper. When he opened it there was a note:

*Perfectly adequate is seriously bad dude. You need to get yourself some skills.*

And just like that, his mind was back on Megan.

# CHAPTER 11

Dimitri took Callum's words seriously. That's why he found himself outside Megan's apartment door at five o'clock the next morning—he'd set up some training. As he knocked on the door, he admitted it was probably a little early to get started, but he'd spent the night tossing and turning, frustrated that things weren't moving fast enough with the case. And what better way to work out his frustration than with Megan.

He paused. He needed to rephrase that. The images going through his head had nothing to do with combat training and a whole lot to do with the two of them in one bed. Limbs entwined. Glistening skin. Desperate moans. He broke out in a sweat at the thought. Maybe hanging out alone with Megan wasn't such a great idea after all. He was just about to abandon his plan, in favour of a cold shower, when the door opened. He wasn't really surprised to find Julia, rather than Megan, frowning at him.

"It's five in the morning," Julia said by way of hello.

Dimitri knew she wasn't quite awake because she looked him in the eye when she spoke to him.

"You're always first in the office. You get up early, what's the big deal?" He walked past her and into the tiny hallway.

"I don't get up this early," Julia grumbled as she shut the door. "Why are you here?"

"I've got a training session with Megan."

Her mouth gaped. "At five in the morning? You must have a death wish."

Dimitri ignored her. He knew what he was doing. Mostly. "Where's her room?"

Julia let out a long huff of air and pointed down the hall. "Last door on the right. I need a cup of tea."

She pulled her thick brown terry robe around her and headed off to what Dimitri assumed was the kitchen, grumbling under her breath as she went. Dimitri shook his head as he watched her go, wondering if the woman owned any clothes that weren't brown. He sauntered down the hall, taking note of every detail of his environment as a matter of habit. Dimitri knew the apartment was one of two on the top floor of the building. Back in the day, this floor would have been the servant's accommodation. Which explained the low ceilings, tiny rooms and narrow hallways. With its cream coloured walls and grey carpet the place screamed generic rental property, which is what the whole building had been before Benson Security bought it.

Without hesitating, Dimitri knocked at Megan's door. There was silence. He banged the door with his fist and called out, "Yo, Buffy, time to train." Nothing. "Megan," he shouted. There was a mumble from inside the room. It sounded a lot like, "Go to hell." Then there was silence.

Guess she wasn't a morning person. With a shrug, Dimitri turned the handle and let himself into Megan's room.

The curtains were shut and the room was dark, but the light coming in from the hallway meant he could see inside the room. Under the tiny window was a double bed. Wedged into the rest of the floor space was a desk and chair, an old armchair, a set of drawers and a rickety old wardrobe. Benson Security needed to take better care of its staff. Although, to be fair, they'd put him up in a nice hotel nearby so he couldn't complain. He wondered why Megan was living here instead of the hotel and made a mental note to ask her later.

He reached for the light switch beside the door and flicked it on. Nothing happened. He looked up and saw the lightbulb had been removed. Huh. With one generous step he was over at the desk and flicked on the pink sparkly lamp. The lump in the middle of the bed mumbled something before blonde hair disappeared under the pillow.

With a grin, he picked up one of the books piled high on the desk. What the hell? His eyebrows shot up at the title: *How to be a bodyguard—personal security, the idiot's guide.* He shuffled through the rest. *Beginners guide to firearms, The dummies' book of spying, Cold War Spy Craft* and *How to make it as a mercenary.*

Dimitri stared at the books dumbfounded. He was actually pretty glad Megan was out cold, because he was speechless. With absolutely no guilt about snooping, he switched on the open laptop to see what else the crazy woman had been doing with her spare time. Sure enough, she had bookmarks to all sorts of YouTube channels. He followed the link to the first one, where a guy in costume store fatigues was explaining what it was like to be a mercenary. Dimitri shook his head. If this guy was private security, Dimitri was Queen of England.

"Buffy, you are filling your head with a serious amount of crap," he told the sleeping lump.

It whined, but didn't move. Enough of this. It was time to get his *partner* on the straight and narrow. The whole mission depended on her pulling this off. Finding his sister depended on her. It was past time to get serious. With one quick move, he grabbed a handful of her bedding and yanked.

She screamed as he tossed the bedding to the floor. Megan was sprawled on her stomach in the middle of the bed. She wore cute pink cut-off shorts and a matching pink tank.

"What the hell?" Megan shouted from under the pillow. "Put the bedding back. My bum is freezing."

"And what a gorgeous ass it is." Dimitri grinned at her grunt of annoyance, but noted she still hadn't moved. "Enough screwing around. It's time to get up. You have training." He folded his arms and worked on looking intimidating —if for no other reason than to get his eyes off her ass.

"Joe?"

Now that rankled.

"Not Joe. Dimitri. Rise and shine, Buffy. It's time to play with the big boys."

She peeked out from under the pillow. Her cheeks were pink, her eyes were dazed with sleep and she had a serious case of bed head. The sight made Dimitri stop breathing. She was stunning.

"Dimitri? What are you doing here?" She looked around as though she'd only just figured out she was in bed and he was in her room. "Why are you in my room? Where's my bedding? Can't you knock?"

Yeah, she was waking up alright.

"I did knock. You sleep like the dead. Now get up. Get dressed. We've got work to do."

Her eyes found the clock on the shelf beside her bed. He spotted the second the time registered, as every muscle in her body went tense.

"It's five o'clock!" It was a screech. "In the morning!"

"I'm partnered with Einstein," Dimitri muttered.

"Oh, hell, no." Megan scrambled up onto her hands and knees and crawled across the bed towards him.

The sight made all the blood in Dimitri's body rush south and for a second he thought he actually saw stars. She was perfect. All curves and lean limbs. All smooth, smooth skin and lushly swaying hips. His hands tingled with the need to touch her. His mouth watered at the sight of her coming towards him and thought fled. Suddenly, he couldn't remember why he was there and he really didn't care. His little brain had taken over. And his little brain didn't want to train. Nope. It didn't want Megan out of bed. Bed is exactly where his little brain wanted to keep the woman. Possibly for eternity.

He shook his head as she reached over the edge of the bed, grasped the bedding on the floor and yanked it back up onto the bed. With an adorable scowl, she wrapped herself in it like the filling in a burrito. Then with a sigh, she burrowed down, closed her eyes and went back to sleep.

What the hell?

The way she was wrapped up tight in the bedding made it impossible to snatch it away from her again. He thought about fetching a glass of water to chuck at her head. Then he had a better idea. With a wicked grin he bent, picked up the tightly wrapped woman and slung her over his shoulder.

"What are you doing? Put me down, right now!"

She wriggled and shifted, but she couldn't fight back—her arms were wrapped up tight in her blankets.

"I told you to get up, Buff. One way or another you're waking up and we're gonna train."

"Let go of me. I mean it. You are going to regret this. Put me back in bed right now. Are you listening to me? This is your last warning."

Dimitri ignored her as he set off down the hallway,

pushing at doors to see which one held the bathroom. Ah, there it was. He caught sight of movement out of the corner of his eye and looked over to find Julia staring at them.

"Got any coffee, Julia?"

She nodded, her mouth hanging open.

"Great, I'll grab a cup while Megan takes a shower."

He knew his grin was evil. He felt it. And he didn't care. With a wink to Julia, he stepped into the tiny bathroom—all the while ignoring Megan's litany of orders and curses.

The showerhead was above the bath. Perfect. He turned the water on to cold and then dumped the writhing bundle into the bath under the spray.

There was thrashing, swearing and screaming as Megan struggled to get free. At last, soaked, she stood on her sodden bedding and turned off the water. Her hair was plastered to her face and her clothing had turned into a second skin. One look at her lush breasts told him the water had indeed been very cold.

"I am going to kill you," she snapped at him. "Dead. Stone cold dead." She pointed at him. "If you don't have a will, write one now. You're going to need it."

With a laugh, Dimitri turned his back and headed for coffee. Just before he closed the door, a bar of soap flew past his head.

"Ten minutes," he shouted at her. "Then I'm coming in to get you."

"Was that really necessary?" Julia asked as he walked into the kitchen.

She was dressed for the day in a shapeless navy dress that came to her ankles. He'd been wrong, she did own other colours. Her honey coloured hair was tied tight in a bun at the back of her head and her wide rimmed glasses were perched on her nose. She looked like a cute little owl librarian.

"Nope." He reached for the coffee pot. "It's wasn't necessary, but it sure was fun."

He really hoped Megan found the shower to be *perfectly adequate* because in ten minutes time they were heading out —whether she was ready or not. He watched Julia shake her head as she walked out of the apartment. Dimitri sipped his coffee as he kept an eye on the hallway leading to the bathroom. He wouldn't put it past the woman to try to sneak back into bed—with or without her bedding.

"THIS WOULD BE SO MUCH EASIER if you'd back off," Megan grumbled.

They'd been in the shooting range for hours and so far she'd only hit the target once. It was humiliating. Not as humiliating as stomach problems during an operation, which was now her gold standard for all things humiliating, but this experience still rated. She probably would have done better if she'd been allowed to shoot more. Instead she'd had to sit through the world's most mind-numbing safety talk—apparently she shouldn't gesture with a gun while she was talking. Like she couldn't figure that out for herself. Men. Now the same idiot man was crowding her space and it was messing with her concentration. It wasn't fair. In a real gun battle she wouldn't have Dimitri plastered to her back. If she didn't have him there now, she was sure she'd do a whole lot better.

"I would back off if you'd get your grip right." He wrapped his arms around her to cover her hands where she held the gun at arm's length. The feeling of his body wrapped around hers was beyond distracting.

She tried to shrug him off, but he was immovable. "Can't you just tell me what to do? Do you need to stand so close?"

"This is better," he said against her ear, making her shiver. A reaction she, unfortunately, couldn't hide.

"Better for who?" she grumbled.

His hands engulfed hers as he moved their position. "Like this."

She couldn't decide what was getting to her more, his scent or the sensation of his muscles moving as he pressed against her back. Scent, she decided. She wanted to breathe it in deep, immerse herself in it and rub up against him like a kitten.

"You're sighting too low." His words made her eyes snap open. Honestly, if Claire could see her now, her sister would laugh until she toppled over.

"I'm serious," she said. "You need to back off and let me get on with it."

"When you're ready. Keep your elbows loose and raise the nose of the gun." He physically moved her into position. All she heard was blah blah blah blah as the feeling of his strong hands on her body short-circuited her brain.

"Yeah, like that," he rumbled. "That way you're more likely to hit the greatest mass of your target."

She snapped her head around to look at him. He was driving her crazy. He needed to back off and take his sexy smell along with him. And what was with the terms he was using anyway? When something was a spade, you called it a spade. Damn it. "You mean body. Why don't you just say body?"

"Because the thought of you pointing a gun at anyone again makes me break out in hives."

She scowled at him. It was very tempting to swing round and point the gun at *his* greatest mass until he apologised for being a dickhead.

"Don't even think about it. Do I need to go over the safety talk again?"

And that was another thing that drove her nuts, his mind reading trick. It wasn't impressive. It was just plain irritating.

Along with his shirt. What was with that T-shirt? It was at least two sizes too small. He wasn't Captain Freaking America. There was no need to flaunt his pecs to the world. Indecent. That's what it was.

"Remember what I told you," he said. "Don't jerk the trigger, ease it softly."

He stepped back from her so she could shoot and her body felt instantly cold. Already she missed his arms around her and it irritated the hell out of her. Her body was confused. It didn't know whether it wanted to kick the man for driving her mental, or kiss him until he took off his annoying shirt and let her loose at his pecs.

Pheromones! That's what it was. Now it made sense. He was oozing pheromones. Essentially, he was drugging her. No wonder she couldn't think straight.

"Are you going to shoot anytime soon?" he drawled.

She glared at him. As she faced the target, her shoulders became solid and her arms stiffened. The gun jerked upwards and she missed it entirely.

"So much for keeping those muscles loose," he mumbled.

Megan spun on him. "I hate this."

"Maybe you should stick to the Taser?" he suggested for the millionth time.

If he mentioned that Taser one more time, she was going to get the thing and zap him until he cried uncle.

"Just because I hate training doesn't mean I won't eventually get there. It takes practice. Distraction free practice. Why don't you run along and play with the other boys while I work on this?"

He shook his head. "Good try, but someone needs to keep an eye on you."

"Have it your way." She turned back to the target, fury building inside her like a fireball. "How about you put your damn pecs away and let me focus? Huh? You want to be helpful, dress in clothes your size."

She didn't take time to perfect her stance, instead she fired angry. Several shots barked out in succession as she cursed the man under her breath.

"Enough." Dimitri's hand covered her wrist. "This is no way to improve. We'll try again once you calm down."

"Telling a woman to calm down is a sure way to get her to aim the gun at your head."

He cocked an eyebrow at her. Then he turned to the target and stopped dead. Megan peeked around him to see what had his attention and felt a slow grin break out. All six shots had hit the dead centre of the paper target. The look on Dimitri's face was priceless. It almost made breathing in his pheromones for hours on end, worth it. And now, she needed to get out of there—before she did something she regretted. Like peeling off his T-shirt and biting into his pecs. She shook off the image. Definitely time to go.

"I'm done here." She placed the gun on the shelf beside her and took out her ear plugs. "I don't need training. I just need to be mad to hit the target." She put her protective glasses beside the gun. "Next time, just piss me off before you hand me a weapon. It will save time. It shouldn't take too much to do it. All you need to do is open your mouth and let your brain run free."

She left him gaping after her as she strode for the door.

"Hey, we're not done here," Dimitri shouted after her.

"Oh, we so are," she shouted back.

"That was a lucky shot," he shouted, undeterred. "You need to be able to replicate it under stress."

He thought she wasn't under stress? The man was an idiot. Honestly. He rubs all over her for hours on end, drugging her with his scent and then dismisses it? Oh, that was not on. She stormed back into the room to give him a piece of her mind on the matter.

Dimitri was reaching for her gun when she strode into the room. He caught sight of her and his eyes darkened. In that second, with that one look, the anger inside Megan switched to something far darker. Something she couldn't stop and wasn't sure she'd want to anyway.

She caught him off guard when she pushed him back against the wall. Without a word, she twisted her hand into his too-tight shirt and pulled his face down to meet hers. Her kiss was punishing. More like an attack than a tease. Dimitri groaned into her mouth. He wrapped his arms around her and she was engulfed in his scent. The same blend of woodland forest and pure Dimitri that was driving her insane not ten minutes ago, now made her delirious with need. She couldn't breathe him in deeply enough. She couldn't get close enough. His taste was ambrosia on her tongue. Addicting. He was addicting.

"More." She grunted the word against his mouth.

His reply was a feral growl. He turned them. Her back hit the wall, making it shudder.

"Up," he demanded.

Megan felt his grip on her ribcage as he lifted her. Her legs wrapped around his waist. She grabbed handfuls of hair and angled his mouth where she needed it to be. His fingertips dug into her backside as he pulled her closer. She felt his hard length rub against her crotch and moaned. Perfect. He was perfect.

Her tongue duelled with his. Because that was what this was, a fight. A sparring match between opponents. Each wanting dominance. Megan bit his bottom lip before sucking it into her mouth to soothe the pain. Somewhere inside her, on a primal level, she wanted to mark him. She wanted to leave evidence that he was hers. She was an idiot, wanting to tag her name on a building that didn't belong to her. She shook off the thoughts as she fisted her hands in the bottom of his offensive shirt.

"Off." She tugged.

He pressed her against the wall with his hips as he fisted his hand in the neck of his T-shirt and yanked it over his head. Oh, yes. Her eyes ran over every perfect dip and curve before her. He was an all-you-can-eat buffet for her senses. She closed the distance between them and licked a line across his pecs.

"Megan," he groaned.

Salty, tangy, Dimitri. She nipped at his shoulder, before nuzzling her nose into the crook of his neck and breathing him deep. Heady. It was heady. She was spinning out of control and she didn't care. Her hands ran over his chest to his stomach, memorising every curve. His skin burned under her touch. She wanted to wrap herself in the heat and stay there forever.

"Babe, if we don't stop, I'm going to take you up against this wall. Are you sure you want that?" Dimitri's voice was a rumble that vibrated through her.

She closed her eyes for a second, revelling in the sensation. It took a minute for his words to penetrate. Megan's eyelids flickered, like she was coming out of a daze. The gun range came into focus. The fact her legs were wrapped around a half-naked Dimitri and his hands were inside the back of her yoga pants registered.

"Megan?"

She looked up into his dark chocolate eyes and all but melted. Gorgeous. She licked her lips as she stared at his mouth. His lips were red and swollen. She smiled in satisfaction.

"You're killing me here, babe."

She tore her eyes from his lips. "We probably shouldn't, huh?" Her voice was hoarse.

His forehead touched hers as he groaned. "You're killing me."

Thought replaced sensation as her brain rebooted. No, this wasn't the place for this. Or the time. Probably. She pushed at his chest and he got the message. He gently lowered her to the ground, keeping his hands on her hips to steady her. His perfect chest filled her vision and she had to fight the urge to sink her teeth into him.

"Not the right place," she said instead.

"The guys have a session booked here after lunch."

She glanced at the clock high on the wall. Soon. That was soon. She hadn't even thought about food, mainly because she was dealing with a very different sort of hunger.

"Wrong time," she said.

He sighed and pressed a kiss to her forehead. "Later. When this is over."

His words made her long, which in turn made her feel vulnerable, which led to irritation. It was the irritation that made her push Dimitri back.

"What makes you think you'll get another chance at me?"

He gave her a cocky grin. "Well, I'm not an expert or anything, but I figured this meant you liked my particular brand of *perfectly adequate.*"

Men. Idiots. All of them.

She pushed past him and strode to the door. "This boat has sailed, Dementor."

"Yeah," he called after her, and she could hear the laughter in his voice. "You keep telling yourself that, Buffy."

She stomped up the stairs to the sound of him chuckling behind her.

# CHAPTER 12

"Benson Security, how may I help you?" Julia made an effort to sound confident and professional although she hated talking to strangers on the phone. Or generally. At least it was a whole lot better than in person.

"This is Commander Tessa Sharp with the Metropolitan police force. I need to speak with Callum. I can't get him on his mobile."

"I'm sorry, Callum is out of the office right now." Julia grabbed a pen.

"In that case, give him this message and tell him to call me back ASAP. Tell him that negotiations have gone better than I thought they would and the timeline for picking up Rudi could move forward."

"No problem. Anything else?

"That's it. I've got a meeting. Thank you." The line went dead.

Julia put the note in her tray for Callum and got back to reading quotes for a new roof. She'd only just started to go through them, when the phone rang again. The sooner they employed a receptionist to man the phones the better.

"Your grandmother has gone missing," were the first words Julia's mother said to her when she answered the phone.

"Hi Mum, no she hasn't. I got an email from her this morning." Julia put aside her work to focus on the conversation. Multitasking wasn't possible when talking to any member of her family. "Her conference finished and she's going to visit Machu Picchu with Alice."

"Oh." The wind went out of her mother. "I wish the old bat would email me too. It would save a lot of worry. I'm not sure about those two travelling alone. They attract trouble. Aunt Alice especially."

"You're one to talk," Julia pointed out. If something disruptive was going on, odds were her mother would be in the middle of it.

"Next time she emails with a change of plans, can you let me know? It will save me from freaking out. I almost booked tickets to go find her and drag her home."

Julia smiled at the thought of the media frenzy that would surround the family's rescue attempt. It would drive her grandmother mad. Although not shy, the woman shared Julia's introverted nature and the last thing she'd want to be was the centre of attention. No, Gran liked to live under the radar—that way she could get away with a whole lot more than she would otherwise.

"How's my baby girl?" her mum cooed into the line.

"I'm twenty six, Mum, hardly a baby."

"You'll always be my baby. Now stop trying to distract me and tell me how the new office is coming together. And I want to hear about all those hunky men you work with. You didn't send me photos. I need photos of the hunky men." There was laughter in her voice.

"Does Dad know you're collecting photos of hunky men?"

Julia knew it was a joke, but she wouldn't put it past her mother to have an actual collection stashed somewhere.

"He encourages it. Makes me randy."

"Mum!" Julia's cheeks turned red and she shook her head. This was one of the reasons she kept her life compartmentalised—the rest of her family had missed out on the shame gene.

Her mother laughed. "How's it going? I want to know."

"Fine, it's going fine." What else was there to say? The building was crawling with tradespeople, the team was completely dysfunctional and she had an aneurysm every time Joe came near her. None of which she planned to tell her mother.

"Mmm," Libby mused. "I think your father and I need to make time to take you out for lunch. You can show us around the building. Introduce us to your colleagues."

"No!" Julia took a deep breath. "I mean not right now. Soon. It's just that it's a terrible mess around here and we're in the middle of a very tense, hush-hush case."

"Are you sure you aren't avoiding us?" It wasn't an accusation. Her mother knew it was a very real possibility and she was concerned. Julia had spent a lifetime avoiding her completely over-the-top family. It had been her survival mechanism growing up. Not that she didn't love them. She did. She adored each and every one of them. Just in small doses.

"Not this time, I promise. We'll set something up as soon as I have a little more time." Something that happened far away from the office. Or anyone she knew.

Lake had made it very clear when he hired her that he'd deal with her many personal issues, but he wouldn't tolerate her family exposing the work of Benson Security to the media. If she wanted to keep her job, she had to keep them away from the office. Which was almost impossible now that she was in the same city as her parents and siblings.

"I'm holding you to that." It sounded like her mother was settling in for a long chat. "Now tell me about the men. Which one do you fancy the most?"

Julia groaned, but was saved by the light flashing that there was someone else on the line. "I've got to go, Mum. Someone else is calling and I'm manning the phone."

"Typical. Just when we get to the juicy stuff. One way or another we're going to weed information out of you, Julia Collins. Okay, go play spy. I love you." She made kissing noises and then hung up.

Taking a deep breath to cope with the whirlwind that was her mother, Julia connected to the other line. For once she didn't bemoan the fact that there wasn't a receptionist to cover the calls.

# CHAPTER 13

Megan found Julia in her tiny office, which was positioned behind the front desk in the entrance area of the building. At some point the team would hire a receptionist. For now, with the building still being modified and the business not officially open yet, Julia was watching the desk. This entailed keeping the front door locked and speaking to everyone via the intercom. Julia had issues, bless her wee heart.

"Hey." Megan plopped down in the lavender-coloured chair on the other side of the desk from her flatmate. "I just kissed Dimitri. Again." Yep, those words had really come out of her mouth.

Julia stopped sticking post-it notes all over a wall-sized whiteboard and turned slowly to stare at Megan. "Are you crazy?"

"I'm beginning to think so." She took out her ponytail holder and ran her fingers through her hair. "One minute he's making me madder than hell, the next I'm playing tonsil hockey with the man. There must be some medication I can take to stop this from happening. Do you think valium would work?"

"No." Julia gave her the same look Megan had received from her older brother over the years. It was somewhere between disbelief and horror.

"It's probably just the stress of the situation," Megan said hopefully. "People kiss each other all the time when they're stressed. Right?"

"I don't."

Julia was not helping and there was no point calling Claire—she'd only ask for details. Sometimes her twin acted like a little devil on Megan's shoulder. So no, she wouldn't be calling Claire. It looked like, for this situation, she was on her own.

"Maybe I should go for a run, work off my stress. If I'm exhausted I'll be less likely to jump Dimitri's bones if the situation arises."

"You don't run," Julia helpfully pointed out.

"I can learn. Seriously, how hard can it be? It's like walking, only faster." She pointed at the wall which was neatly covered in Julia's project management timetable. "They have spreadsheets for that."

Julia shook her head as though coming out of a daze. "I know, but they don't have screens this big. I like being able to see every detail of the project in one glance." She gave Megan a shy smile. "The renovations are ahead of schedule. The team will start on our flat at the beginning of next week."

"Fab." Megan helped herself to a chocolate mint from the bowl Julia kept on her desk. "Are you still keeping two flats on the top floor?"

That was the set up now, but there had been some talk of changing it. Megan had no doubt that whatever was decided the newly renovated space would look amazing. Julia had great taste in décor. Once the building was finished it would be a subtle melding of blue, lavender, cream and silver. The furniture was functional, but modern and stylish. She'd even managed to weave in a little bit of accent pattern throughout the place. Overall it gave the feeling of a discreet, upscale, professional business. She doubted the guys who owned the business would notice how classy it was, but Megan was sure their clients would.

"No. We'll have one self-contained flat—the one we're in —and the rest of the floor will be converted to hotel style en suite rooms. That way operatives will have somewhere to stay overnight, or short term if need be, while retaining a unit for those of us who are between accommodation and need to stay a bit longer. If the people in the rooms need to use a kitchen, they can come down and use the one on the office floor."

"Operatives." Megan grinned. "I'm an operative. How cool is that? Maybe I should get it on a T-shirt."

"Maybe." Julia smiled at her before sitting at her desk.

She had two computer monitors and three open notepads, all perfectly aligned on her desk. Even her pens and sticky notes were colour coordinated. She was the same way in the flat they shared. The first time Megan had opened a kitchen cupboard and seen the colour coordinated labels on the containers, she almost ran. She knew from experience there was no way she could be as neat as Julia expected. Fortunately, Julia had patience. Lots of patience.

"I suppose we should find another place to live, at some point." Megan sighed. "I don't want to move. I like living here. It's close to everything and I don't need to get up early for work."

The house was situated on a stately street in Westminster, near Victoria train station. It was close to the shops, the London attractions and the river Thames. There was no way Megan could afford to live in this area unless the company provided the accommodation.

"I spoke with Callum and he said he's in no hurry for us to move."

"Does that mean we can stay indefinitely?"

"I don't think he meant that." But Julia's tone said she hoped otherwise. Megan knew that for Julia, being in the building where she worked, in an environment she controlled, was reassuring for her.

"I bet if we live quietly, he won't even notice we're here."

Julia laughed and shook her head. "This place is so big I doubt anyone would notice if we hung around."

She had a point. The Regency era townhouse was set up like the Tardis—much bigger on the inside than it appeared on the outside. It was tall, narrow and deep. The basement was the biggest floor, housing more than enough space for the gun range, training room, gym, swimming pool, changing areas and a couple of seriously illegal holding cells.

The ground floor held reception, the conference room, two interview rooms, a bathroom, the kitchen and the office they were currently sitting in. There was also a lovely court-yard outside the kitchen, with another building at the end of the garden. That part used to be the old carriage house, but was now a separate house where Callum lived. One that Julia was not allowed to renovate. Callum insisted on taking care of the planning and work on his own.

The first floor held offices—in the process of being reno-vated. The second floor would hold the computer division once it was finished. And the third, and last, floor was for accommodation. With its huge windows and grand propor-tions, the building had a stately feel to it that would have been intimidating if the place wasn't full of rough and tough mercenaries.

"Day dreaming again?" A deep voice jarred her back to the present.

Megan looked up to find Joe standing in the doorway, a

folder in hand. He flashed those dimples of his that would have made her weak at the knees, if she wasn't a teeny little bit wrapped up in a man who refused to take her seriously.

"Hiding," Megan said. "I'm worried if I show my face, Dimitri will have more training sessions for me."

"Training? Is that what the kids are calling it these days?"

"Har-de-har-har." Megan threw one of Julia's mints at this head.

He snatched it out of the air, unwrapped it and popped it in his mouth. All while smiling knowingly. Men.

"What are you up to?" she asked him.

"Meeting with Callum."

"I didn't see him come back in," Julia said, more to her desk than anyone else. "Can you take a message to him? It's from Tessa Sharp and sounded important."

Joe cast an anxious glance at Megan. It made the hairs on the back of her neck stand on end. "Where is it?"

Julia pulled a piece of paper out of a tray marked with Callum's name, but instead of handing it over she read it. "I think he needs to call her back urgently. She said..."

"Thanks." Joe snatched the piece of paper, making Julia's eyes snap up to him.

Megan sat up straight. She definitely didn't miss the "oh shit" look Joe flashed in her direction this time.

"Joe, I was going to say her message may have an impact on Friday's meeting with Rudi. She says the timeline for picking him up might move forward."

The hairs on Megan's neck stood to attention. "What timeline? What's this got to do with Rudi?"

Joe looked at the ceiling for guidance. A bad sign. A very bad sign that Megan wasn't going to like what she heard. "Callum had a meeting with the Special Investigations Commander at the Met and she wants to hold off on taking

Rudi down until she has everything in place with her sister organisations."

"Oh," Julia whimpered as her hand flew to her mouth. Her eyes shot to Megan and she had that look people get when they know they've given something away they shouldn't have.

Megan felt everything within her still. "How long?" she said to Joe. "How long before Rudi is arrested?"

"It makes sense to take down the whole operation at the same time, you know…" Joe started.

Slowly, Megan got to her feet. She stepped into his space and poked him in the chest. "How long before that asshole is behind bars? How long before Claire is safe?"

His shoulders fell in defeat. "A few months." He glanced at Julia who was watching them both. "Maybe less, going by this message."

Megan didn't say a word. She couldn't speak. She was too damn angry. They'd been planning this behind her back. Scheming about things that concerned her and her sister, without so much as a word of consultation. Not only that, but they were shirking their end of the deal. The deal where Megan used her face to get them access to Rudi and in return he was removed from Claire's life. A white hot flame of fury engulfed her. She couldn't hear whatever Joe and Julia were telling her. She didn't care about anything else they had to say anyway. She'd heard enough. There was only one person she wanted to deal with.

Without a word, she turned on her heel and stormed to Callum's office.

# CHAPTER 14

Dimitri had his head together with Callum, going over the plans for Friday, when his office door slammed open to reveal a livid Megan.

"Months." Megan bit out the word.

Dimitri cast a worried glance at his boss. There was no need to guess what this was about.

"Months." Megan stormed towards them, her face flushed and her fists clenched at her side. "Months until Rudi is put in jail. Months that my pregnant sister will have to hide, afraid he'll get her. Months." She strode across the room, slapped both palms on the desk and glared at Callum. "When were you going to tell me?"

"Calm down." Callum used the words no man should ever say to an angry woman, proving once and for all that there was a very valid reason the guy was still single.

"Calm down?" It was barely a whisper. Megan's hand shot out and she grabbed a glass paperweight on the corner of Callum's desk. An instant later it was flying at his head. Only Callum's quick reflexes saved him.

"What the hell?" the man roared.

Dimitri rushed around the desk and grasped Megan in a bear hug, before she could throw anything else.

"Calm down," she shouted. "You're telling me to calm down." She struggled in his hold, kicking her heels against his shins. Damn, that stung. He was going to have bruises. He squeezed her to get her to stop. She didn't spare him a glance, instead she stilled long enough to fume at Callum.

"You promised me. You said we'd deal with the threat to Claire. That it would be over as soon as we got to Rudi."

"Things change," Callum said.

"Not helping," Dimitri told the man.

Megan roared, punching at Dimitri's arms to get him to release her. He held tight as Joe rushed into the room. His face paled when he saw Megan.

"She was in Julia's office when a message came through from Tessa. Looks like it might take less time to get everything in place to pull Rudi in."

"It's still months." Megan went ballistic in Dimitri's arms. He understood her reaction—they'd told her the problem would be dealt with during the meeting Friday. If they'd done that to him, he'd have thrown things at Callum too.

She was going to make herself sick getting this worked up. Dimitri tightened his grip and put his lips to her ear. "Stop it," he snapped.

"Go to hell," she shouted.

He squeezed her. "Stop it before you hurt yourself. Listen to what we have to say. There are good reasons for the delay."

She froze in his arms. She turned to look at him over her shoulder. "You knew?"

*Oh hell.* "Yeah. I knew."

Wow, he could have sworn her eyes actually flashed. "So, what? Your sister is more important than mine? It's okay to save Katrina but not okay to protect Claire?"

He felt his own fury build. "That is out of order and you know it."

"As out of order as hanging my sister out to dry and not even having the courtesy to tell me?" Her eyes went wide. "You didn't want me to pull out of the meeting on Friday. That's why you didn't include me in this new plan."

She went crazy in his arms again, cursing him at the top of her voice. Dimitri spotted Rachel, Ryan and Julia appear outside the door. Callum caught his eyes as he held Megan tight.

"Conference room," Callum said.

"Let me go, you lying son of a bitch. Let me go right now." Megan tugged at his arms.

She was too mad to think things through. The Megan he'd seen in action in the alley would have had him disabled by now. Callum ordered everyone to the conference room and Dimitri followed, carrying Megan.

Ryan pulled out a chair for Dimitri and he sat in it, holding Megan on his lap, securing her in place with his arms and legs.

"Isn't that overkill?" Rachel raised an eyebrow at him.

"I value my balls." And he sure as hell wasn't going to let Megan loose to get at them.

"From what I heard, you value them more than the Donaldson sisters," Rachel said, making him glare at her.

"Not helping."

"But truthful."

"Enough," Callum barked.

Megan's eyes were on Callum. He could feel the fury hum throughout her body.

"There are reasons for this decision. Good reasons. And your behaviour right now is exactly why you don't know about them." Callum turned to Joe. "Educate her." He thumped down into a chair.

"Jules," Joe said. "Put up the photo of Rudi's top men."

The lights dimmed and a photo of three men filled the wall behind Callum. It was obvious Rudi hadn't picked them for their looks.

"As we all know," Joe said, "Rudi keeps his business close to his chest. There are three guys who work closely with him. They each deal with a different level of the flesh trade. One of them is in charge of shipping women to brothels run by customers who put an order in for new merchandise."

"Women," the indoor plant corrected. "Girls. Not merchandise, Joe."

Joe nodded his agreement at Julia's gentle reprimand. "The middle guy is in charge of running the in-house escort business. It's more high-end than the brothels they ship the women off to. The last guy deals with private sales." His dark eyes looked at each of them in turn. "Personal slaves."

The impact of those words made Dimitri want to vomit, but he kept his focus on the furious woman in his arms. This was about her. Not about him.

Joe continued, disgust clear on his face. "Rudi deals with special customers personally. By special customers I mean rich guys with a public reputation who don't want it sullied by anybody finding out about their sick hobbies. I tried to get some names but nobody was talking. All I could find out was that Rudi made a lot of trips to Dubai, Monaco, Indonesia and the US. Apart from his special customers, he's hands-on with all areas of his business. Nothing happens that he doesn't know about."

He looked at Megan as he pointed to the screen. "These guys are the reason you can't take Rudi out of the equation on Friday. If we chop of the head of the organisation, another will rise to take its place. They'll just start over, building on the contacts they already have and continuing the work Rudi started. If we want to stop future women being sold, raped and tortured, we need to take down the whole organisation in one fell swoop. Not only that, if we don't hit it all at once, we risk a chance that parts of the organisation will scatter and we'll lose the women who need to be saved." He dragged his fingers through his hair, making it stand on end. "That's why we need to wait for the police to do their thing. I wish I didn't have to say this, but this is way bigger than eliminating the threat to Claire. It's about finding Katrina *and* ripping apart the whole damn operation. And that can't happen until all the appropriate players are in place, in all the different countries Rudi's organisation touches."

There was a moment's silence before the image disappeared and the lights went back on.

Callum's dark gaze pinned Megan. "It isn't just about your sister. It's about all those other women who are trapped in hell right now. It's about stopping it from happening again. This organisation has connections in too many countries to take it out in a piecemeal fashion. We need to hit the whole thing in one go and we need to hit it hard. That's why we have to wait before Rudi is arrested, we can't risk them running to ground. We can't risk the lives of all those women."

"And what about Claire?" Megan's voice was husky, strained from shouting. She seemed calmer, but Dimitri didn't dare loosen his hold. If there were two things he knew about Megan it was that she was unpredictable and volatile.

"We'll protect Claire until this is over," Joe said.

"But you can't guarantee her safety, or the safety of her baby." It wasn't a question. Megan knew as well as anyone in the room that there were no guarantees.

"There may be another option." A hesitant voice came from the plant. "I-I'm sorry, but there's a story in Rudi's file.

Two, in fact. Twice he was targeted personally and both times he backed off."

Joe grinned proudly at the plant, making Dimitri wonder all over again just what the hell was going on between those two.

The men started to shake their heads but Rachel spoke up. "The bully principle. Hit him harder. Make sure he stays down. It could work."

"No." Callum folded his arms over his black shirt. "Too risky. We stick with the original plan."

Megan relaxed in Dimitri's arms. The rage leached from her eyes leaving behind hopeless dejection. He didn't relax his hold on her, although now it was for a different reason than self-preservation—he was offering her comfort.

"But," Megan said, "if we hit him personally, rather than through his business, and we hit him hard, surely he'll get the message and leave Claire alone? Plus we'd still have the information we need to find Katrina. And the authorities would still have what they needed to take down the whole organisation in one fell swoop. We'd all get what we want."

Rachel nodded, surprising everyone by taking Megan's side—again. "I agree. From everything we know about Abramovich, I don't see why a personal message wouldn't work on him. It makes sense that Claire's family would strike out at him to make him back off. I don't see how that would have repercussions for a police investigation."

Callum ignored Rachel and addressed Megan. "I know you want this to end for your sister. You need to trust me that that's exactly what we're going to do. It will just take a little longer than we envisioned."

"And in that time, Claire gets to worry about Rudi coming for her while she's pregnant. We can't watch her every single minute of every day. The risk is too high. If we don't make it clear that Rudi needs to back off now, we take a risk with the lives of Claire and her baby."

"You have to trust us. We know what we're doing." Callum would not be moved on this point. "Hurting Rudi, because that's what you're talking about here, will only make him suspicious. It could jeopardise the whole plan. It's a risk we can't take."

Megan wriggled in Dimitri's arms before turning to him. "Let me go. I won't hit anyone."

He didn't want to, but he opened his arms. Megan pulled up a chair and sat right beside him, her thigh touching his as though needing the warmth to ground her. Dimitri placed a hand low on her back and rubbed his thumb to soothe her. She relaxed a fraction more, but didn't acknowledge his touch in any other way.

"I really don't see how it could jeopardise the police side of things," Rachel said. "There is no way to connect Dimitri and Megan to the police. If they should warn him off Claire, while they have their meeting with him, it would only come across as a personal response by a family member to a personal threat. I don't see how he could connect it to his business in any way."

"We can't take that risk," Callum said again. "Getting his business records and getting out in one piece is more important than anything else." He looked at Megan. "That's if you're still on board."

Dimitri wanted to smack Callum for asking the question. It showed how little he knew of the woman. He felt her stiffen under his hand. Her chin shot up and her eyes were dark.

"I'll do my part. Unlike some people in this room, I keep my word." She stood, her posture rigid as though she was clinging to her control by sheer will.

Callum nodded. "I had to ask."

"No, you really didn't." Megan shook her head in disgust and left the room.

"You're making a mistake," Rachel said to Callum once Megan was gone. "You should trust her, trust your team to pull this off without jeopardising future arrests."

"You don't know what you're talking about, Rachel."

Dimitri winced at Callum's words. He saw Rachel's lips thin and her eyes narrow. The temperature in the room seemed to drop by several degrees. And Dimitri wondered if they'd made a terrible mistake by tying Megan's hands. He, more than anyone else in the room, knew exactly how far a person would go to protect someone they loved. And he knew Megan was nowhere near her limit.

# CHAPTER 15

"This isn't going to work," Megan complained for the thousandth time since Julia had suggested they head across London to Rachel's flat for a private girl meeting. Her anger had worn off and now all she was left with was a sickening sense of betrayal that made her want to vomit. "She hates me. She won't help."

"Have some faith," said the woman who hid behind office plants.

"Either way, it should be entertaining," Elle added, as she adjusted the yellow headband she'd pulled from her bag. It matched her skater dress perfectly and made her look like a punk Doris Day.

They entered the lobby of Rachel's swanky apartment building on Hyde Park Corner and approached the concierge desk.

"We're here to see Rachel Ford-Talbot," Megan said, mainly because Julia was pretending to be invisible again and Elle was too busy checking out the decor.

"One moment, madam," the guy in the tailored suit said as he reached for the phone. "Whom shall I say is calling?"

"Her nemesis, her pet hacker and the invisible office manager," Megan said.

Julia poked her in the back. Megan rolled her eyes. "Megan Donaldson, Elle Roberts and Julia Collins."

"Very well." He dialled Rachel's apartment.

"Ms Ford-Talbot, you have guests here to see you. A Ms Megan Donaldson, Ms Elle Roberts and a Ms Julia Collins."

There was a moment's silence while the guy listened to Rachel. Megan tried to work out Rachel's end of the conversation from the completely blank look on his face, but she didn't get very far.

"Ms Ford-Talbot would like to know what business you have with her this evening?" the guy said at last.

"We're staging a revolt and thought she'd like to be in on it," Megan said.

He repeated her statement word for word then listened. "Of course, madam."

He replaced the phone while Megan waited to be kicked out of the building. There was no way Rachel would entertain them. The woman only thought about herself and had made it perfectly clear that she considered everything else, beneath her notice.

"You may go up. Apartment five. Use the last elevator on the left."

For a second Megan stared at the guy, unable to believe they had gained entrance to the princess's tower, then she felt a tug on her sweater.

"Thanks," she said as she followed Julia and Elle to the lift.

"Do you know that the cheapest apartment in this building goes for thirty-seven million pounds," Elle said.

"No way!" Megan's jaw dropped and she wondered if she should wipe her fingerprints from the elevator buttons. Or even better, erase her shabby presence from the building all together.

"Yep." Elle nodded. "This is one of the most elite addresses in the world. And I can tell you for a fact that Rachel's apartment is not the cheapest in the building—she's in one of the split-level penthouse apartments."

"How long has she lived here?" Megan wondered if she'd bought the place from the money she'd earned working for her cousin's IT company. And if so, she wondered just how much Harry was paying his staff.

"She's owned this place about three years. Before that she owned a house in Chelsea." Elle smiled. "Right next door to her parents' mansion."

"Ah," Megan said. "Silver spoon, huh?"

"Platinum spoon," Elle corrected.

"I think I'm going to be sick," Julia said, and sure enough her face was grey.

"Hey." Megan wrapped an arm around her friend's shoulder. "It's only money. Don't be intimidated."

Julia looked up at her as she swallowed hard. "It's not the money. I met lots of wealthy people when I worked in television. It's Rachel." She leaned in and whispered. "She's terrifying."

Megan couldn't disagree. "Stay behind me. I'll protect you."

"This should be fun," Elle muttered.

A few minutes later they were standing on plush burgundy carpet outside the door to Rachel's flat. Megan noted it was the only door in the hallway. It figured Rachel would have her own elevator—she probably had her own butler too. The door opened without them having to knock and to Megan's surprise they weren't greeted by the help, but by Rachel herself.

"You must be desperate if you came to me," Rachel said by way of hello.

"No kidding," Megan said.

Julia's arms shot out. She thrust a box of cupcakes in Rachel's direction. Her face had turned a deep shade of red but no words came out of her open mouth. She seemed petrified in place.

"We brought cupcakes." Elle took the box from Julia's outstretched hands.

Rachel looked at it as though the sugar would jump out and bite her bony backside.

"Oh for goodness sake, it's just cake. We'll eat them. Rachel is afraid the calories will cling to her." Megan rummaged around in her bag, bringing out some carrots and dip. "I got you carrot sticks and carb free, fat free, flavour free dip." She shoved the lot into Rachel's hands. "You're welcome." She pushed past her and into her flat.

No, not a flat, this was something else. The room was a vast open plan experience, with polished dark wooden floors interspersed with thick white carpets. There was space enough for three large sofas and two armchairs, all shades of white and cream, but with different patterns and textures. The cream walls had a plethora of modern art, some of it Megan even recognised. The paintings were original, expensive and added colour to the room. But the best part of the whole space was the wall of floor to ceiling windows that showed a panoramic view of Hyde Park and the lights of London.

"Holy hell," Megan hissed. "Just how rich are you, Rachel?"

"It's crass to ask someone about their wealth." Rachel sauntered past her to the cool white marble-topped breakfast bar between the living room and the kitchen. The kitchen cabinets were a deep, reflective red. Like blood. Megan shuddered. It suited Rachel to a tee.

Megan dumped her hobo bag on an armchair wide enough for two people and sauntered past the baby grand piano to look out the windows. "On a scale of one to Kardashian, where do you sit?"

"Trust you to compare me to the Kardashians. As I was saying—crass. Let's just say I'm comfortable and leave it at that."

"Comfortable?" Megan burst out laughing.

"She's a trust fund baby." Elle threw herself into the middle of one of the large, soft sofas and propped her pastel blue Doc Martins on the glass coffee table in front of her. "Her family own TayFor Pharmaceuticals. Her father still holds the majority share and is on the board. Her brother is the current CEO. Rachel is the wild child, believe it or not, because she didn't go into the family business." She cocked an eyebrow at Rachel. "I'm still trying to figure out why you didn't?" When she got no response from Rachel she carried on. "Her estimated worth is round about the six-hundred million mark."

Megan felt her jaw drop. "I should have let you buy your own carrots." She curled up in the big armchair and stared out into the darkness at the blinking lights of Central London.

"Get your feet off my table." Rachel pointed at Elle.

For a second Megan thought Elle would argue, instead she plopped her feet onto the white shag rug.

"Why are you working for my cousin if you're so rich?" Megan asked.

Rachel gave her a look that said she thought Megan's IQ had taken another dip. "Do you expect me to spend my life drinking tea and discussing Harry's love life?"

"Why would you discuss my cousin's love life? I thought you hated his wife."

"Not Harry your cousin. I'm talking about the prince. William's brother." Rachel let out a sigh. "Grandson of the Queen. *That* Harry."

"You know Prince Harry?" It was a good job Megan wasn't the type of person to feel easily intimidated because this conversation would have caused some serious inferiority issues.

Rachel shrugged. "Doesn't everyone?"

"Uh, no, Rachel, we don't all know Prince Harry personally." Megan thought about it for a second. "But some of us aren't against being introduced to the guy." She batted her eyelashes and gave Rachel her best pleading look.

It didn't work. "I'll make sure to schedule an introduction for the first of never," Rachel said. "Now tell me why you're here and what you want."

Megan wasn't quite ready for that conversation just yet. She was done dealing with disappointment for the day. If Rachel was going to kick them out on their ears, she'd rather it was delayed. "Do you have a pool?" she asked, because it seemed like exactly the kind of thing Rachel's apartment should have.

"Of course. It's upstairs." Rachel sauntered towards them. She was dressed in white silk yoga pants with a matching cropped top. Her hair was tied in a high ponytail on top of her head and her feet were bare.

"Great," Megan said. "Then, do you have a spare room? I'm looking for an alternative place to stay in case I get kicked out of the office." She let Rachel gape for a beat. "Don't panic, I was joking." Still... "But if you ever want someone to look after the place for a few days while you're away, keep me in mind."

Rachel's expression was easy to read—it said Megan was the last person she'd let loose alone in her home. In fact, from the way she was standing, arms folded in the middle of her living room, she was being pretty clear about not wanting her there at any time.

"What do you want?" Rachel said.

"Believe it or not, we're here to ask for help."

"I don't believe it."

"Trust me," Megan said. "Neither do I." She pointed at Julia who'd scurried over to the seat furthest from everyone. In this case it was the piano stool. "It was her idea. She said you have connections that we could tap into."

"Connections like?" Rachel cocked one perfectly groomed eyebrow, which made Megan wonder if she had staff on hand to keep her looking like that.

"Do you have a stylist? A staff of spa people? A live in chef?"

"Do you have ADHD? That would explain why you can't focus for more than ten seconds at a time. Read my lips—what connections are you talking about?"

"Your pharmaceutical connections of course," Elle said as she rummaged around in the kitchen area. She came up with a bottle of white wine and four glasses.

"Help yourself," Rachel said sarcastically.

It washed right over Elle, who said thanks then started pouring the wine.

"Why do you need access to my family's company?" Rachel asked Megan.

"Well, it's like this. After this afternoon's briefing, and the news that Claire is being hung out to dry, we," she motioned to Julia, Elle and herself, "decided to take matters into our own hands."

"And exactly how do you plan to do that?" Rachel looked so bored she was almost comatose.

"I'm going to warn Rudi off Claire."

Elle wandered over, handing out wine glasses to each of the women. Megan noted she'd removed her Doc Martin boots and wore silver rings on most of her blue painted toes.

"And where do I fit into your planning?" Rachel surprised Megan by taking the glass Elle offered and sipping from it without comment. "I won't be a party to anything that will endanger the team. One of us has to be sensible here."

"They're morons, Rachel, but I don't want them to get hurt. We'll make sure they're otherwise occupied while I deal with Rudi." Megan sipped her wine. It was good. She bet it cost a bomb.

At last, Rachel showed a spark of interest. "You're taking on the bully? Tell me you're going to hit him harder than he could ever hit you." She looked at each of the women in turn.

Julia whispered a yes, Elle grinned widely and Megan nodded.

"We're going in hard and fast and we're leaving as much damage as we can when we're done," Megan added. "We won't do anything to interfere with getting the information Dimitri needs, or tipping Rudi off about the investigation and arrests. This is purely about getting him to back off Claire. About standing up to the guy. About making him pay."

The cold smile that spread over Rachel's face made Megan shudder. "In that case, ladies. Count me in."

Elle whooped and held her glass out to Rachel for them to toast her decision. Megan eyed her fellow conspirators. Between them they were smart, resourceful and courageous. The men really shouldn't have locked them out of the planning.

Megan sat up straight and grinned. "How about we move this meeting to the pool? And don't forget to bring the cupcakes."

"The women are definitely up to something," Dimitri said the following morning, as he watched them through the glass window in Julia's office door.

"Yep." Joe folded his arms over his black wifebeater. It was good to see he looked as disturbed as Dimitri felt at the sight of Megan, Julia, Rachel and Elle with their heads together.

"They're plotting."

"Yeah, but what?"

Dimitri glanced over at Joe. "You don't think they're going to do something stupid that will interfere with the op, do you?" To be honest, if he was in Megan's position, that's exactly what he'd do. Although he completely understood her rage at discovering her sister wouldn't be safe for months yet, it didn't mean he'd let her screw things up.

Joe frowned in the direction of the women. "They wouldn't, would they? Haven't they been paying attention? They can't mess with this op, or this guy. He'll chew them up and spit them out."

"Yeah, but look at them. Rachel is in there and I don't hear shouting. That isn't a good sign." Dimitri cocked his head as he studied the women. "Maybe we should remind them exactly how dangerous this guy is? Knock this on the head before it causes problems."

"I like how you think." Joe grinned at him. "I know just the thing. We'll give them a slideshow they'll never forget. Get them to the conference room in ten."

"And if this doesn't scare them straight?"

Joe's eyes turned to flint. "Then we corner the weakest link."

They looked over at the women.

"Julia," they said at the same time.

As Joe jogged off, Dimitri headed past reception and into Julia's office. Laptops snapped shut when he opened the door. Yeah, that wasn't suspicious at all. Amateurs.

"Would it kill you to knock?" Megan frowned at him.

At the sight of her pink pouting lips, Dimitri was momentarily derailed. It felt like an eternity since he'd had a taste of her and even though he knew it was best to keep it that way, he still couldn't help but suffer withdrawal symptoms every time he saw her.

"What do you want?" Rachel demanded, bringing him back to the issue at hand.

"You're needed in the conference room." He noted Julia's face turning beetroot red. Definitely guilt. Interesting.

"There isn't a meeting scheduled." Rachel stood tall in her spiked heels and tailored suit. She folded her arms and tapped her red talons on the grey sleeve of her jacket.

He wasn't intimidated. "Scheduled or not, there's still a meeting. Hop to it, ladies." He flung the door wide and gestured for them to leave.

Elle gave him a sunny smile, Rachel tried to incinerate his head with her glare, Julia couldn't look at him and Megan frowned.

"You're up to something," she said as she came level with him.

"Funny, I was thinking exactly the same thing about you."

She gave him a cute little growl and stomped after the rest of them. Dimitri cast his eyes around the empty office. There was no time to search the place, but his sixth sense, honed from years with the US army rangers, was screaming at him that there was trouble ahead. He hoped to hell it wasn't the sort of trouble that got them all killed.

"Bloody meetings," Megan grumbled as they filed into the conference room. "All we do is hold meetings. I'm seriously over being a mercenary. It's boring."

"Amen, sister," Elle said as she plopped down into a chair.

"Can we hurry this along?" Rachel's icy voice demanded. "We have things to do."

"All in good time," Joe told her. "We have a little Power-Point presentation for you. Shouldn't take too long."

"Joe?" Julia's voice trembled and Megan willed her not to give the game away. "I wasn't told about a meeting. I don't have anything on file for this presentation."

"I'm running the media today, Julia." Joe's voice was firm. A tone he never, ever used with Julia. It set off alarm bells. "You sit down and pay attention."

Julia ducked her head and grabbed a seat, far from Joe and close to the wall. Megan watched Joe as he in turn studied Julia. Something was definitely up. When she saw the guys share a speaking look her stomach flipped. They were on to them. She was sure of it. She pulled her phone out of her pocket and sent a text to Rachel and Elle. Not to Julia, the woman didn't have anything even resembling a poker face.

The text said: *They're suspicious. Do NOT leave Julia alone with them!!!*

She didn't have to add anything else. They all knew who would cave under pressure. She caught a subtle nod from each of the women.

The lights went out and Joe's baritone filled the room. "We thought, seeing as the op is less than twenty four hours away, that it would do us all good to have a reminder of what we're dealing with."

A photo flashed on the screen. It showed a beaming blonde woman in her graduation gown. "This is Becky Marshall. She graduated from Florida U with a degree in childhood education. She went missing while she was backpacking through Eastern Europe with her cousin. She turned up three months later when German authorities raided an illegal brothel on their eastern border. This is what she looked like when they found her."

Another photo appeared on the screen and Megan felt the blood drain from her face. Julia gasped. Elle swore. The woman on the screen was a shadow of the beaming blonde. She was naked, bloody, broken and bruised. Someone had cut words into her stomach. Her eyes were glassy.

"She was alive." Joe's tone was deadly. "If you can believe it. She was drugged out of her mind and the hospital didn't think she'd had a decent meal in weeks. She'd been raped repeatedly. Beaten. Cut."

Megan heard a soft sob coming from Julia and her fists clenched. "What's the point of this, Joe?"

Joe carried on as if she hadn't said a word. "The brothel was owned by Rudi Abramovich. The only reason we know this is because the authorities were lucky during the raid and managed to detain someone high up in the organisation." The screen flashed to show a man hanging in a cell. "He killed himself after mentioning Rudi's name. There wasn't enough evidence to pin it to Rudi after that. Charges were never laid. But then, you need to catch the bastard in the right country to charge him with anything."

The photo changed again. This one was taken in a hospital. The woman was sitting on a gurney. Her face wasn't in the photo. Her torso was covered in bruises, some old, some new. There were small circular scars on her breasts. "Those marks are cigar burns. Rudi thought it was a good punishment for his wife after she didn't smile at his associates during dinner."

"That's Hope?" Elle whispered.

"Yeah." Joe sounded tight, like he was about to roar. "That's Hope. Those photos were taken in the hospital after we got her out of Romania."

Julia's sobs became more strangled. Megan stood up and blocked the projection with her body. "Enough, Joe. What's this all about?"

The lights came on, making everyone blink hard for a few seconds. When their vision adjusted it was to see Dimitri and Joe standing shoulder to shoulder, arms folded, staring at them.

"This is about making sure you realise what's at stake here," Joe said. "We know you're scheming something. Whatever it is, you'd better think again. We can't take any risks. This man," he spat the word, "gets off on hurting women. He doesn't see them as people, they're possessions, objects to do what he wants with. He tortures, rapes, kills. He's done it personally and he sanctions it when the people who work for him do it." He took a step towards Megan. "This isn't a game. Nobody's playing here. This is dangerous. You, especially, are in danger."

"Don't you think we know that?" Megan snapped at him. "We read the report just like you did. We saw the photos. Heard the taped testimonies of women who survived. Don't you think it would have more of an impact on us than it did on you? Look around you, Joe. We *are* women. We know the fear of being hurt. Of being raped. Of being taken. It's a fear you can't understand because you don't live with it every single bloody day."

She threw up her hands in exasperation as she turned her back on him.

"I don't think—" he started, but Elle stood and glared at him.

"No, you don't think," she said. "Neither of you do. Look at the two of you. You're huge, over six feet of solid muscle and attitude. You walk out of here at night and it never even occurs to you that someone would look at you and think you'd make a great victim. You've never been on a date where the guy won't take no for an answer. You've never had someone you trust turn on you just because they know you can't fight back."

Rachel stood. "You've never been out for an evening and taken a drink someone has tampered with and then lived with the gap in your memory and the possibilities of what might have happened during it."

Julia sobbed again. "You've never cowered because you knew that even if you hit back it wouldn't make an impact."

"Jules." Joe's voice sounded strangled. He took a step towards Julia, but she turned her face to the wall and he looked as though he'd taken a blow.

Megan took a deep shuddering breath full of fury. "You two are doing what you do best, I get it. You're knights in shining armour, desperate to ride to the rescue. You're big, you're bad and you can be terrifying. But one thing you will never be is a woman at the mercy of a man. To answer your question, we're taking this very seriously. We're taking it very personally. And we will make sure that this man pays for what he's done." She sneered at them. "Even if we have to deal with you two idiots to get the job done."

She looked at the other, equally furious women. Elle had her arms around a sobbing Julia.

"We're out of here," Megan said to them.

"My place," Rachel said. "We need a night without testosterone stupidity."

"Amen, sister," Elle said.

"We'll be back in the morning. Maybe you should spend tonight thinking about how insulting your little slideshow was and how bloody arrogant you were to think it was a good idea." Megan gave them one last disgusted look before following her friends. As she left she heard Dimitri's voice.

"That didn't go as planned," he said.

"No kidding, Einstein," Joe said. "I think we may have made things worse."

Megan rolled her eyes. She was dealing with idiots.

# CHAPTER 17

Dimitri wished he had a hangover. But instead of spending the night getting lost in a bottle, after the spectacular failure in the conference room, he'd spent it going over the details of the op. In between stressing, double-checking and worrying, he'd managed to grab a couple of hours sleep. He'd done more complex jobs on less, but he still felt like hell.

"Let's go over this one more time from the top," Callum said as he stood at the front of the conference room.

There was an aerial map of Rudi's house pinned to the rolling whiteboard at the side of the table.

"Ryan and I will take up sniper positions, here and here." He pointed to the positions they'd scoped that covered the two main entrances to the property. Callum's vantage point in particular gave him a good view right to the front door and behind one of the garages.

"Joe will be on the ground, here." He pointed at the driveway two properties over from Rudi's house. The owners were out of town and Callum had pulled strings to enable Joe to park his car there without private security blowing his cover. He was close enough to get to them should they need someone covering their backs fast.

"Dimitri and Megan will drive up to the property in the Ford Sedan we bought for that purpose." Callum looked at everyone in turn. "The car cannot be connected to Benson Security. It has no tech in it. That's because we know it will be searched and scanned. Most likely tagged as well. You won't touch that car after you leave the property." He rubbed his face. "You will also be scanned for bugs when you enter the property, that's why you aren't being wired for this op. It would never make it past the first checkpoint." He pointed at the guardhouse inside the gate. "Your phones will be confiscated along with anything else that's even remotely electronic. You'll lose your weapons. From there on in, you're on your own. Naked in a hostile environment."

"I really hope you don't mean literally naked," Megan piped up, pulling a smile from one or two people.

Her anger from the previous day was gone and she didn't seem to be bearing a grudge. Which was suspicious. The Megan he'd come to know was real good at bearing a grudge. He eyed her thoughtfully and earned a sunny smile. Maybe he was reading too much into the situation. Maybe. Wrenching his eyes from her, he concentrated on Callum.

"You have twenty minutes to get in, get the information and get out." Callum studied Dimitri and Megan. Dimitri read everything he couldn't say in his eyes. This wasn't a good situation. They were literally walking into the lion's den without backup or weapons. "I can't give you more than that."

"Why not?" Megan said. "What if it isn't long enough to get the ring? What if Rudi keeps us waiting in the hall for the whole twenty minutes?"

Callum stared at her. "Then you leave. Twenty minutes is

all you get. If you don't succeed in that time, then we try again another way."

"But why twenty? It doesn't seem long enough." Megan looked worried.

The sight melted Dimitri's resolve to keep his distance. For some reason he hated it when Megan experienced discomfort of any kind. He reached over and covered the back of her neck with his palm. He rubbed tiny circles in her tense muscles with his thumb, gratified when the gesture seemed to comfort her.

"Twenty minutes," Dimitri told her, "is the maximum he can give us in case we're injured and need help. Any more than that and we might not survive a trip to the hospital. It's also the minimum amount of time it would take Rudi's security to fully mobilise." Well, they could probably do it in less than twenty minutes, but they were accounting for the time it would take before the alarm was sounded.

Her beautiful blue eyes held his. "What if we're badly injured and twenty minutes is too long?"

"Anything you can't survive for that amount of time would kill you anyway."

She licked her dry lips and held his gaze for a moment longer before turning back to Callum. "Got it, twenty minutes and then the cavalry storms the castle."

"We have got to work on your metaphors," Dimitri told her. "Cavalries don't storm castles."

"Yeah, correct me, because that's the most important part of this discussion." She frowned at him and he couldn't help but chuckle. It felt good. It felt normal. It was reassuring. He dropped his hand back to the table in front of him, wishing he still held Megan. And calling himself all kinds of a fool for wishing it.

"Twenty minutes from the second you enter that house,"

Callum said again. "You both have watches on. Use them. If we don't see you exit on twenty, we come in, guns blazing, and get you out of there."

Dimitri nodded. "Once inside Rudi's office, I disable the guards while Megan uses the tech Elle gave her to copy the information on the flash drive. Then we get out of there before they wake up."

"Painting a target on our backs and leaving Claire hanging in the wind," Megan said.

"One thing at a time, Buffy. First we get the info, then we swoop in for the kill."

"Yeah, right," she muttered. "We swoop in *months* from now."

"Okay." Callum ignored the dig. "We ready to head out?"

There was a round of nods as one by one, people left the room. Dimitri watched as the women wished Megan luck and Julia gave her a shy hug. The strange actions made him realise more than ever that Megan, in fact none of the women, were trained for this sort of thing. They didn't know what to expect. They didn't know how to react. And Dimitri knew it was far too late to worry if they were asking too much of them.

They headed down to the garage at the back of the house as the rest of the team left to get into position. The meeting was scheduled for noon and they had plenty of time to get to the house. Megan was wearing faded jeans that were ripped at the knees. As agreed, her face was makeup free and her hair was rumpled as though she hadn't been able to fix it. The T-shirt she wore had a hole ripped in it and a black smudge. The intent was to look like they'd been on the road for a couple of days and there had been a struggle when he'd taken her.

"Give me a minute," Megan said, heading for the bathroom.

"We're on a schedule here," Dimitri shouted after her.

"I'll be right back."

Dimitri closed his eyes and mentally went over the plan. He had no doubt he'd be able to subdue the guards inside Rudi's office, or that he'd be able to knock Rudi out so Megan could duplicate the information on the ring. What worried him was getting out without setting off alarms. The timing was a problem. They'd need to work fast. Otherwise the security team would discover their boss unresponsive and the house would be locked down tight. He rubbed his temples. So much could go wrong. If Megan got hurt…No, he couldn't think like that. The question wasn't whether she could take care of herself or not, it was whether she'd follow orders or go all maverick on his ass.

"I'm ready."

Dimitri opened his eyes and promptly forgot to breathe. His jaw opened and closed a couple of times before words came out. "What the hell?"

Megan stood in front of him, her hand on her cocked hip, her eyes gleaming. She wore a red mini dress that fit like a second skin. It left nothing to the imagination. Her hair was tied in a high ponytail. Her lips were painted red, her eyes were outlined in black. Her only jewellery was a black wrist-watch and an oversized ring in the shape of a black rose. Her feet were clad in mile-high black pumps.

"What the hell?" he said again, because his brain was fried.

Her smile was slow, wide and full of evil intent. "The girls and I decided this outfit would cause more of a distraction than the poor, victimised woman outfit."

His eyes snapped away from tracing her curves. "Is this what you were planning in the office yesterday?"

"You'll never know." She sashayed towards him. "Because instead of asking politely, you decided to educate us. Shame the only thing we learned was just how arrogant you guys are." She smiled at him. "Let's go or we'll be late. Wouldn't want to keep Rudi waiting, now would we?"

She climbed into the car. So much for not going maverick on him. At least the worst she'd done was change clothes. He could cope with that. It would be fine. He hoped.

It took all of Dimitri's self-control to focus on getting the car out of the garage and into traffic. He kept getting distracted by the steaming hot blonde sitting beside him. Rudi's house wasn't that far from their office as the crow flies, but with London's roads and heavy traffic it would take time to get there. As he drove, his brain rushed over the plan, trying to see where her new look would ruin things. Apart from questions about why she was in such a great state, he couldn't think of any problems. In fact, it might even work in his favour. He could tell Rudi he cleaned up the merchandise for the meeting. Yeah, that would make him look good. He relaxed. Slightly.

It took a few minutes for him to realise Megan wasn't talking, which wasn't normal. She sat quietly beside him, clutching her stomach and looking nervous. Dimitri did a double take—Megan never looked nervous. It suddenly occurred to him that she may have been hiding her anxiety about the op. He should have talked to her about it. It was normal to feel anxious the first time, even for a trained operative.

"It's going to be okay." He tried to reassure her. "Just stick to the plan and everything will be fine."

"I'm okay. Don't worry."

He wasn't reassured. As they pulled into a quiet leafy street near Rudi's house she suddenly bent double.

"Pull over. I'm going to be sick." She slapped a hand over her mouth.

"Hold it together," Dimitri barked.

"I'm sorry. I need to stop. I'm going to be sick." She looked around frantically. "There. Over there. Pull into that drive."

He looked where she was pointing. It was a discreet tree-lined entrance to a private clinic. Dimitri swerved the car into the drive and pulled up on the grass behind the wall.

Megan scrambled out of the car. She ran to the back of it, bent double and started retching. Dimitri pulled out the throwaway cell phone they'd bought for the car. He dialled Callum.

"We're a few minutes behind. Megan's being sick."

Callum swore. "Nerves?"

Dimitri clasped the back of his neck. "Yeah. Shit. I don't blame her. But…"

"Aye, but. You've got time. Not much. Sort her out and get back on track. We're in position. Nothing unusual happening at the house. Call me if there's a problem. If she can't hold it together we'll need to abort."

Dimitri swore loudly. "I'll make sure she holds it together."

He shut off the phone and threw it on the dash. This was a complete and utter balls up. He was so close to finding out where his sister was and now this. He took a deep breath and went round to the back of the car to pull Megan together. She was tough, smart. She could do this. It was just nerves. It happened to all of them first time out. Once he assured her she was safe with him, she'd be fine.

He hoped.

He found her bent double, clutching the boot of the car.

"Hey." He ran a hand over her back, in what he hoped was a patient and soothing gesture. "You okay?"

That's when he noticed something was wrong. It took a second for his brain to register it, but by then he was too late.

As fast as lightning she spun towards him. His vision blurred and a prolonged agonising pain made his body spasm and freeze. Then everything went black.

# CHAPTER 18

"This is all your own fault," Megan told the writhing hulk as he thrashed around in the boot of their car.

Dimitri grunted loudly against the pink ball gag she'd bought especially for him. She had her twin sister to thank for knowing about ball gags and restraints. Claire was going through a cowboy-BDSM romance novel phase and seeing as they shared a Kindle account, Megan got to read what Claire read. Hence her knowing to buy a soft leather harness for Dimitri that neatly tied his hands and feet behind his back without putting too much pressure on his joints. It was amazing what you could find in a good lingerie shop these days—especially one in Soho. Since kinky sex had gone mainstream it was trendy to stock things like pink ball gags. The world was a strange and delightful place.

"I should have bought a different type of gag," she told him as she placed some cereal bars and a bottle of water beside his head. "This one causes you to drool and it isn't attractive."

She was pretty sure the words he shouted from behind

the gag were curses. She patted his head to comfort him and then reached behind him to the small black clutch bag Julia had put in the trunk earlier. She pulled out her mobile phone and sent a text to the rest of the women.

*Dimitri disabled. Plan on track.*

Rachel replied. *Callum getting anxious. Speed things up.*

Julia replied next. *Taxi on its way. 2 minutes.*

Lastly she heard from Elle. *Am in position.*

Megan sent a smiley face and a thumbs up to all of them. Then she eyed the man beside her and took a couple of photos of him. After she sent them to her email account, to add to her memory book later, she ran to the front of the car to retrieve the disposable phone. Once back at the boot she swapped out her cell phone for the throwaway one. She wasn't stupid enough to take her own phone into a dangerous situation.

"I know you're a big bad ex-army ranger and you'll probably figure out a way to get out of your restraints before someone comes to rescue you, so I've left you a snack and drink for while you wait. I'm sending Callum a text telling him you need to be picked up. You shouldn't be in there too long. Just enough time for me to get into the mansion."

There was more muffled shouting and cursing. Dimitri liked to give orders. Pity she couldn't hear him—she'd bet these ones were particularly creative and very alpha male. She didn't worry about anyone hearing the noise he was making. They'd parked in the side entrance to the private clinic and Elle had been out to disable the nearest security cameras the evening before.

Dimitri grunted a panicked question. His eyes were wide and there was sweat on his brow. She checked his ankles and wrists to make sure she hadn't cut off circulation. Nope, he was good. He was just being a drama queen. He shouted the muffled question again and she was pretty sure he was demanding to know what she was doing. He didn't need to know.

"Okay, babe, I'm going in. Wish me luck." She patted his cheek. He went crazy under her touch. "How do I look?"

Dimitri exploded again, struggling against his bonds and hitting his head off the side of the car. "Yeah, I know. Freaking awesome. Right?" She grinned at him. "Now stop thrashing around, you'll hurt yourself."

She flicked her phone on and sent a message to Callum—remembering to write in full sentences as he didn't speak text.

*Dimitri needs rescuing.* She added two smiley faces, the photo she'd taken of him earlier and the address.

Callum's reply was quick. *What the hell?! Stop whatever you're doing. Now!*

"Callum seems worried," she told Dimitri.

She leaned forward to place a kiss on his stubbled cheek. Her bag spilled into the boot. "Oops." She grinned as she stuffed everything she needed back into the bag. Not the most reassuring of starts to her first job as an undercover gun-for-hire, but whatever.

With one last smile at the man, she closed the boot. Megan straightened her dress, ignored the thuds coming from the car and headed through the gate as her taxi pulled up. She climbed in the back, gave the driver Rudi's address and settled in to watch the cherry tree lined street pass by. It was the middle of March and spring had hit London early. It was still chilly though, and Megan wished she'd planned for a coat in her disguise. Part of her brain acknowledged she was focusing on the mundane to stop herself from freaking out. She shoved that part down deep.

She saw the large ornate gates before she spotted the no-neck behemoth guarding them. He was dressed in a black suit, black shirt and black shades. He didn't smile when she climbed out of the cab. Megan didn't let it faze her. She looked up, up, up at the man and cocked her head.

"Take me to your leader," she ordered.

And then she grinned.

# CHAPTER 19

Dimitri fought and struggled against his bonds. He was going to kill her when he was free. No. He was going to torture her, then kill her. What was she thinking? She was untrained, inexperienced. She was going to get herself killed. Fuck. *She was going to get herself killed.* He'd lose her. The same way he'd lost Katrina. No. No.

His forehead fell to the carpeted interior beneath him. Okay. He needed to think. She was only a few minutes ahead of him. He just had to get out of the car, get to her and put a stop to this insanity. He concentrated on the feel of the leather straps around his wrists. They weren't too tight. Sure, they were attached to ankle straps and there was a ball gag in his mouth, so that made it difficult. He had a sudden flash of an image of a pig on a spit roast with an apple in its mouth, and groaned. He needed to get out of there. Get out. Save Megan. Then kill her personally.

His muscles were still shaky from the Taser blast, but he pulled at his restraints, focusing on the weak points. Nothing happened. He let out a blaze of curses and tried again. Nearly there. Nearly there. He'd just about dislocated his shoulder when the boot popped open. The light made his eyes scrunch tight.

"Well, that isn't something you see every day. You've got yourself in a bit of a spot there, son."

"You shouldn't mess with women. It never ends well."

Dimitri blinked as his eyes adjusted to the light. Bill and Bob Granger were staring down at him with matching grins. Dimitri shouted at them to set him free. The words were a garbled mess, but the old men got the point. As Bob unclasped his gag, Bill worked on the buckles holding the rest of his restraints.

Bill held up the pink leather harness as Dimitri climbed out of the car. "Mind if I keep a hold of this?"

"I don't give a crap what you do with it," Dimitri snapped.

"The missus might get a kick out of this kinky stuff," Bob said. "You can keep the gag though. That's just unsanitary."

"You're lucky we were at the office," Bill said. "You could have been stuck in there for hours and that would have been murder on your back."

Bob nodded. "When Callum called we were happy to help out. This job is the most fun we've had in years."

"And we can keep an eye on young Ryan," Bill said.

Bob nodded. "That boy needs supervision."

"We need more men," Dimitri muttered as he reached into the boot for the phone Megan had tossed in beside him.

"What are we? Chopped liver?" Bill demanded.

Dimitri stared at them as he hit the speed dial for Callum on his throwaway cell. "Security specialists. We need more security specialists."

"Well why didn't you say that?" Bill grumbled.

"What the hell happened?" Callum shouted in Dimitri's ear.

"She Tasered me and took off on her own." Dimitri could barely get the words out of his mouth, he was so furious. But rage was good. Rage was better than the fear that threatened to overwhelm him and leave him helpless.

"You let her get the drop on you? Did you learn nothing in the rangers?"

"I know." It was all he could say.

"She just climbed out of a taxi in front of the house. They've taken her into the guardhouse."

Dimitri's jaw clenched so tight, he thought a tooth might crack. "She's going to get killed. We need to get her out of there."

"We can't. We'll put her in more danger if we rush in now. She has twenty minutes, like we agreed."

"You can't give her twenty minutes. You know what can happen in that time." Images Dimitri didn't want in his head flashed in front of his eyes. The ones from yesterday's impromptu slide show were uppermost in his mind. They had to get her out of there.

"Interfering with her plan will jeopardise her more. We need to let this play out." Callum didn't sound any more pleased about that than Dimitri felt. "The boys have gear for you. Suit up and get over to Joe. You two will be first in if there's trouble."

"*When* there's trouble," Dimitri corrected.

"I'm going to kill her," Callum said.

"Get in line." Dimitri ended the call and tossed the phone back into the boot. He turned to the two men. "What you got for me?"

Bill handed over a bag. Relief hit him when he saw his gear. He took off his denim jacket and tugged on his shoulder holster over his T-shirt. Once he'd shrugged back into his jacket, he filled the pockets with extra clips. Next he strapped his knife, in its leather holder, to his ankle under his jeans. He grabbed the earpiece, switched it on and inserted it in his ear.

"Dimitri on," he said.

"Glad you could join us," Joe drawled. "Now get over here so we can cover your girl."

"On my way." Dimitri nodded at the two old men and climbed into the driver's seat. "What's happening?"

"Nothing," Joe said. "She's still in the guardhouse."

"This is a total clusterfuck." Dimitri pulled out into traffic and fought the urge to speed all the way to Joe's position.

"You said it," Joe mumbled.

"I can't get a response from any of the women." Callum's tight voice cut in.

"None of them?" Joe's tone was deadly.

"None of them," Callum confirmed.

"They're all in on this," Dimitri said.

"Even Rachel?" Ryan joined the conversation.

"My last communication from the women was a text from Rachel telling me to calm down, that they had it under control."

The men spoke all at once as curses filled the line. Dimitri spotted the house Joe was parked in front of and pulled his car in beside him.

"You okay?" Joe asked from his position near the gate.

"I will be once this is over." He moved to stand beside Joe, pulling his gun from its holster as he did so.

"I see movement." Callum's voice made Dimitri's stomach roil. "She's being escorted to the house. She's smiling. Looks relaxed. The guards look relaxed too."

Good. That was good. It bought her more time. She'd made it this far. She had to be okay. He closed his eyes. What if she didn't get the info on his sister? His whole world was lying in the hands of a twenty-three year old ex-hairdresser with no sense of fear.

"Breathe," Joe ordered. "You need to be on your game."

"I'm good." He could compartmentalise with the best of

them. With one deep breath he tucked his emotions away to deal with later and concentrated on the task at hand—to be ready when Megan needed him.

THINGS WERE GOING MUCH MORE SMOOTHLY than Megan had expected. The guards had taken her into their building, where they'd gone through her tiny clutch bag. They'd removed her phone, keys and wallet, but left the roll of bright pink tape (although that one got a confused look), the sparkly pink marker pen, the half dozen condoms and her red lipstick. The guard examined her cheap little MP3 player before tossing it back into her bag. It was a relief when she realised she wouldn't have to argue to keep the thing.

Her bag was tossed through the x-ray scanner near the desk. A guy monitoring the screen studied it.

"All clear," he said.

Slowly, the bodybuilder ran his eyes down the length of her body. "We need to check you out. Stand with your legs apart and your arms wide."

He ran a metal detecting wand over her body without problem. He placed the wand on the desk behind him. The guy was big, and didn't have much of a neck, but if she'd seen him in a nightclub she would have given him a second glance. Pity he was one of the bad guys.

"I need to check physically," he leered.

*Of course you do.*

Feigning interest in him, she cocked a hip. "Be my guest."

It took concentration to look relaxed when all she wanted to do was vomit at the thought of him touching her. What happened to chivalry? Wasn't he supposed to find a woman to pat her down?

"Step out of your shoes," the bodybuilder ordered.

When she did, he passed them to his colleague to be put

through the scanner. Megan concentrated on the guy in front of her. His fingers wound through her ponytail. Looking for pins? She wasn't sure. They trailed down her neck, over her shoulders and straight to her breasts—surprise, surprise. She worked hard to keep her body relaxed and a half smile on her face while he groped her in the name of security. And he was thorough in his groping. What he thought she was keeping in her G-string, she didn't know. She forced herself to smile when all she wanted to do was kick his dick into next week. When this was over, she'd have to shower with Lysol. Even then, she wasn't sure she'd ever wash the memory of his touch from her body. Instead of gagging, she tried to look as though his assault was turning her on. No point in making an enemy this early in her plan. As her mother always said—you catch more flies with honey.

When he'd finished, she resisted the urge to shudder and instead winked at him. He handed over her shoes and bag. Deliberately holding on to his arm she put the shoes back on, she let her hand trail over him before she released him.

"Maybe later, when I'm finished with your boss, you and I could have a private meeting all of our own." One where he helped her escape, maybe?

"I'll escort you to Mr Abramovich," the big guy said.

His grip was firm on her arm as walked her to the front door of the house.

"You must work out." Megan batted her lashes at him. "I bet you're just mouth-watering without a shirt on."

The bodybuilder's eyes darkened as he looked down at her. He opened the door and gestured for her to go on through. As she did, she glanced in the direction she knew Callum was perched and winked.

With a deep breath, she walked into the house.

# CHAPTER 20

The house was a palace. Marble and gold leaf everywhere, but still remarkably tasteful. Uniformed staff scurried about the place, dusting, carrying trays and generally keeping busy. Guards were posted at various points. There weren't as many as expected. By the time she reached Rudi's office she'd only counted four. They were dressed in black, armed and wired for communication. She pretended they didn't exist for the most part, but smiled when one caught her eye.

A hand at her elbow led her through the house, past the staircase to a large wooden door on the right hand side. Another guard stood outside the door.

"I'll take it from here," he told her protector.

With a nod, she was handed over. Megan smiled at the bodybuilder as he left, hoping her flirting would help her get out of there later. Twenty minutes, that was all she had before the guys came storming in. A glance at the face of her cheap plastic watch told her she had nineteen minutes left.

The door swung open and Megan swallowed her nerves. Clutching her bag with shaking hands, she was led into the room. She reminded herself to swing her hips and act relaxed. Yeah. Not easy. Especially when, behind the vast wooden desk that dominated the room, Rudi Abramovich stood watching her, like a lion stalking prey.

After a moment, he nodded to the guard to leave and she was alone with him. His ex-wife had been right. When the women called asking for advice on how to handle this meeting, Hope had been certain Rudi would want to be alone with her. His arrogance wouldn't allow him to see Megan as a threat. Hope said he'd want an opportunity to toy with her. That he always toyed with his prey.

Megan scanned the room as she faked nonchalance. It was decorated in blues and creams. Tasteful. Elegant. On the desk was a laptop. On her left, against the wall, was a cabinet that functioned as a bar. The top held crystal decanters of whisky. There were two sofas flanking a coffee table. French provincial—her brain supplied the style as her eyes skimmed the room. On the wall beside the desk were three monitors. One showed the interior of the guardhouse.

"I watched your entry." Rudi rounded the desk. "I was expecting you to arrive with a colleague of mine. Dimitri Petrokov."

Megan shrugged. "Dimitri had a little run in with a Taser. He's currently locked in the boot of his car." She leaned in to him and whispered. "Between you and me, I'm hoping he rots there."

His eyebrows arched. "So, you manged to escape your jailer. Why didn't you run back home to your husband in Scotland? Why come to me?"

"When I found out you were looking for me and realised who you were, I knew my options would be considerably better with you than with Grunt." She sneered the name of her sister's husband.

"Is that right?" Amusement, instead of suspicion, oozed from him. "And did Dimitri tell you the plans I have for you?"

Megan channelled the cheap seductive moves of every reality TV bimbo she'd ever seen. "I'm hoping we can come to an agreement that will make you keep me around instead of giving me away."

"You're risking a lot on this hope."

"I think it's worth the chance," she purred. What woman purred? None. That's who. She was making herself nauseous. "You're a very handsome and powerful man. We'd be good together."

It was beyond surreal, standing in front of the man who hunted her sister. A man who was very good at pulling on the veneer of sophistication while nurturing the evil within him. He granted her an amused smile and she was struck once again by his model looks. He was elegantly dressed in a Savile Row suit. Grey silk, subtle and tasteful. He wore an open-necked white shirt beneath it. His hair was tousled but expensively cut, and his eyes were mesmerising. He was gorgeous. George Clooney gorgeous. Which actually helped her focus on the situation instead of drooling over the beautiful package of evil before her. Clooney was way too old for her. If he'd been Chris Hemsworth gorgeous, she would have been in trouble.

"Why should I believe that you would give up your husband so easily?"

She licked her lips as she slowly looked him over, head to toe. "Trust me when I say, I'd rather be here. Grunt is so..." She pretended to cast around for a word then supplied the one Hope had given her. "Unsophisticated."

His eyes flared with approval. His ex-wife had been right. The guy was seriously into himself. When she got out of this, she was going to send Hope a huge hamper filled with chocolate.

"Well, Claire." His charming façade firmly in place, he

held out a hand. "It *is* lovely to meet you, at last. You are much more than I expected you to be."

"Thank you, so are you."

As soon as she clasped his hand, the hidden compartment in her ring triggered. The pin prick made him jerk back slightly. Megan pretended she didn't notice, refusing to let go of his hand as she stepped towards him. All she needed was a few seconds for the chemical to enter his system.

He smiled and it lit up his face, making him even more dazzlingly handsome. "Now that you're here, what do you want?"

"I want the same thing you want," she said seductively. "I want to make Grunt pay."

"Is that right?"

She gestured to the sofa. "May I sit?"

"By all means." He swayed slightly as he took the armchair beside her.

He was toying with her, exactly as Hope said he would. Megan reached into her handbag and pressed the record button on her MP3 player.

"If you tell me why you want Grunt to suffer," she said, "I'll tell you why I want the same thing."

He was amused by her guile. "It is very simple. The man took something from me and I wish to take something from him." With a slight shake of his head, he gripped the wooden arms of the upholstered chair as though to steady himself.

"You like to keep your possessions," she said with her own smile. "He stole from you."

The amusement fled from his eyes. "I worked hard for my possessions. I will not have anyone take what is mine."

Evil made his features ugly and Megan's blood chilled. *This* was the man who tortured and killed without remorse. The rest was just packaging. Underneath the pretty exterior was pure, unadulterated vileness.

He blinked and the dark ugly thing that was his true heart disappeared. His eyes were glazed. "What have you done to me?" The words were slurred.

"The same thing you like to do with the women you take. I've drugged you to make you easier to handle."

When he worked hard to focus on her face, Megan knew he wasn't really seeing her anymore. He was seeing whatever his mind supplied and she hoped they were visions full of the horror he deserved.

"You should be proud. I got the idea for the ring from you." Megan pulled the roll of pink tape out of her bag. "Clever, huh? Very *Man From Uncle*."

He mumbled something, but it was incoherent. Too drugged and out of it to call for help, he was still able to make noise and that wouldn't do. She ripped off some tape and made a cross shape over his mouth. Then she wrapped the tape around his wrist and secured his hand to the wooden armrest. His head lolled to the side with a muted groan.

Megan rooted around in his pockets for his phone. As soon as she found it she snapped off the back. The SIM card went into the slit she'd cut in the hem of her dress. The battery was removed and slipped under the couch. Taking the two skin-coloured elastic bands out of her hair, she used them to attach the phone to his hand. With his elbow on the other armrest, phone positioned against his ear, she secured him in position with the tape—making sure it was wrapped around his wrist under the cuff of his shirt, so you couldn't see it. If anyone peeked in the door they'd see his back, sitting on the chair with his phone in his hand.

Good.

He groaned. She ignored it. It was exactly the kind of sound effects the guard outside the door would expect if he was having sex. Well, if he was having bad sex. She was pretty sure she made way better noises than that. She glanced at her watch. Twelve minutes. Megan tugged the ring off his finger and ran to the laptop, pressing buttons randomly to boot it up.

"Come on, come on." She removed the hidden USB cable from the hollow heel of her modified shoe, where it had been made to look like part of the shoe design. After she attached it to her MP3 player, she connected it to the laptop.

Ten minutes. Her fingers flew over the keyboard as she typed in the commands Elle had drilled into her. Music from her MP3 player filled the room. Good. That was good. She laughed loudly and called Rudi's name for the guard listening outside the room. All the while she typed, opening the programme Elle had installed into her modified MP3 player. Using Hope's directions she hit the secret button on Rudi's ring to reveal the micro USB connection. She plugged it into the laptop. Elle's programme would do the rest. It would copy the information, wipe the ring clean and upload a virus that would be transferred to Rudi's cloud account—and hopefully downloaded to his secure information box in Switzerland as well.

Eight minutes. Elle said the programme would take at least six.

She glanced back at Rudi, only to see he was sliding off the chair. Running barefoot back over to him, she knew there wasn't enough tape on the roll to secure him to the seat. There had to be another option. He wasn't wearing a tie. There were no cords or sashes in the room. She glanced down to check the time and it hit her. She whipped her dress over her head, then removed her bra, before putting the dress back on. Pulling tight, she wrapped the bra around Rudi and the chair, straining to clasp it. She felt particularly grateful that the cheap elastic stretched far enough. Done. She hoped the elastic left a mark. With his jacket draped over the back of the chair, you couldn't see it at all. Perfect. She even tugged the cups up to make it look like he was wearing it. Just because.

Dance music thudded through the room. Megan added some Meg Ryan orgasm noises into the mix as Rudi's head lolled and his eyes closed. Nope, that wouldn't do. She wanted him awake for this part. She smacked his cheek to get his attention. When his drugged eyes looked up at her she held his chin to keep him in place.

"Just how many women have you raped and killed, Rudi? How many have you let other men rape and kill? You really didn't give a crap about any of those women, did you? I know you didn't and you deserve to pay for everything you've done. But, see, here's the thing." Megan pulled the last elastic tie out of her hair, letting it fall loose to her shoulders. "I can't kill you. Mainly because I'm not a killer and I honestly don't think I could live with your sorry death on my conscience. No matter how much of a service I would be doing the world. In saying that, I really do think you deserve to be punished."

She held up the elastic ring. "See this? It's my version of a docking band. We use docking bands in the Highlands to remove sheep tails. The ring tightens and tightens until the appendage falls off. This one was made just for you. Can you guess where I'm going to put it?"

He shook his head, but it lolled around on his shoulders. She checked her watch. Five minutes. With an air of detachment, she unzipped his trousers and pulled him free. Hope was right, he was tiny. She snapped the band on at the base of his penis, tugged it as tight as possible and fastened it, the same way you would a zip tie. Okay, so it was nothing like a true docking band, but it would certainly do the job. The only way that sucker was coming off was if it was cut off, but doing that would cause some serious damage. Although, to be fair, probably not as much damage as leaving it on. She fastened the trousers back up. Hopefully nobody would find the ring until his penis had fallen off.

The computer beeped behind her and Megan ran over to it. Done. Good. She tapped some more keys and Rudi's voice rumbled out of the machine, repeating the short conversation they'd had earlier. She left it on a low loop. Loud enough for people to know he was talking, but not so loud they could make out what was being said.

She quickly unplugged her MP3 player and cables, and stuffed it all back into her bag. The ring was forced back onto Rudi's finger, knowing that the drugs would mean he didn't even remember her taking it off. Lastly, she fished around in her bag for the permanent marker. The casing might have been pink and sparkly, but the ink part was jet black.

It was so tempting to write the truth about him across his face. Rapist. Murderer. Slave trader. Wife beater. Oh how she wished the words could be tattooed into his skin. The ugly core of this man *should* be evident on his exterior. Unfortunately, she couldn't risk anyone seeing the words and guessing she'd messed with other parts of him.

Opening his shirt wide, she wrote her warning across his chest: *leave Claire alone or else.* Not exactly Shakespeare, but he should get the message. A cold rage overtook her as she remembered the woman in the photos from the day before with words sliced into her body. Her hand twitched with the need to grab a knife and do the same to Rudi.

A noise outside the door reminded her she was on a schedule. She fastened Rudi's shirt. Fluffed her hair, wiped her lipstick off with the back of her hand and pinched her cheeks to make them look flushed.

Two minutes.

She arranged Rudi's clothes so they would look dishevelled from behind, then opened the door. The stony faced guard immediately blocked her exit.

She forced a smile. "He's on an important phone call. He told me to come back another day."

The guard frowned. He looked over her shoulder at Rudi while Megan held her breath. This was it. Life or death. The moment of truth. He would either see a man rumpled from sex and making a call, or he would see a scene staged for him. If he saw the latter, her life was over. Her palms began to sweat and there was a strange tingling in her legs, which she thought might be her body preparing to run. Breathing was hard. Waiting harder. Eternity. It was an eternity.

"Okay." The guard nodded and Megan almost passed out from relief. "I'll escort you out."

"Thank you." She kept her eyes down and tried to look helpless.

Hope was right. Rudi had been too arrogant to let his minions know who she was and how much he wanted to own her. Otherwise they would never have let her walk out of the house.

"He said he's not to be disturbed until he's done with the call. He seemed kind of mad."

The guard nodded once, held her arm and escorted her out. Heart pounding, muscles tingling and fighting the urge to hyperventilate, Megan let him lead her through the building. When she walked out of the door, she winked in the general direction of Callum's hiding place and hoped he got the message.

The bodybuilder was waiting at the gate for her. "I'll call you a cab," he said.

She shook her head. "Don't bother. I fancy a walk." She ran a fingertip down the centre of his chest and her heart pounded so fast she thought she might pass out. "It's been very nice meeting you."

Her stomach was flip flopping continually and she felt like she was going to vomit. Or pass out. Neither option was a good one. As she turned towards the gate, she spotted someone out of the corner of her eye and her world stopped dead.

Reynard Durand.

The guy she'd shot in the backside in Scotland. The guy who'd terrified Hope. The guy who knew who she was and wanted to get his hands on her to win favour with Rudi.

That guy.

He stood beside a car at the corner of the house, talking to another man. Megan ducked her head and tapped her bag against her leg. A nervous gesture, she hoped the body-builder wouldn't notice. It was impossible to stay still when every cell in her body was screaming for her to run.

Slowly, oh so slowly, the gate began to open. She heard movement behind her. Footsteps on gravel. She couldn't hear anything more. The sound of her own blood rushing through her veins drowned out everything else. She couldn't tell if the footsteps were coming towards her or going away.

At last, the gate opened enough for her to squeeze through. Smiling at the guard one last time, so as not to raise any suspicions, she ducked her head and pretended to fish around in her handbag as she walked away.

A voice called out behind her. "Wait. Miss. Wait."

She kept on walking. Picking up speed. Trying hard not to run. Not to hurry too much. She just had to make it to the end of the street. Around the corner, Elle was parked waiting for her. She just had to make it to Elle.

She heard footsteps thudding on the pavement behind her and held her breath. Her team were out there. Callum, no doubt, had his gun trained in her direction. They could see what was happening. They wouldn't let Durand hurt her. She was sure of it.

A hand on her arm. Her vision blurred. A body appeared in front of her.

The bodybuilder.

It was the bodybuilder. He held up her phone. "You forgot this."

"Thanks." Her voice was breathy from anxiety, but she hoped he read it as lust.

"I programmed my number. It's under C for call me."

*Ew! Yuck. Yuck. Yuck.* "You know I will."

She turned on her expensive, but modified, heel and sauntered to the end of the street, putting an extra swing into her hips, just in case.

As soon as she rounded the corner she bolted for the bright blue Mini Cooper, parked illegally in front of the entrance to someone's house. Elle was behind the wheel. Megan threw herself into the car.

"Go. Go. Go." She slouched down in the seat as Elle pulled out into traffic.

"You okay?" Elle said.

"I think I'm going to vomit."

"Understandable. But don't do it in the car."

"You're all heart."

"I know." Elle gave her a manic, near hysterical, grin. "You can get up now."

Megan sat up in her seat and fumbled with her seatbelt. "My hands are shaking."

"Adrenalin." Elle cast her a sideward glance. "Or fear. Just how terrifying was it?"

"Not so bad while I was in there. I had to focus on the job. But now..."

"Yeah." Elle turned into the main road, heading to Rachel's house as they'd prearranged.

"I need a shower." Megan watched the busy shopping street pass by. It was filled with people who were having a normal Friday afternoon. The sight made everything Megan had just done, even more surreal. "I have to wash away the stink of Abramovich." She didn't even want to think about the part of him she'd touched.

"He deserved it." Elle's lips thinned.

"I know, he deserved that and more. Damn, Elle, when I close my eyes all I can see are the photos of the women he hurt. I keep thinking that could be Claire and then I remember that it *is* Katrina." She went to rub her eyes but remembered her hands were dirty. Invisible dirt from touching Rudi. "You got any wipes?"

"Glove compartment."

Megan pulled out the antibacterial wipes and used all of them cleaning her hands.

"Do you think he'll stop going after Claire?" Elle turned into Rachel's road.

"I hope so." Surely, even Abramovich would heed this warning? "Stop the car."

Elle swerved to the kerb and Megan threw open the door. She emptied her stomach in the gutter, much to the disgust of a passer-by. When she sat back in her seat and closed the door, Elle handed her a bottle of lemon flavoured water.

"I'm sorry," Megan said as she gratefully took it.

"Don't be. I couldn't have done what you did."

"We did it together." She gulped the water. It was the truth. She may have been the one to walk into the building, but without the rest of the women it wouldn't have happened.

"I just hope the guys understand."

"I hope Dimitri understands."

"He will once he realises you got the information he needs."

Megan wasn't so sure. In Dimitri's eyes she'd put his sister at risk. Megan didn't see it that way. She was certain the level of risk in the plan she'd just pulled off was less than it would have been if she'd gone in with Dimitri.

She knew now that there was no way the two of them could have disabled the guards and then walked out of there. It would have been chaos. And, assuming Dimitri was even able to knock Rudi out long enough for them to get the information on the ring, Rudi would have known as soon as he came to that they'd accessed his records. The police wouldn't have had a chance to plan for a raid. Rudi would have shut things down. Megan rested her forehead against the cool glass of the passenger window as Elle used the fob Rachel had given her to open the security door to the private garage.

No, this way was better. She just hoped Dimitri would come to understand that.

"Come on," Elle said after she'd parked the car in one of Rachel's spots. "You need a cocktail."

"After a shower."

They climbed out of the car and headed to the elevator. Before the doors opened, Megan turned to her friend and confessed. "I was terrified I would screw the whole thing up."

"It's okay." Elle pulled her into a tight hug. "It's okay."

And then they rode together up to Rachel's apartment.

# CHAPTER 21

Elle was right. Cocktails did help. So did the long, steaming hot shower Megan took where she scrubbed her skin red to remove the memory of the body search. Unfortunately, it would take a lot more than expensive body wash and a loofah to rid her of the memory of touching Rudi.

"When do you think the guys will calm down?" Megan sat on the edge of Rachel's pool, sipping a blue cocktail with a cherry in it. Elle said the drink was called: *She got away with it.* Megan wasn't sure the name was legit, but the taste was heaven.

"Duh, never," Elle replied from the bar in the corner of the pool room, where she was mixing more drinks from her imagination.

"They might calm down a little when they realise how successful the operation was." Julia sounded more hopeful than convinced. "Maybe Rachel should send them a text to let them know we have Rudi's records. They must be worried about it."

"Bad idea," Elle said. "Better not to contact them until we know they're calm and rational."

"Which might happen faster if we keep them informed."

The sight of Julia gently arguing with Rachel made Megan do a double take. She was overwhelmed with a surge of pride and had to fight the urge to break into a cheer.

Elle cast a sceptical glance at Julia. "And they'll forgive us for cutting them out of the loop, they'll then offer to cater to our every whim and we'll all live happily ever after."

Julia let out a heavy sigh. "Okay, I get the point. But I don't like shouting and there will be shouting when we see them."

"Earplugs," Rachel announced. "Discreet and effective. Put them in, think of something you can cope with, like puppies, and smile politely no matter what happens."

"Helpful," Megan said.

Rachel inclined her head. "It's a gift." She took another sip of the luminous blue liquid. "For heaven's sake, Julia, put on a swimsuit."

"I'm fine, thank you," Julia said, as though she was being offered another cup of tea rather than being criticised. Amazingly, the tactic shut Rachel down.

Megan looked at her friend. While the rest of the women were in swimwear they'd borrowed from Rachel's vast selection, the best Julia had managed was to take off her brown woollen dress. She sat beside the pool in her white utilitarian underwear and a full length beige slip. Seriously. A slip. Megan thought they'd stopped making those in the fifties. As soon as this mess was over she was taking Julia shopping for some lingerie designed in the twenty-first century.

Elle plopped down beside Megan and swished her feet in the water. "Don't you worry the pool will crack and you'll drown in your sleep?" she asked Rachel.

Rachel reclined, elegantly, on a white lounger. Her eyes closed. "No."

"Come on." Elle pointed at the pool. "There's a glass

ceiling between your bed and a tonne of water. You can't tell me you don't lie there awake at night looking for cracks."

"I like looking at the water at night. It's relaxing." Rachel didn't open her eyes, but took a sip of her cocktail.

"But you're *under* the water." Elle just couldn't get her head around this. "It's unnatural."

Rachel opened her eyes. "So is your hair."

Megan held up a hand. "Hey, remember you promised to retire your inner bitch for the evening."

"I apologise," Rachel said, in a tone that conveyed she couldn't care less.

"I like my blue hair." Elle fluffed her bob. "It's groovy."

"Do people still say groovy?" Julia asked.

"Julia, hon, you need to join this century," Elle told her, mirroring Megan's thoughts. "Retro is in again."

Julia looked down at her slip. "I'm not very good at being in this century."

"We can tell by your wardrobe," Rachel said.

Elle frowned at her boss. "Don't worry, Julia. Tomorrow we'll take you shopping and help you out. We'll get you a cool new wardrobe."

"Makeover!" Megan held her glass aloft as she grinned.

"I don't know…" Julia chewed her bottom lip.

"It will be fun," Elle declared.

Julia blushed. "Okay. We can do that."

"After we deal with the men," Megan pointed out.

"Yep," Elle said. "After we deal with the men."

"And just how do you think you'll deal with us?" said a baritone behind them.

Megan squealed and jumped into the pool, still holding her cocktail glass. She spluttered as she brushed her wet hair from her face, only to find Elle and Julia in the water beside her. Rachel was still lounging on her seat, her position unchanged. The woman had nerves of steel.

"Who let you in?" Rachel barked at them. "This building has security."

"We let ourselves in. The security is pants." A vein throbbed in Callum's neck. Not a good sign. "Put on a robe and go deal with your concierge. He thinks we're here to attack you."

"Are you?" Rachel stared at the men coolly.

"No. Sort him out. We have things to discuss."

"What's to stop me going down there and summoning the police instead? I'm sure they'd be happy to remove you from my home."

That vein throbbed again. "Don't test me, Rachel."

Megan swallowed hard. It was very clear they'd pushed the man to his limit. Even Rachel was wise enough to back down.

"Fine. I'll be back shortly." She grabbed a plush white robe, slipped into it, along with some designer flip-flops, and headed out of the apartment.

Megan noticed that only Callum watched her leave. Joe was staring at Julia, who was now cowering behind Elle. And Dimitri was glaring at Megan. Fury vibrated off the three men. This wasn't good. She would have much rather dealt with them when they'd calmed down—in a couple of months. Maybe. She tried to casually glance around her, looking for an exit that didn't take her past the men.

"Please," Dimitri said. "Try to run. I dare you."

Her eyes snapped back to him. The sight of his tense muscles and death ray glare made her decide staying in the water was a better plan. She wasn't a coward by any stretch of the imagination, but she still took a step closer to Elle. Safety in numbers and all that.

"Get out of the pool," Callum ordered. "We need to debrief."

Megan caught Elle's eyes, and saw the same surprise she

felt at Callum's term. Debrief sounded very civilised. Perhaps he wasn't that mad after all.

"By debrief," Joe said, "he means find out why you scrapped the operation, went AWOL and put the life of one of your teammates in danger." He pointed at Megan. "You could have been killed. You went in there alone, unarmed, to face off against a guy who's known for hurting women. Not cool. Seriously, not cool."

"You kept your team in the dark," Dimitri said. "You kept your partner in the dark. You risked lives. Yours. Claire's. Mine. Katrina's."

Okay, so not so civilised.

"Out. Now." Callum's voice was deadly low. The kind of tone no one dared argue with.

With slumped shoulders the women moved in a line towards the stairs. Dimitri grabbed a couple of towels and threw them at her and Elle as they climbed out of the pool. Julia, who had just noticed her slip and white underwear had turned transparent, was trying to cover herself with her hands while her face turned pink. Joe took the last towel, stepped up to Julia and wrapped it around her. She held it tight as she stared at his feet.

"Living room." Callum barked.

He stepped to the side to let Megan and Elle pass. Megan could have sworn she heard his teeth grind together. They obviously weren't moving fast enough for Joe, who picked Julia up and strode from the room with her in his arms. She squealed her protest, but Joe ignored her.

Megan caught Dimitri's eyes and opened her mouth to explain. He held up a hand, fury emanating from his very pores. "Don't. I'm so mad at you I can't think straight."

She snapped her mouth closed and hurried after the other women. By the time Rachel came back everyone was downstairs in the living room. The three women were sitting in a row on one of her huge expensive sofas, clutching their towels around them. The London skyline was behind them and the men were standing, arms folded, staring at them.

Rachel sashayed into the room and stood behind the sofa, folding her arms to mirror the men. No one said a word. A few seconds later the door banged open and Ryan ran in.

"What'd I miss?" He sounded particularly gleeful, which made all of the women frown at him.

Callum cast him a cool glance. "We haven't started yet."

"Cool. Time to grab a snack then." He headed into Rachel's kitchen.

"I didn't say you could help yourself, Ryan," Rachel told him and Ryan just grinned as he opened the fridge.

"Okay," Callum said. "Before we get into how stupid…"

"Irresponsible…" Joe said.

"And dangerous…" Dimitri added.

"Your stunt was today," Callum continued. "You four are going to start at the top. I want every detail of this plan. Now."

Megan shared a glance with Elle. Julia was studying her feet, her shoulders hunched as she curled in on herself.

"Now!" Callum shouted.

Megan took a breath. Seriously, what was the worst that could happen here? The guys were mad, sure, but they wouldn't hurt them, so the worst they were looking at was some shouting and posturing. She squared her shoulders. Years of dealing with her cop brother had made sure she was immune to angry posturing.

"It started when you lot decided to hang Claire out to dry," Megan said, and all eyes snapped to her.

"And let a rapist carry on with his business," Rachel added.

"When I signed up for this, it was on the assurance that Claire would be made safe during this operation." Megan glared at the men. They were angry? Well so was she. "You lot broke your end of the deal."

"I told you Claire would be safe," Joe said.

"Eventually. The key word here is eventually. I want my sister safe now."

"So you jeopardised my sister to make it happen?" Dimitri's anger was barely contained, breaking through in the tight white lines around his mouth.

"Exactly the same way *you* jeopardised *mine* to get the information you needed on Katrina."

"You put yourself at risk." Dimitri took a step towards her. Callum slapped his palm in the middle of Dimitri's chest. "It better have been worth the risk. You and the rest of your girl gang better not have fucked up getting the information we need on Katrina's whereabouts." Dimitri's eyes were pure black.

Megan felt her indignation evaporate. She'd mess around with him over many things, but not this, this was too important. And she, more than anyone else in the room, understood his fear.

"Elle," she said.

"We have everything," Elle said. "My laptop is decrypting it now. We'll know where your sister is very soon."

The air went out of Dimitri. As though his knees couldn't hold him, he sank to the chair behind him.

"You're sure?" he asked Elle.

"Absolutely."

The lines around his mouth faded as he looked back at Megan with eyes too dark to read.

She held his gaze. "I wouldn't screw up something that important."

"But you could have," Dimitri said.

She shook her head. "No, not that part. All I wanted was a chance to sort out the problem for my sister at the same time as getting the information you needed on yours. Is that so much to ask? You know what I'm fighting for here. You more than anyone else."

With a reluctant air, Dimitri gave her a stiff nod.

"How did you do it?" Callum asked. "How did you immobilise Rudi and the guards without Dimitri to help you?"

Megan glanced at her friends. "Well, Hope said if I went in there alone and played to his ego, he'd dismiss the guards to spend time with me. That's exactly what happened. I amused him and he didn't see me as a threat. He told the guard to leave. I drugged him and then I got the information we needed."

There was silence. Four guys stared at Megan with identical expressions. She wasn't sure what the expressions were, stunned maybe? Worried? Nope, it was too hard to tell. Time ticked by and still no one spoke.

Elle clapped her hands and stood. "Great, well I'm glad we cleared that up." She gave Megan a "what the hell?" look. "How about we order pizza?" She headed towards the phone.

"Sit." Callum ordered.

Elle didn't argue. She sat.

"You drugged him?" Callum's voice sounded strained.

"Yes."

"Explain." It was another order. Megan was beginning to get a bit cheesed off by the many orders coming her way.

"Okay," Megan said. "It's like this. We knew from our many, many team meetings and briefings, that I wouldn't be allowed to take any tech into the building. So we went old school." She couldn't resist a grin at Elle and Julia—who was still staring at the floor. "Julia spoke to a guy she knew in the props department at the BBC. He found the coolest ring for me. It'd been used in a spy movie and was hollowed out, to hold liquid. It even had a little injector spike that shot out when you shook hands." She couldn't stop the excitement that seeped into her voice. So sue her, that ring was seriously righteous. "Anyway, Rachel tapped her family connections, who are in the pharmaceutical business, and we filled the ring with a ketamine and rohypnol cocktail."

"I need to sit down for this," Callum muttered as he perched on the edge of the armchair behind him.

"It was totally cool. The ring worked perfectly. As soon as Rudi shook my hand, it activated and he was injected with the drug. If you think about it, it was poetic. A ring to knock him out and get the ring with the records."

"I just realised," Elle said. "You had the ring to rule them all."

They fist bumped.

"Holy crap." Joe ran a hand over his head. "It's like hearing about a train wreck after the fact."

"You dosed the guy with date rape drugs?" Callum said.

"I need a drink." Dimitri headed for the kitchen where Ryan pulled out a bottle of whisky.

Megan scrunched up her nose. "I didn't sexually abuse him or anything, if that's what you're thinking."

"No. I wasn't thinking that." Callum took the glass of whisky Dimitri handed him and emptied it in one swallow. "What did you do to him?"

"I secured him to his chair. And then I used the micro USB connection lead that was hidden in my shoe heel to connect to his laptop." She grinned widely. "Julia's friend, the prop guy at the BBC, modified my shoes for me. He did such a great job, the modifications didn't even turn up when they ran my shoes through their scanner."

The men just stared at her. Megan didn't know what to make of that. In the end, she decided they were awed by the brilliance of the plan. She elbowed Elle, signalling it was her turn again.

"While Rudi was a slobbering mess," Elle said, "Megan

downloaded the information on his ring to an old MP3 player I'd modified. She then wiped the data from the ring and uploaded a virus to it that should travel through Rudi's cloud account to his data storage unit in Switzerland."

"Holy shit," Ryan said. "You can do that?"

Elle stuck her nose in the air. "Of course." She sighed. "Fine. I *may* have asked Harry to work on the programme. I *may* have told him it was a hypothetical situation. I *may* have made it into a challenge so he'd write the code by the time we needed it."

Callum held his glass out to Dimitri who took it and went for a refill.

Elle cleared her throat. "It's not that I couldn't have written the code myself. It's just that Harry is a freaking genius and did it way faster."

"He doesn't know you used his code to break into a secure facility, does he?" Callum asked.

"To be clear," Elle said. "It's not the whole facility, just the storage area Rudi uses. It will wipe out everything there, but it won't spread."

Callum took the refilled glass from Dimitri and nodded his thanks. He downed it in one go again. "Do you four realise how many international laws you broke doing that shit?"

"Yes, but *we* didn't do it." Elle was trying to look innocent. She nearly pulled it off. "Harry did it. Hypothetically speaking."

Megan had to clench her fists to stop from giving the woman a high five. But Callum's eyes were on her. He stared at her long enough to make her squirm.

"That isn't all you did, is it, Megan?"

She wasn't going to deny it. The reason she went in there was warn Rudi off Claire. She'd done her job. Nothing more. "No. That isn't all I did." From the looks on the faces around the room she wasn't sure she wanted to tell him the rest.

"Spit it out," Callum ordered as Dimitri's eyes burned laser holes through her skull.

"I simply carried out the rest of the plan. I warned him off Claire." She crossed her fingers and hoped that was enough information.

"How?" Dimitri asked.

Megan took a deep breath. "I wrote the warning across his chest in permanent marker." She paused, wondering if they'd let her leave it at that. She was guessing from the death glares that they wouldn't. She took a deep breath and confessed the rest. "Then I used a modified version of a docking band on his penis."

The men froze at the word penis.

"A docking band?" Ryan sounded more than a little hesitant.

"It's basically a thick elastic band. It cuts off the blood supply to whatever you tighten it around, making it numb, die and fall off. It's commonly used on sheep tails."

"No!" Ryan called out in horror.

As though choreographed, each of the men covered their crotches with their hands. Megan looked at Elle to see if she noticed and they burst out laughing. Rachel joined in from where she stood behind them.

"That is sick." Ryan shook his head. He looked kind of pale. "You have an obsession with damaging men's packages. You need counselling, woman."

"Really?" Rachel snapped. "Is it as sick as raping and murdering women? As sick as selling young women, barely more than girls, to brothels where they are raped repeatedly? As sick as beating his wife to the point where she would have rather died than endure another punch to her stomach?" Rachel's voice vibrated with anger. "Tell me Ryan? Is it wrong, when a man uses his penis as a weapon, for someone to remove that weapon from him?"

"I think I'm going to vomit," Ryan said.

Rachel pointed to the corridor off the lounge. "Toilet is first on the left."

"How the hell did you manage to get out of there when you'd left Rudi drugged and, and, you know…" Joe looked a little green himself.

"I staged it to look like he was on the phone and then I walked out." Megan shrugged like it was no big deal. The last thing she wanted was for the men to know how close she'd been to losing her mind to fear with each step she took out of there.

"Are we sure we got all the information we need to shut Rudi's operation down for good?" Callum asked.

Elle pointed to a laptop on the table in the corner of the room. "Before I started messing around with the code to decrypt the sections that needed it, I made several complete copies and sent them to the office. We have a lot of information already from the stuff that wasn't encrypted. More than enough to decimate his organisation."

"Great, that's great," Callum said as he stood. "Unfortunately, it doesn't change things at this end." He pointed at Megan. "You are lucky to be alive." He stared at each of the women in turn. "The rest of you are lucky this didn't go belly up. We could have lost Megan along with the information needed to retrieve Dimitri's sister." He glared at them as he folded his arms. "Luck. That's what this comes down to. Not field expertise or skill or training. Luck. That's not how this team works. We don't rely on luck. And we certainly don't have space on this team for people who don't play by the rules. We're taking over from here on in. You lot can pack your bags. You're fired."

# CHAPTER 22

"What?" Megan shot to her feet, letting her fluffy white towel crumple around her ankles. She put her fists on her hips and glared at Callum. It would probably have looked more intimidating if she wasn't wearing a leopard print bikini, but whatever. "You're firing us?"

"You can't fire me," Rachel said. "It's in my contract."

Callum gave her a cold look. "There's nothing in your contract that says I can't suspend you indefinitely. I'm happy to keep on paying you to stay out of the office and out of my business."

"You're firing us?" Elle demanded. "For getting the job done? For getting you information? For stopping Rudi in his tracks? For protecting Claire? You're firing us for that?" Her outrage was tangible.

Megan pointed at her. "What she said."

"Oh, no. Not again," Julia muttered. "I can't lose another job. I just can't. I can't."

Megan looked at the woman who had her head between her knees and was rocking slightly as she fought a panic attack. She pointed at Julia.

"You broke Julia! That is not on." She stomped over and patted Julia's back while she looked at Joe. "You're going to let him fire Julia?"

Joe's lips thinned. "This is his company. His call."

"That's it. I'm calling my cousin." Megan stalked towards the breakfast bar where she'd left her phone.

"Call Harry," Callum said. "It won't change anything. You lot endangered yourselves and the rest of the team today. You," he pointed at Megan, "especially, are way out of line. You Tasered your partner and locked him in a trunk. You endangered the whole operation. You could have cost us the chance to find out where Dimitri's sister is stashed. You're irresponsible. Reckless. You're dangerous. And you don't give a crap about your team. Tell your cousin that while you're on the line to him. Yeah, you got the job done. But that wasn't a guaranteed outcome. It was luck. The end doesn't justify the means when you betray your team to achieve it. This could have gone badly wrong. And you want me to congratulate you? Okay then. Well done. Your rash and selfish actions didn't get you killed. Well done indeed."

The room was silent—only Julia's panicked breathing could be heard. Callum's words sliced through Megan's anger. A huge wave of guilt washed over her and she fought not to drown. She glanced at Dimitri, unconsciously seeking reassurance. His silent, unflinching stare was a condemnation in itself.

"You treat this like a game." Joe was clearly disgusted. "It isn't a game. People's lives are on the line. Nobody wants someone on the team they can't trust to have their back. You might have gotten the results this time, but what about next time? Will your maverick behaviour mean someone gets hurt? Or the mission gets compromised? Or a teammate dies? I'm not prepared to put my life in your hands. I don't trust you."

It was as though she'd been slapped. Her face actually stung.

"He's right," Rachel said, making Megan feel nauseous. Rachel stared at Joe. "You're right."

There was nothing else to say.

Dimitri shifted in his chair, then stood and stalked to the window. He stood at the opposite end of the room from Rachel, his arms folded, glaring out into the night. Although Megan knew he was coping with his own feelings—anger, betrayal and hope at getting one step closer to finding his sister—his actions still felt like rejection. Stupidly, she wanted the man to stand up for her when she didn't deserve it. She wanted to hear that he forgave her, that he understood. Instead, she looked at the tense line of his back and felt bereft.

There was no getting away from the fact that Callum was right. She'd been lucky. Her inexperienced team had been lucky. And relying on luck was no way to stay safe in the long run. She'd let her own arrogance blind her to the risks. She hadn't really considered what would happen if things went badly. She hadn't let herself believe for one second that she wouldn't get the information Dimitri needed to find his sister. But that hadn't been confidence rooted in skill, it had been arrogance. The truth was, she could easily have blown it for him. She could have set his search for Katrina back months. Which meant she would have been responsible for everything Katrina suffered in that time. Why hadn't she seen that before now? The answer hit her hard as Joe's words beat at her soul. A game. She'd treated the whole thing like a game where having fun was more important than staying safe. How foolish and arrogant she'd been. Shame covered her like an early morning frost, making the joy that had bloomed in her success become brittle and break.

Her tongue stuck to the roof of her mouth, but there were

words that had to be said. "I didn't think…" No, that wasn't right. She had thought. Just not enough, not about the right things. Selfish. Arrogant. Flippant. Those words were closer to the truth.

"The end doesn't justify the means," Callum said again. His even words didn't come from anger this time, they came from pity.

"No." Megan swallowed hard. "No, it doesn't." She felt young and stupid and painfully aware of being exposed. "I'll pack up and head to Scotland. But will you think twice about the rest of the women? I was the one who led this revolt. It was my idea, my plan. I roped them in. Let them keep their jobs." She felt tears bite at her eyes. Reckless. She'd been reckless. With her life. With Katrina's. With Claire's. She looked at Dimitri. She'd been reckless with his trust. A last blow that hurt most of all. And it was nothing less than she deserved.

Callum heaved a sigh. He folded his arms. "I need people on this team who respect each other. Who take things seriously, follow orders and work well together. I don't think that applies to any of you."

"I'll go." Rachel surprised them all. "Elle should stay. I *am* her direct manager. I'm responsible. I'm sure if I'd vetoed her involvement, she would have listened." Having said her piece, she turned her back on all of them to stare out at the glittering lights of London.

Megan blinked back tears that would only humiliate her further.

"I appreciate the sentiment, Rach," Elle said. "But you're wrong. I would have gone behind your back and helped Megan." She looked at Callum. "I'll go too."

Julia clutched her stomach, her face grey. "You are absolutely right. I am as much to blame as Megan. I helped plan this from the beginning. I suggested we call Hope and that we use Rachel's family connections. May I stay in the flat over the weekend? I need time to sort out somewhere to live."

Callum gave a terse nod.

"Damn it," Joe said. "Callum…"

They stared at each other, silent communication passing between them. Callum shook his head slowly.

Joe let out an exasperated sigh. "We all stuffed up when we first started out in this business. We all got caught up in the adrenalin rush and did stupid things that put team members in danger. They did get results and they look like they understand what they did wrong."

They stared at each other, while Ryan sat silently at the breakfast bar and Dimitri stared out at the city. Megan looked down at her phone. She couldn't call Harry. She *wouldn't* call Harry. This was her fault and she needed to take the consequences like an adult. She let out a tremulous breath. Being an adult sucked big time. She didn't want to go back to Invertary. She didn't want to go back to hairdressing, or nannying, or baking cakes. She wanted to be a private security specialist. She wanted it badly. And she'd blown it.

"I got a teammate shot first time I went out on an op," Ryan said softly.

Everyone looked at him. Megan saw, for the first time, that underneath his boy wonder exterior was the hardened core of a warrior. She knew then why Lake had picked him for his team. Ryan's lips were tight as he stared at Callum and Joe.

Joe nodded. "We're at fault too. We didn't let the women in on the planning. We assumed they didn't have anything to contribute because they don't have our training. It was dumb. They're smart and skilled. It's just not what we're used to. We should have listened. If we had done, we might have come up with something that worked for everybody."

"It doesn't change things," Callum said to both men. "None of it does."

There was nothing else to say or do. She needed to get out of there. As she scrolled through her contacts looking for the taxi number her phone vibrated with a reminder that she had unread texts and stored voicemail messages. She opened the texts expecting to see Claire's name and hoping for comfort from her sister. Instead she saw an unknown number. She opened the message without thinking and stopped dead as she read it.

Slowly, she looked up at the people in the room. Faces were stoic. Nothing was being said. The tension was fog thick.

"Um, Callum." Megan flinched under his dark gaze, heavy with disappointment. "Remember that guy I shot in the backside in Scotland? The one trying to kidnap Claire for Rudi? Durand?" Of course he remembered. Stupid question. It was nerves talking. Or maybe shock. Who knew?

His shoulders tensed. He nodded once. Sharp.

Dimitri turned back from the window, his attention on her. Megan felt the weight of it, but strangely found it to be more reassuring than oppressive. She cleared her throat as she held up her phone.

"Yeah, well, Durand texted me."

# CHAPTER 23

*Megan, I know where you are and I'm coming for you.*

The words were burned into Dimitri's eyelids. He saw them each time he blinked. Elle had grabbed the phone, taken out the battery, removed the SIM card and plugged it into her laptop. Her fingers were flying over the keyboard, trying to reverse trace the message while they talked.

"Do you think he, like, literally knows where I am?" Megan asked as she came back in from the changing room beside the pool, a pile of clothes in her arms. "I mean, as in the address of this apartment."

"I don't think you need to worry," Rachel said. "This building has excellent security. Nobody is getting in here."

"We got in here," Joe said.

"Good point. I'll arrange hotel rooms for us until we know my home and the office are secure." Rachel picked up her phone from the coffee table, leaving the room as she dialled.

"I'm running a programme that will let me know if he hacked the phone or accessed the GPS," Elle said without looking up from her laptop screen. "We'll know in a couple of minutes if he has this physical location."

"We need tea." Julia scurried into the kitchen and put on the kettle. She was still wrapped in a towel.

"I got your clothes," Megan told her and Dimitri could almost feel the relief that was visible on Julia's face.

Julia hurried back across the room, nabbed her clothes and headed out of the room, all under Joe's watchful eye.

Dimitri watched Megan as she pulled on the red dress she'd worn to Rudi's house, over the bikini she'd borrowed from Rachel. Dimitri wanted to tear the dress from her body and rip it into tiny shreds, just because he knew Rudi Abramovich must have lusted after her while she was wearing it. The thought of her in that house alone with that monster made him want to pummel something until his knuckles bled.

He'd shut down when he heard her story. There was too much to process. He'd never been so close to panic as when she'd gone off on her own. Twin fears had assaulted him, ripping him in two. Anxiety over missing an opportunity to find out where Katrina was being held and terror over what Rudi might do to Megan. The complete and utter helplessness he'd felt had almost brought him to his knees. Only the ability to fall back on his training kept him standing.

Megan pulled her hair back into a messy bun, securing it with an elastic band she'd found in the desk. Delicate, she was delicate. Sure, she might be fearless and have skills that could help her in a crisis, but physically she was delicate. Soft skin, so easily marred. Long limbs, so easily broken. Damn it, he didn't know how he would have survived if something had happened to her. The thought made everything within him still—Megan Donaldson was important to him. Important in a way no other woman had ever been. She'd wormed her way into the heart of him. Sneaking under his crusty shell with her wit, intelligence and insanity. No. He couldn't lose Megan. His hands suddenly felt empty because he wasn't touching her.

"Tell me how Durand managed to get your number and why he's texting you." Callum perched on the edge of the armchair. He'd sent Ryan down to update the building's security team about the possible threat. Ryan would stay down there until Callum decided he was needed elsewhere.

"I saw him at the house. He didn't see me. I'm sure of it. He probably saw me on security footage after I left." Megan fluttered around the room while she spoke. Nerves keeping her on the move. She was worried about Durand. She should be—the guy was a grade A nutjob.

"By the sounds of it, they've discovered Rudi," Joe said. "That's the only way they'd know to check the security footage."

Callum nodded his agreement. "How'd he get your number, Megan?"

She cast a nervous glance at Dimitri that had his chest tightening. *What the hell had she done now?*

"My phone was confiscated. I flirted with one of the guards—as part of my cover," she hastily added. "Before I left he said he put his number in my phone. I assume he took my number too. Durand could have gotten the information from the guy."

There was a pause. Dimitri groaned and Joe exploded. "You took your personal phone on an op? Are you nuts?"

Megan's cheeks turned red. "It was an accident. I intended to take the cell from the car, but they got mixed up when I was dealing with Dimitri."

"You mean when you tied me up and stashed me in the trunk of the car." There was a good chance, even if they lived to a hundred, that he was never going to let that go.

"Sorry?" she said with a nervous smile.

"I want to know how you got him in the boot," Elle said. "He's almost twice your size."

"When I Tasered him he was standing at the boot, I just threw it opened and toppled him into it." She shrugged like it was nothing. At least that explained the lump on the top of his head and the crick in his neck.

Callum pinched the bridge of his nose. It was his go-to move when the stress was getting to him. Dimitri thought it was also what he did when he had the urge to shoot everyone around him.

Megan paced the room, unable to sit still. It was like trying to interrogate Tinker Bell. Dimitri couldn't take it anymore. He needed to touch her. He needed the solid reassurance that she was in one piece. As she walked past his perch on the arm of the sofa, he grabbed her. Pulling her into the V between his knees, he clamped his arms around her. Better. Much better. She wasn't making him dizzy anymore and he felt much more relaxed knowing he had a hold of her.

Dimitri caught sight of Joe smothering a smile as Megan squirmed in his hold.

"Stop it," he ordered against her ear.

The shiver that coursed through her body made him want to purr.

"Let go of me." She bit out the words, but he noticed she wasn't fighting that hard to get free.

"No." He nipped at her earlobe and felt justified when her jaw dropped in outrage.

"I can't believe," Elle grumbled, "that after all the planning we put into the tech side of the op, you blew it by taking your phone?"

"I told you, I had two phones. I left the wrong one in the car with Dimitri. It was a mistake. I was in a hurry to get out of there and picked up my usual phone."

This was exactly the kind of thing the guys were talking

about. She relied far too much on chance and not enough on planning and training. That kind of attitude was a sure way to get yourself killed. In this business there was always a certain amount of risk, but training, planning and good backup minimised it. He was going to make damn sure Megan realised that fact.

"You and I are going to have a long talk later about all the risks you take," Dimitri said against her ear. "Privately."

She swallowed hard, but only made a token effort to get out of his grip.

"Just how big a threat is this guy?" Callum looked to Dimitri for the answer.

"Big." Durand fit comfortably into the category labelled sociopath. "Story I heard was that, a few years ago, a guy in the States stole from him. Durand tracked him down. We're talking bloodhound stuff here—he hunted the guy for months until he found him. Then he cut off his fingers, toes and tongue before slitting his throat. The guy was alive for days learning his 'lesson'. Afterwards Durand made sure the message spread that no one gets the better of Reynard Durand. He will always find you and he will always exact revenge."

Megan's heart raced under his palm and he brushed his lips against her neck to reassure her. Durand would have to go through him to get to Megan. Delicate fingers curled around his wrist and she subtly shifted closer.

"Scotland," Joe said. "He won't forgive her for shooting him in the ass."

"No." Dimitri rubbed his thumb against her hip. "I was hoping he'd assume she was Claire and back off to let Rudi deal with her, but now he knows she's Megan the chances of him leaving her alone are slim."

"Great, we've got a psycho out for Megan. Just what we need." Callum massaged the back of his neck.

"I can go back to Scotland," Megan said. "Maybe if I just slip back into my old life, he won't bother with me."

Joe shook his head. "It's too late now. He's already warned you he's coming. You'll be more exposed in Scotland."

"You're staying here." Dimitri made sure she heard the flint in his voice. There was no way she'd make him stand around helpless again while she was in danger. He was going to protect this woman whether she liked it or not.

"Bossy," she grumbled, but stroked his arm at the same time.

"Got it!" Elle stopped typing and looked over at them. "He tracked her GPS. He has this address." Her lips thinned. "Someone downloaded her contacts this afternoon. They know who she works for and where the office is. They also hacked her email and phone accounts."

Dimitri heard a buzzing in his ears and it took him a minute to register it was his blood beginning to boil.

"I'm such an idiot," Megan muttered to herself.

He cupped Megan's chin and tilted her face back to his. Guilt. Her eyes were full of it.

"Yeah, this time you are." He gave it to her straight.

She nodded, taking it on the chin and making him proud.

"We're compromised. We need to get out of here. Pack it up." Callum stood as he gave the order.

Rachel came back into the room, trailing a carry-on suitcase behind her. She was dressed in cream slacks and a cream off the shoulder sweater and her usual dominatrix heels.

"I heard," she said as she walked into the middle of the room. She shook her head at Megan. "Idiot."

"I know," Megan said.

"I'll get Julia. We'll catch up with you downstairs." Joe stalked past them, no doubt in order to search all of Rachel's closets for their office manager.

Dimitri felt Megan slump against him. Defeated. Her spark had taken a hit, but these were lessons she needed to learn if she was going to work in the field. He eyed Callum. "What about them being fired?"

Callum clearly wasn't happy with the situation. "Nobody's fired. Yet. We need to sort this mess first before we deal with anything else. Let's go."

Elle grinned and shot Megan a thumbs up gesture, but Megan barely smiled in return. Good. She needed to take this seriously. She needed to feel the impact of her actions and decisions.

"I've booked two suites at the Savoy," Rachel said.

Savoy? Dimitri arched an eyebrow at the woman. "We're hiding out at one of London's most exclusive hotels?"

Rachel gave him a cold look. "I don't do slumming."

"Savoy it is then." He looked down at Megan, noting how perfectly she fit in his arms. He could tuck her under his chin and surround her. Protect her. He silently scoffed at his thoughts. Like Megan would ever let anyone protect her. Still, he filled his lungs with her strawberry scent. She didn't need to know she was being protected now, did she?

"I need my shoes." Megan pushed against his arms. Reluctantly, he freed her and then watched her dress cling to her backside as she bent down for her shoes. It showed every sensually perfect curve. Yeah, he really hated that dress.

"Rachel?" he called.

"What is it now?" Rachel snapped.

"Has the Savoy got any shops? Megan needs some new clothes."

"Yes." Rachel stuck her nose in the air. "There are a few boutiques, but I doubt very much Megan would find anything to her taste."

"You mean I wouldn't find anything I could afford," Megan said. "Honestly, Rach, you are such a snob."

"Yes, but I'm an accurate snob."

Megan rolled her eyes as she looked at Dimitri. "Can we swing past the flat at the office so I can pick up some stuff?"

"Too dangerous."

"Well, can we go to the Savoy via Oxford street? There's a sale on in Top Shop."

Dimitri just stared at her. Seriously?

"No shopping," Callum barked.

"Oh for the love of all things Prada." Rachel let out a dramatic sigh. "I'll pay for some new clothes at the hotel."

Knowing how independent Megan was and how much animosity was between her and Rachel, he expected her to refuse. Instead she grinned widely.

"I'm going to need one of everything," she said as she followed Rachel out the door. "All I have on me is this dress and the bikini I stole from you."

"What happened to your underwear?" Rachel said.

"I left it at Rudi's house," Megan said.

And Dimitri had to hold the wall for a second until he got that image out of his head. She'd stripped for Rudi Abramovich? Yeah, they were definitely going to have a very long, private chat once they got to the hotel.

Right after he burned that dress.

# CHAPTER 24

Julia rushed down the hallway into a darkened room. When she flicked on the light switch she saw it was Rachel's home office. Julia didn't care what room it was, only that it was empty. She dumped her dress and shoes onto the desk and unwrapped the towel around her. Her slip was still wet from jumping into the pool like a scared rabbit. Only rabbits would burrow, not jump in water. She shook her head. The slip had to go. She could pull on her dress over her damp underwear. Not perfect, but there was no way she had the confidence to walk back out there without any underwear on.

She tugged the knee length slip over her head and looked around for somewhere to put it that wouldn't be ruined by the water. That's when the door opened. She squealed and scrambled for her towel, just in time to hold it in front of her before Joe stepped into the room.

"Joe! I'm getting dressed here." Her cheeks burned and she unconsciously backed up until her hip hit the desk.

The room seemed to fill with his presence as he stepped inside and closed the door behind him. Julia felt her heart race. Her eyes flicked between Joe and the door. Without being able to stop herself she cast around for somewhere to hide. Her only option was under the desk. She took a step to the side, ready to run around the large wooden corporate desk and duck under it.

"Don't even think about it, Jules," Joe rumbled.

She froze in place. She knew her eyes were wide and she had the terrified look of a rabbit in headlights. It was just another one of the many things she'd change about herself if she could. Maybe, once this whole mess was over, she'd use her unemployment time to check into a clinic where they could reprogram her brain. Cognitive behavioural therapy. She'd tried it years earlier but had been told she was trying to change her personality, not her behaviour and it wouldn't work. The therapist had been a lovely man. He'd told her there was nothing wrong with her. She'd laughed hard until she cried and he'd comforted her. All she could think was, if there was nothing wrong with her then why did she have so many problems doing things other people took for granted. Maybe another clinic would be willing to give her a go.

"Whatever you're thinking," Joe said, "stop it."

She blinked at him before her eyes shot down to stare at the cream carpet. "You can't read minds. You don't know what I'm thinking." She paused, realising that wasn't what she meant to say. "I mean, I'm thinking that I need to get dressed and you need to leave for me to do that."

"No." He folded his arms and turned into a wall.

"No?" It came out shaky. Did he want to watch her getting dressed? That was all kinds of wrong.

"We're heading out and I need a minute to talk to you."

"I need to get dressed."

"Then do it. I'm not stopping you."

Her face was so hot she felt like her hair might catch fire. "I can't do that in front of you."

"Fine." He turned and gave her his back. "Get on with it. I want to look in your eyes when I say my piece."

Julia just stood frozen to the spot.

"Julia." His voice seemed to drop an octave. "Get dressed or I'll do it for you."

His words jerked her into action. She dropped the towel and fumbled for her dress, pulling it over her head and hoping the dampness from her underwear wouldn't seep through the material. Although, the ugly brown fabric probably wouldn't show the marks. She smoothed her hand down the dress. It was crinkled, but it covered her from below the knee to under her chin. It was her invisibility cloak. She'd bought it especially so as not to attract any attention to herself.

"You done?" Joe's voice jerked her back to reality with a thump.

"Ah, yes." She slipped into her low heeled brown pumps. The last time she'd seen her sister, Belinda had pointed out that the Queen wore exactly the same shoes. She then threatened to take Julia shopping. It had taken half an hour to talk her fashion junkie sister out of that idea.

Joe turned slowly and Julia waited nervously for whatever he had to say. It had to be about the plan she'd helped Megan execute. She was under no illusion that she was as much to blame as Megan. In fact probably more so. They'd all had a role to play in the planning: Rachel's had been oversight and pharmaceuticals, Elle's was tech and getaway car, Julia's was ideas, coordination and strategy and Megan, well, she was the muscle.

"I know what you're going to say." Julia held up a hand in the hope it would keep him where he was, which was close enough. "I shouldn't have helped Megan. It was irresponsible."

"Yeah, it was, but that wasn't what I was going to say." He stalked towards her.

Julia backed up until she almost bent backwards over the desk.

"Joe?" She hated that her voice was a trembling squeak.

He placed a hand on either side of her, palms flat on the desk. His face was inches from her, his eyes dark with an intensity she had no experience in reading.

"Joe?" It was a whisper.

"Here's the thing." His voice was chocolate smooth. "Yeah, you were in the wrong, but I get why you did it. I do."

Then why didn't she feel reassured by his words? And why was her mouth suddenly dry? Dealing with Joe was akin to living in a country where she didn't know the customs and didn't speak the language.

"Good?" she whispered. "Thanks?"

His eyes crinkled. Amused. Yet still intense. It was disconcerting.

"I realised something today while you four were off playing renegade."

"Okay?" Her fingers curled around the edge of the desk.

"I realised that I'm done being patient. When I heard what you lot had done, when I saw Megan walking in there alone, I was angry. I'll admit it. But mainly I was scared out of my mind that you'd put yourself on Abramovich's radar."

His words sucked the air out of her lungs, making it hard to breathe. "Why would that make you scared?"

"Because…" Joe's head fell forward, his eyes closed. "You would have been in danger. Even more so than you are now. And Rudi Abramovich isn't someone you want after you."

"I understand," she said. It was his need to protect that had taken a hit.

"No, you don't." It was a low, obstinate drawl. "You and me, there's something there."

"W-what?" Oh, she *needed* badly to run and hide. Her fingernails bit into the desk as she held on tight.

"I've been taking it slow. Waiting for you." He looked up at her through those thick lashes. "I'm done waiting."

She was going to faint. Pass out. Possibly die. She knew it. Her heart was racing so fast it would have been impossible to count the beats. It was impossible to breathe. Her lungs didn't work. They'd seized. She was trapped by Joe's dark eyes. Paralysed in a gaze that seemed to see right through her.

"I'm putting you on notice," he whispered. "You and me? We're going to happen."

Slowly, oh so slowly, he closed the distance and his lips brushed hers. Julia sucked in a breath, a gasp that made her dizzy. Her lips burned where he touched. Gently, softly, he rubbed his lips across hers. It set off a chain reaction. Tingles from her lips straight to her fingers and toes. Julia couldn't think. She couldn't move. She just stared at the man in front of her.

"Get ready." She felt his words as a breath on her lips. "I'm coming for you."

Leaning back, he kept his eyes on hers. It was as though he could see deep inside her. With one last, dark look, he turned and sauntered from the room, as though he hadn't just reduced her to a puddle of confused need and fear on Rachel's cream carpet. With trembling fingers, Julia lifted her fingertips to her lips. She still felt him there and that's when she realised it wasn't a kiss, it was a brand.

Joe was coming for her. He'd lost patience in his pursuit *of her.* She hadn't even known he'd been pursuing her. Her mind couldn't cope with this. It had officially overloaded. She forced her body to move as she gathered up her slip and towel.

"Get a move on, Jules," Joe called. "We need to get out of here and the team are waiting downstairs."

She hurried out of the apartment, clutching the sodden towel and slip to her. She kept her eyes firmly off the man beside her as they rode the elevator down to the garage. It didn't matter what he thought would happen between them, or what he wanted. It didn't even matter that Joe had a starring role in most of her X-rated dreams. Or that one smile from him made her heartbeat stutter. All that mattered was one irrefutable truth—there was no way she could handle a man like Joe Barone. No way at all.

# CHAPTER 25

"I can't believe I'm in the Savoy," Elle said as they were escorted to their suite of rooms by a butler.

Megan was sure that if it had been under any other circumstances than her putting the team in danger, she would have been excited too.

"You can borrow my phone if you want to send some pics to Claire," Elle said.

"Maybe tomorrow."

Callum shot her a tight glance. "Or maybe never. I don't think we need to put our location on Instagram, do you?"

Yeah, that shot hit its mark. "Seriously? You think I'm dumb enough to go public with our hideout?"

"I have no idea exactly how dumb you are," Callum said. "To be honest, I'm hoping I never find out."

"Are you Jeeves or Wooster?" Elle asked the butler. "And who wrote those books again?"

"The author was P.G. Wodehouse, madam," the butler said. "Jeeves was the butler and Wooster was his employer." He looked thoroughly bored at the question and Megan wondered how many times the guy had been asked it.

"See?" Elle looked over her shoulder at the frowning faces of her teammates. "I knew he'd know."

"Oh for the love of Chanel," Rachel muttered.

If Megan had been in a better mood, she may have found it funny that the princess of darkness was swanning through one of London's most exclusive hotels with a group of ragamuffins in tow.

The butler stopped in front of a door and addressed Rachel. "Ms Ford-Talbot, as per your request we have joined two suites together to meet your requirements. I apologise again, on behalf of the hotel, that the Royal Suite wasn't available for you at this time."

"Not at all." Rachel strode through the group. "It was a last minute decision on my part. I'm sure the accommodation you've arranged will be more than adequate."

The butler nodded and opened the door. Megan followed everyone into the suite as the man waxed lyrical about the amenities. She felt her jaw hang open. The guy called the décor Elizabethan. Megan wasn't sure what that meant, but to her it looked like they were staying in a castle. From the French style armoire, to the velour-covered chaise, the room was a study in elegance—which made her standing there in her mini dress, sans underwear, beyond tacky. She felt like Julia Roberts in *Pretty Woman* when she'd turned up at the Beverly Hills hotel in her hooker outfit. It wasn't a good feeling.

"I'm afraid these rooms do not have a private dining area large enough to accommodate your party. If you would like, I could reserve one of our private dining rooms for you and your group this evening." To give the butler credit, he didn't bat an eye at the fact Rachel's group would have fit in better at a backpackers' hostel.

"A private dining room would be wonderful. We don't have a preference in regards to the restaurant." Rachel looked at Callum. "Half an hour?"

"Make it an hour. I have some calls to make first." Callum made no attempt to appear friendly to the help.

"Excellent." The butler actually bowed. A tiny little one, but still. Megan wanted to wrap him up and take him back to Scotland to show her sister. It would be nice to have a souvenir of her time as a mercenary. One that didn't make her feel bad.

"If there is anything more I can help you with, please do not hesitate to call," the butler said.

Rachel inclined her head and the man left. Leaving the team standing in a set of rooms that were designed for aristocracy.

"Okay," Rachel said. "There are four bedrooms. I'm taking one of them. I don't share."

"What a shock," Megan muttered.

"The rest of you can fight over the other rooms." Rachel turned on her heel, wheeling her suitcase behind her.

"I want a river view room!" Elle shouted and raced off. She threw open a door. "This one is perfect. There are two beds. Who's with me?"

"I am." Julia sounded determined as she kept her head down and hurried after Elle.

The door closed on the sound of Elle whooping loudly about the view.

That left two rooms, three men and Megan. She looked at the three men in front of her.

"One of you needs to take the sofa." The sofa was a formal, upholstered design with delicate carved wooden legs. "It looks comfy."

She didn't wait for an answer. Instead she headed for the bedroom near Rachel, hoping that it too had a river view. She was lucky. The view was perfect. Closing the door behind her, she made a beeline for the windows. Lights flickered on the gently lolling waters of the Thames. The London Eye across the river was lit up, a strange big wheel of fairy lights in the city skyline. Boats chugged up and down the river, people strolled along the walkways lining the Thames. To her right she could just make out Parliament building, but Big Ben was too far back to see. She wondered if Rachel's room had a view of the world's most famous clock.

The door opened making her jump.

"Hey, roomie." Dimitri strode inside.

"I'm not in the mood to argue with you. There's only one bed, I got here first, you need to find somewhere else to sleep." She was in no mood to deal with Dimitri. She felt as though she was bruised on the inside.

Dimitri completely ignored her. There was snick sound as the lock turned.

Megan had to fight a sudden urge to run. "What do you think you're doing?"

Dimitri leaned back against the door. He folded his arms over his grey T-shirt and lazily crossed his ankles. Only the calculation in his eyes and the fact he was barring her exit betrayed that he wasn't as relaxed as he seemed.

"I'm tired." It was an understatement. She was emotionally exhausted. A limp rag version of her usual self. "Can we do this, whatever it is, tomorrow?" Or never, which would suit much better.

The infuriating man didn't answer. Instead he just stood there, staring at her. Thinking so loudly she could practically hear him. Slowly, purposefully, he pushed away from the door and stalked towards her.

Prey. She felt like prey.

Before she could stop herself, Megan stepped back and felt the chill of the window press against her back. Dimitri came to a halt in front of her. He placed his hands palms down on the window above her head. His face was close enough for their breaths to merge.

"You and I are gonna have that talk now." It was a rumbled order.

"Now isn't a good time for me." It was the understatement of the year.

Her defences had been broken apart by the realisation that her actions caused more problems than they'd solved. The soft underbelly of her soul was exposed. The wounds from words hurled at her earlier in the evening were raw. There was no space inside her for more of the same.

"I can't." It was a whispered confession. She closed her eyes at the truth of it, as accusations from earlier that evening flooded her mind.

*"You're irresponsible. Reckless. You're dangerous. And you don't give a shit about your team."*

*"You treat this like a game. It isn't a game. People's lives are on the line. Nobody wants someone on the team who they can't trust to have their backs in a situation."*

"What do you want?" she whispered. "To make me bleed?" She held up her hands, wrists out. "Trust me, I'm already bleeding." You couldn't see the blood that poured from her wounds, but she hoped Dimitri could feel it. Could recognise it.

His jaw clenched, tight. His eyes blazed. "You nearly cost me my sister."

Another slash. Another wound. She wasn't sure how she managed to stay on her feet.

"I know."

There was nothing else to say. No apology great enough. She'd chanced a woman's life because she'd thought she knew better than everyone around her. And although she'd convinced herself that she acted to protect Claire, she'd also done it to pander to her own ego. She was beginning to see that the damage she caused by acting then thinking, was long lasting. There were always consequences—for her and for the people she dragged into her plans.

"You took risks with Katrina's life to protect Claire." Another accusation.

That one bristled. She met him eye to eye. "You did the same."

He shook his head. "No. We always intended to protect Claire. The only thing that changed was the timeline."

That reasoning would never be good enough for Megan. "She's my twin."

He moved closer, the length of his body pressing against hers. There was no personal space from this man—he wouldn't allow it. "It doesn't excuse what you did. You put yourself in danger. You took risks you're not equipped to deal with. You took your phone into a dangerous situation and gave a sociopath the ability to track you. You relied on luck and charm to get you out of there alive. You were unprofessional. Nothing you did was smart or sane."

He was breathing hard when he finished. Megan couldn't say anything. He was right. They were all right. She'd gone in armed with bravado. The fact she'd gotten out again was pure luck.

"You put yourself in danger." His words were barely a growl. "You went in there without backup."

Unable to look at him, she turned her face. Her hands fell limply at her side.

"That is *not* acceptable." Dimitri rumbled the words against her throat.

It was unacceptable because she was an amateur. Because she was untrained. Unskilled. Inexperienced. Because she'd been playing at being a mercenary, while the people who actually knew what they were doing were left in the dark.

There was nothing she could say to change things. She deserved every angry word fired at her.

"Do you have any idea how crazy I was, knowing I couldn't watch your back? Knowing if something happened I wouldn't be able to get to you in time? You left me helpless." He hissed the word. It was the final insult to him, the fact she'd taken away his ability to protect.

Megan blinked back tears that threatened. It hurt to swallow. Her throat was tight with words she couldn't say. Words she had no right to say. What was the point of an apology now? Empty words, offered too late.

"It was the longest twenty minutes of my life," Dimitri said on a growl. "Waiting for you to come out of there. I felt every second. You can't be in danger. It drives me insane when I know you're in danger." Dimitri's nose rubbed up her throat. He nipped her earlobe. A chastisement that had her jerking within the cage he'd made of his body. "It can't happen again. I won't allow it." His forehead fell to her shoulder. "*Megan.*" There was agony in the word. "How could you make me choose like that?"

Megan stilled. "Choose?"

"You or my sister," he whispered. "Save you and ruin the chance to get at Rudi's records. Or let you get hurt in the hope I'd get another chance at the records down the line." His eyes closed slowly. Megan stopped breathing. Slowly, his eyelids fluttered open. The black depths of his eyes held emotion she was terrified to name. "You made me choose. Don't ever do that again."

"You didn't have to choose," Megan whispered, her heart beating so loudly she almost couldn't hear her own words. "I made it out. I got the information. We're both going to be fine."

He shook his head slowly. "No. I had to choose. I had to

be prepared. I had to know what I would do if you didn't come out on time, if something went wrong. I had to know."

She couldn't ask. She didn't want to know what his choice had been. The fact he'd had to make one was enough. Pain enough. Promise enough. She felt her bruised heart crack open and she felt Dimitri slip inside.

He bit her bottom lip. Hard. It wasn't the teasing caress of a lover, it was the reprimand of a man on the edge.

"Never." His words came out as a breath. "Never again."

Unable to take her eyes from his, Megan reached up with a shaking hand and cupped the back of his neck. She tugged him to her, closing the scant distance between them. And then she poured her promise into a kiss.

# CHAPTER 26

The beast inside Dimitri, the one that had been barely leashed since Megan walked into Rudi's house alone, broke free. She'd taken his control from him when she'd removed him from the operation. Now he wanted it back. But only she could give it to him. Only she could ease the fear that had been riding him, hot like rage, since she'd walked away from him and straight into danger.

Her nails scraped his scalp as she threaded both hands through his hair and tightened her hold. Flattening one palm to her nape and the other low on her back, he pressed her against him. She burned with the heat of her intensity. That fearlessness of hers, which was dangerous when she was in the field, made her unrestrained in her passion. Their kiss was a tussle of wills. A fight for dominance. A battle of untempered need fought out in clashing teeth and tongues.

He needed to feel her skin against his. He needed her naked. He needed it now.

Keeping her pinned against the cool glass, he fisted his hands in the neck of her dress at the base of her throat and ripped. The material was no match for his strength. Megan wrenched her lips from his, but her fingers remained tangled in his hair. She looked down, then back up at him. Her eyes sparkled, the blue luminous.

"You owe me a dress." Her hands fell loose at her sides. What remained of her dress slid down her arms to the floor, leaving the woman dressed in a leopard print bikini.

She was all lean muscle, rich curves and satin smooth skin. He trailed a fingertip from the hollow of her throat, down through the valley of her breasts, across the satin cream expanse of her stomach to hook in the top of her bikini bottoms. She watched his progress, her cheeks flushed a perfect rose. Brilliant blue eyes turned black as she looked up at him through her lashes.

"What now?" It was a challenge.

"Take this off." He barely recognised the low husky timbre of his voice. "Unless you want me to buy you a new bikini too."

Her shrug was slight, but he felt it. "It isn't my bikini. Rachel can afford another one. Do what you like with it."

He didn't have to be told twice. He hooked his thumbs into the thin elastic at her hips and tugged. A fleeting glimpse of delectable blonde curls protecting paradise, before his attention turned to the fine elastic straps keeping her bra top on her shoulders. He tugged. They broke.

"You like ripping my clothes from me." It wasn't a question. And from the flush in her cheeks and the dark need in her eyes, he would say she liked it too.

He snapped the clasp in the middle of her back and the top of her bikini fell away, leaving her gloriously naked—except for the high heeled black pumps on her feet. He took a tiny step back to look at her, folding his arms over his chest to stop from grabbing at everything he could reach. She stole his sense. What little he had left of it.

"Kick off the shoes." Another order. He wondered if she'd

humour him enough to obey. One way or another the shoes were going. Abramovich had seen her in those shoes and he didn't want that evil son of a bitch in the room with them. Not now. Not for this.

She steadied herself by gripping his biceps and kicked off the shoes. Once they were gone, she leaned back against the window. One leg bent lazily at the knee, she ran her fingertips down his chest until they hit his folded arms. Her touch burned through the cotton of his shirt.

"You're still dressed, Dimitri."

"You're not."

He looked his fill. His eyes traced the curves of her body before returning to caress her full perfect breasts. And his look was a caress, he made sure of it. One filled with heat and promise.

"I'm losing patience," his little cat said, making him smile.

He glanced at the picture window behind her. The lights flickering in London's night. "People can see you."

A glance at the darkened room and a shrug. "It's dark in here and we're high up."

His lips began to curl. This woman was full of surprises. "Turn around."

She considered him for a moment. "This is the last order I follow." But she turned, letting it be known through her easy grace and cheeky smile that the only reason she was doing so was because she wanted to.

Her attitude made him so hard it was painful, and then he caught sight of her perfect ass and his jeans almost cut off his blood supply. He groaned in appreciation. She placed her hands high on the glass in front of her and arched her back, lifting her ass towards him like an offering.

A seductive glance over her shoulder. "Better start touching, Soldier Boy, or I'll get bored."

Yeah, right. Confident that she loved every minute, he let his eyes feast.

"I'm giving you until the count of three and then…" The steel in her voice didn't match the mischief in her eyes.

She was perfect. And she was his. Tonight. Forever. He didn't give a shit if she fought him on it. It was a done deal.

"One." Her Highland lilt was husky.

Dimitri caught sight of her breast as her hard little nipple grazed the icy cold glass. He bet that felt good.

"Two."

Her heart shaped ass swayed enticingly in front of him.

"Three." She pushed away from the window.

And fast as lightning he fitted his front to her back. His arms caged her, pressing her to the glass. He felt her shiver at the dual sensations of cold, smooth glass against her front and the rough heat of his jean clad thigh pressed between her legs.

"You are perfect." He fought his way into the crook of her neck, because Megan wouldn't give up control easily. If at all.

He pressed his thigh into her warm, wet core as he nuzzled the sensitive spot where her shoulder met her neck. How was it possible she smelled like a warm spring day on a cold dark night? She widened her stance and pressed herself against his thigh. His muscles flexed. Her backside wriggled against his erection making him groan. His hands squeezed between Megan and the glass to cup her breasts. They overflowed his grasp as he warmed the chill left behind by the window.

No longer able to resist, he bit her shoulder muscle, then soothed the mark with his tongue. She groaned and writhed against him, making it clear that she was letting him play. For now.

Reluctantly he released her. "Done sharing, Buffy." He reached out and pulled the curtains closed in front of her. He was more than happy to indulge her exhibitionist side—another time.

He turned her in his arms, wrapping her tight against him as he opened his mouth over hers. Luscious. Delicious. His arm clamped around her waist, keeping her in place as his other hand cradled the curve of her backside. Fingers tugged at his hair as she angled his mouth to suit herself. The sensation of her tongue against his drove away the last of his anger. All that was left was need. Need for this woman who had turned his world upside down. The woman who was fast becoming an addiction for him. His woman.

She twisted fast, out of his grasp. Dimitri spun, taking a step towards her, but she held up a hand to stop him as she backed up to the bed.

"I'm getting into bed now. If you want to join me, you'd better get naked." She pulled her bottom lip between her teeth. "Give me a show."

He grinned, delighted at playing with her. "What do I get for making the effort to entertain you?"

She turned to climb on the bed and he almost crumpled to the floor. Knowing full well the effect the sight of her crawling onto the bed would have on him, the vixen looked over her shoulder at him.

"You get me."

As he pulled his tee over his head, the sound that came out of his mouth was barely human. And the witch threw back her head and laughed.


OH THE WICKED, wicked things she wanted to do with Dimitri. Megan's mind was full to overflowing with them. She hadn't had many boyfriends and only a couple of serious ones. Ones she'd let into her bed. But it hadn't gone well—she tended to scare them away. Whereas Dimitri seemed to delight in her wild side. It was a gift. One she didn't plan to squander.

His T-shirt hit the floor, but Megan's eyes were on the dusting of dark hair that highlighted his mouth-watering pecs. She lingered over the gentle definition of his abs, imagining how they would taste when she got her tongue on him.

He groaned. "That look in your eyes. It's enough to make a man lose his mind."

She smiled at him. "Who's stopping you?"

Dark, heated gaze. His fingers sped up as he unfastened the button fly on his jeans. Megan licked her lips. He'd gone commando. "The commando commando," she muttered, her eyes firmly on the prize.

He barked out a laugh. "You aren't entirely sane, are you?"

"Nope." She hooked a finger at him. "Come here."

His jeans, boots, socks disappeared in record time and he stalked towards her, strong muscled thighs flexing with easy grace.

"Wait." She held up her hand.

"What?" Her heart melted a little as he did what he was told, stopping mid-stride to stand before her. "You okay?"

And just like that it melted entirely. She was a puddle on the bed. Megan didn't want to think about what that meant. Later, she promised herself, later.

She made a circular motion with her hand. "Turn. Let me see all of it." She batted her lashes at him as she fought back a laugh. This was fun. So much fun. "You saw all of me, it's only fair that I get to see all of you."

Grinning, he did as he was told. *Le sigh.* The man was a masterpiece. She couldn't decide what she wanted to take a bite out of first—his strong wide shoulders, or that tight hot backside of his. Acting on instinct, she sprang to her knees and wrapped her arms around him. Her hands splayed on his stomach as she delighted in the tactile sensation of all that muscle against her breasts. Her teeth sank into his shoulder and she actually felt dizzy at the taste of him.

"Hey! No biting."

She bit him again as she wrapped her fist around his hard length. Satin smooth and deliciously solid.

He shivered under her touch. "Okay, maybe a little biting."

Megan chuckled against his skin as she slid her hand up and down his length, learning him. He tolerated it far longer than she thought he would before his hand clasped her wrist.

"You keep that up and I'm going to blow."

"And what if I want you to blow?"

"You don't always get what you want." He spun on her and she squealed as she suddenly found herself lying on her back.

Dimitri lay on his side, pressed along the length of her. One arm curved above her head, his fingers playing with her hair, the other smoothing down the curve of her stomach to the flare of her hip.

His dark eyes studied her, equal parts heat and amusement. The perfect combination.

"Kiss me." She ran the nails of her left hand down his back. Scratching hard.

"Where?" the devil demanded.

Her right hand reached for his cock, prepared to make him break the control he seemed to value.

"Nuh, uh." He shifted fast, grasping both of her hands and stretching her arms over her head. He held both her wrists in one huge hand, immobilising her.

"Not fair." She pouted as she tested his hold. It was steel.

"Quiet. You're disturbing my concentration." His head bent and he sucked one of her nipples into his mouth.

"Yes!" She arched off the bed.

She felt his smile against her breast before he proceeded

to drive her insane with his tongue and teeth. When she started to see stars, she fought back. There was no way she'd lose her mind alone. Swinging her leg over his hip, she put all of her strength into flipping him. He landed on his back with an oomph. Megan straddled his stomach, trailing her nails down his chest.

"My turn."

Strong hands reached for her breasts—she batted them away. *"My turn."*

Deep laughter rumbled from his chest and straight through her body. "How about we both take turns together?"

"No." The feeling of warm skin and firm muscle that rippled and tensed under her fingertips needed her full attention. "You distract me and I need to concentrate."

He laughed harder at having his words thrown back at him. Megan bent forward and ran her tongue around one of those tiny hard nipples, over his pecs and up to his neck. She sucked, and bit and licked. Dimitri's huge hands grasped her hips, holding tight enough to leave bruises. It was delicious. Megan pressed up from his chest to look at her handiwork.

"That's going to leave a mark." It was a proud declaration.

In reply, he tightened his grip on her hips. And then she was flying. Up his body to sit astride his wicked, wicked mouth.

"Hold on tight, Buff." The words were a sensual purr against her most private of places. "I'm going to blow your mind."

Holding the polished wooden headboard, she looked down at the man. "Unlike you, Soldier Boy, I don't think with that part of my anatomy."

He barked out a laugh, making her wonder if she wasn't the only crazy person in the room. Then his tongue swiped all thought away. Megan's fingers curled into the warm wood, her head fell back and she lost herself in his touch.

Dimitri's hands clenched on her backside, pulling her closer to him. Muscles tightened. Tingles ran up from her feet to her back. Breathing became a series of desperate gasps.

"Oh, yes, yes…"

Dimitri rumbled against her most sensitive spot and her body froze. A second, suspended on a precipice. Then it snapped and she was flying, with only his hold to keep her tethered. By the time she'd floated back down, she found herself lying back on the bed. Dimitri was cradled between her thighs, supporting his weight with a hand either side of her head.

"Ready?" He cocked an eyebrow at her.

"I'll deal with your attitude when I can breathe again." It wasn't a lie—her words were delivered on gasps.

"Good to know." He took her mouth in a punishing kiss, releasing her just as fast as he'd taken her.

She barely had time to fill her lungs again before he surged into her.

"Yes!" Megan screamed as she wrapped her legs around his hips.

Dimitri's head went back. The tendons in his neck flexed. A gasp. A shiver. His length flexed within her. Her fingers danced over tense shoulder muscles, then up to tighten in his silky hair. When she tugged his face down to hers, his gaze was feral. A man barely in control. And it was perfect. Megan didn't want control. She wanted all of him, raw and strong and limitless.

"Move," she said. "Fast. Hard. Now."

"I'm gonna deal with your attitude when I can breathe again," he said on a groan. "Oh hell, Megan, you're perfect."

"I know." She kicked his backside with her heels, hard. "Now move."

And, with a grin, he did.

# CHAPTER 27

Dimitri woke to banging on their door. Megan was sprawled on top of him. It made him chuckle. The bed was huge, but his girl had him pinned.

"Playtime's over," Callum shouted.

Dimitri checked the clock. They'd missed the team meal. His stomach rumbled at the same time as he wondered why no one had come to get him.

"Make g'way," Megan muttered, but her eyes didn't open.

So it wasn't just mornings when she had a problem waking, it was any time she fell asleep. Good to know. He smoothed a hand over her silken hair.

"I'll get it."

A grumble and a wriggle and her head disappeared under a pillow. Dimitri delighted in the sight before pulling on his jeans and opening the door. His boss was even more stony-faced than usual.

"Get dressed. The office has been hit."

And just like that, Dimitri's languid state was gone. He looked over at his grumpy Scottish girl. "What about Megan?"

"She's safe where she is. Joe's staying here. He'll watch the women while we check the damage."

As Callum spoke, Dimitri pulled on his shirt and boots. He cast one last glance at the woman he'd sexed into an unconscious state, then followed Callum out the door.

Elle looked up from where she was sitting at a desk in the corner of the living room, tapping at her laptop as per usual. Dimitri actually tripped over his feet at the sight of her. She was wearing a pyjama onesie, like a kid would wear, only in her size. Going by the colour, pattern and hood, she was supposed to be a giraffe.

"Hey, Dimitri. When you get back we need to start going over some of the info I've decoded."

"Don't you need sleep?"

Her answer was to lift a waste paper basket which was filled with empty energy drink cans. She waggled her eyebrows at him, then the giraffe lowered its head and she went back to work.

"You saw that, right?" Dimitri felt the need to ask Callum. It'd been a long couple of weeks and he was seriously sleep deprived. It wouldn't surprise him if he'd started to hallucinate.

"I'm pretending I didn't." Callum pressed the button for the elevator. "Otherwise I'll institute a uniform policy for the business." He gave Dimitri a sidelong look. "Guess we're not in the army anymore, Toto."

The doors slid open and Dimitri followed him inside. "Did you just make a joke? It's kind of hard to tell when your face never changes."

Callum stared at him until he dropped the subject. It didn't take long.

"What's the word on the building?"

"Cops called me. One of our neighbours alerted them when they saw masked men in the office."

"No alarm?" Dimitri felt his eyebrows rise. They were a security firm. The first thing they'd put in was an alarm system.

"They hacked it." Callum's jaw turned to granite. "It was a skeleton system. We planned on putting in the full framework when the renovations were complete. Right now there are too many workmen going in and out all hours to make a full system feasible."

"Anybody hurt?"

The elevator doors opened onto the plush lobby. "No word on that. They were still checking the building when they called."

They strode through the Art Deco interior, with its black and white tiled floor and geometric decoration. "How come no one got us for the team meeting?"

"I cancelled it when information started to come in from Rudi's flash drive."

Dimitri stalled briefly. "Anything I need to know?"

"Not yet, but I had to spend time making calls, pulling in favours to check out some of the threads Elle unravelled." He gave Dimitri an even look. "We'll go over it all in the morning, but as soon as we have a bead on your sister's location, you'll be the first to hear about it."

It wasn't anything Dimitri didn't already know, but the waiting was harder the closer he got to knowing the truth about Katrina.

"We need to get her back." The words were out of his mouth before he could stop them.

"We will." It was a promise. One heavy with deadly intent.

By the time they'd made it to the front door, their car had been brought around and was waiting for them, key in the ignition.

"You drive," Callum barked. "I need to call Lake and

Harry. Let them know that this new business of ours is going to hell."

Dimitri didn't think Lake would be surprised or upset. In the few years the ex-SAS specialist had lived in the Highlands he'd managed to set fire to a shop, ruin a Christmas market and have a shootout at the castle. There was a reason Lake didn't blink when things went south—he'd seen it all before.

They made it to the office in record time, driving through central London fast enough to set off every speed camera in their path. They found a place to park down the street from the office and fought their way through the crowds of onlookers. The police had cordoned off an area outside their building. Yellow tape, flashing lights. The whole shebang.

Callum strode up to the familiar face that was clearly in charge.

"Tessa," he said. "What's the damage?"

This time the tall woman was dressed in a pristine uniform, making her rank clear. She inclined her head. "Vandalism. Your new renovations are trashed." Her eyes narrowed. "We thought it was a robbery until the bastards fired at my guys. Then boom. You've lost your ground floor reception area."

Dimitri glanced around him, noting the armed response unit in amongst the rest of the group.

"Trouble seems to follow Benson Security," the woman said to Callum. "Want to tell me who's behind this raid?"

"We had the meet with Rudi this afternoon." Callum kept his voice low. "Megan took things into her own hands. Let's just say Rudi won't be raping anyone again."

Tessa's body visibly tensed. "Dead?"

"No, Tess, she…" Callum trailed off. He looked at Dimitri. "Help me out here."

"Nuh, uh. I can't even think about it."

With a look of disgust, Callum turned back to the police

commander. "It had something to do with a very tight elastic band and a piece of his anatomy."

Dimitri watched Callum's hands twitch as he fought the urge to cover his crotch—exactly as Dimitri was doing.

"Is she insane?" Tessa said with a hiss.

"Aye."

"Hey!" Dimitri snapped. "I'm the only one who gets to call her nuts. Back off."

Two identical, incredulous looks were his response. As Megan would say, whatever. Folding his arms, he glared at them, making it clear they had better back off Megan. The Scottish lunatic was his.

Tessa muttered something about Neanderthal men, while Callum turned his attention to the building.

"This could be a guy called Reynard Durand. He worked for Rudi. Muscle mostly." Callum eyed Tessa. "You heard of him?"

She shook her head. "I'll look into it."

"Commander, ma'am," a voice called out, making Tessa's attention snap to the cop. "We've found two men hiding in the basement. They're saying they work for Benson Security."

With a shared look, Callum, Dimitri and Tessa headed into the building. Reception had been reduced to rubble. Julia's precious whiteboards were firewood and the files from her desk were scattered over the floor. Dimitri's boot trampled a photo of Rudi on his way to the basement stairs, a sight he delighted in. Fortunately, the blast had been small, contained to the front of the ground floor. It could have been a whole lot worse. As they jogged down the stairs to the training room Dimitri heard a familiar voice.

"Get your hands off me. I'm old. My bones are brittle. If you break any of them I'm suing you."

"The Granger brothers," Dimitri said.

Callum's jaw clenched as he pushed open the door to the training room. "What the hell are they doing here on a Friday night?"

"No social life?" Dimitri's comment was awarded a death glare.

"These men work for you?" Tessa asked as she strode in behind them.

Dimitri stopped dead at the sight before him. The two old men were dressed in white y-front underpants with white vests tucked into them. They still wore brown socks and brown loafers. They looked like the scrawny chickens you found hanging in windows in Chinatown.

"We found them locked in one of those rooms." The taller of the two officers holding on to the Granger brothers pointed at the interrogation rooms.

"Those bleeding rooms only lock from the outside," Bill grumbled. "Who the hell planned that?"

Dimitri didn't think it was the time to point out that if you were in those rooms, you weren't meant to get out on your own.

"Callum, tell these idiots to release us." Bob tugged at his arm where the officer held him in a tight grip.

"Where the hell are your clothes?" Callum barked.

The brothers at least had the decency to look embarrassed.

"We were fighting." Bill pointed at the two long poles on the mat. "Ninja style."

Dimitri turned away, becoming suddenly interested in, well, anything, while he fought the urge to laugh.

"Are these two with you?" Tessa sounded incredulous.

"Unfortunately." Callum pinched the bridge of his nose. "They're our contractors. Carpentry."

"That doesn't mean they weren't working with the team

that attacked our men," Tessa pointed out, her focus completely on the brothers.

The Granger brothers took one look at Tessa's terrifying demeanour and put their hands in the air.

"We didn't do nothing," Bill said.

"Idiot," his brother snapped at him before looking at Callum and Tessa. "We just wanted to get away from our wives. They're having a ladies night at the house. The bloody place is overrun with chattering women. We thought we'd come here and get some work done in peace. Without you lot under our feet."

"Then we thought we'd have a tea break," Bill added.

"And during tea, we got to thinking about all the workout equipment down here and how we should give it a go." Bob pointed to the gym room.

"Only, once we were down here, we saw the wall of death." Bill waved at the combat weapons used for training. "Next thing you know, it's Rumble In The Jungle, Granger style."

There was silence. The two young officers holding the men struggled to keep straight faces.

"I was winning until all hell broke loose," Bob grumbled.

"Were not, you bloody liar." Bill glared at his brother.

Callum put a hand up for silence while Tessa heaved out a sigh.

"You two share a house?" Okay, Dimitri knew it wasn't the most important thing to take from Bob's statement. So sue him.

Callum glared at him and Tessa looked at him like he was an idiot.

"Come on," Dimitri said. "Don't tell me you didn't think that was interesting?"

"The house is plenty big enough for two couples," Bob said. "Big enough for privacy when you get noisy with the missus and don't want anybody to hear." He waggled his eyebrows. "If you know what we mean."

Bill rolled his eyes. "Everybody knows what you mean. It wasn't subtle." He looked at Dimitri. "When the kids moved out we thought of selling, but we liked the house. Bob and Dianne didn't mind sharing. It works out great. Except during ladies nights."

"Okay." Callum stared at the ceiling. Dimitri imagined he was praying for strength. After a few seconds, he faced the brothers. "Now that we've got your living arrangements sorted out, how about you tell us what the hell happened here?"

The two men obviously decided they weren't in trouble any longer and jerked their arms from their keepers.

"I need a seat." Bill tottered over to bench against the wall and plopped down. A second later his brother did the same.

"We were down here," Bill said, "when there was a crash upstairs. We thought it was one of you coming back and opened the door to shout up to you, let you know we were down here."

Bob nodded. "We didn't want to scare the women if they caught us in our underwear."

"You could have just got dressed," Dimitri pointed out.

Bill shook his head. "We were in the middle of a fight."

"That I was winning," Bob said.

Bill pointedly ignored his brother. "Anyway, we heard shouting. Somebody said to do as much damage as possible. It took us a minute to figure out what was going on."

"There was another order, this time telling them to sweep the building." Bob looked confused. "That's how he put it. Seemed weird, but never mind. We could hear everything because they were in the stairwell at that point and this building is like a big echo chamber when it's empty."

"We knew we had to hide." Bill shared a look with his

brother, before turning to Callum. "We already told Julia this, but you lot need a panic room. Make that several panic rooms. One on each floor. For the people who can't run fast to the other ones."

"Like us," Bob patted his belly. "I need to cut back on my cooked breakfasts."

"We ran into the nearest interrogation room and planned to lock ourselves in there."

"Only we discovered that the bloody door automatically locked when you entered and only opened from the outside. Which left us stuck in a room, with no way out and a building full of bad guys."

"It's a design flaw." Bill waved his hands around. The reason for all his gesturing was unclear. "What if there's a fire? How is a person supposed to get out of there?"

"Nobody is supposed to be in there without supervision," Dimitri pointed out. "If there was a fire, your handler would get you out."

Bob wasn't mollified. "We thought we'd be safe. Instead we were trapped. It would have been like shooting fish in a barrel." He glared at Callum. "You're getting a panic room. I don't care if you don't want one. You're getting one."

Dimitri had to shake his head to clear it. "You're carpenters. What are you going to do? Build a panic box and shove it in the corner of the room?"

Bill pointed a bony finger at him. "That's the sort of attitude we'd expect from the younger, more ignorant generation. Don't you think we have connections in the business, son? We can tap our sources and get a state of the art panic room installed tomorrow. We've been at the building game longer than you've been out of nappies. Bloody insulting, that's what your attitude is, bloody insulting." He clasped his hands on top of his round belly and huffed.

"Back to the intruders." At the strained sound of Callum's

voice, Dimitri placed himself between his boss and the wall of death. Just in case Callum snapped and decided to put the Granger brothers out of *his* misery. "What else can you tell us?"

"The guy in charge was looking for somebody," Bill said. "He told his men to bring the blonde to him."

Dimitri's muscles locked in place as the old men stared at him.

"Guess that means they're after your girlfriend," Bob said. "She's the only blonde in the building."

"What did she do this time?" Bill said. "Has this got something to do with this afternoon? Did she Taser some other poor idiot after she knocked you out?"

Tessa cocked an eyebrow at him. "Your girlfriend Tasered you?"

"It's how she shows she cares." Dimitri wasn't about to explain his complex and highly violent relationship to a stranger.

"Why didn't you two phone for help?" Callum was back on track.

Bill waved a hand at his underwear. "Does it look like I'm keeping a phone in here? Anyway, we don't abide by them mobile phones."

Bob nodded. "They fry your brain."

"Landlines," Bill added. "They're the only phones that're safe. The other ones send microwaves in to destroy your mind." He pointed at each of them. "Brain tumours. Mark my words. Get rid of your phones before it's too late."

"The intruders," Callum said through gritted teeth. "What happened with the intruders?"

"The morons were crashing around when the cops arrived. Then all hell broke loose." Bob looked at his brother.

Bill nodded. "They came charging back down the stairs. Then some idiot on the ground floor fired at the cops."

"Through the window. We heard the glass shatter."

"Bloody idiots," Bill said. "The guy in charge shouted at them to stop and get out the back. Ten seconds, he shouted. It seemed like a weird thing to shout at the time. We didn't have a clue what he meant."

"But we only had to wait ten seconds to find out," Bob said. "That's when the blast went off."

"I'm serious about a panic room. You really need it," Bill said. "One with a toilet. I almost crapped my pants when that blast went off."

"Heart attack material." Bob patted his chest. "I nearly died."

Tessa turned her back on the brothers, effectively dismissing them. They didn't like that at all.

"They had a car waiting at the back of the house," she said to Callum. "They were gone before the smoke cleared. We tracked them on CCTV but they swapped cars and we lost them. No distinguishing marks. There were four of them, decked out in black with gloves and balaclavas. There won't be any prints. We need to check your security footage, see if we get anything that might help identify these assholes."

Callum hung his head. "There isn't any. We're on a limited system and the cameras aren't operational yet. I'll tap our sources. See if we can find out who's behind this."

Tessa stared at Callum for a long time. Any other man would have shifted nervously under her gaze. Callum just waited, daring her to say something. Which, of course, she did.

"You know this is a security firm, right? You'd better hope this doesn't get out, or your business will tank. If you can't even monitor your own property properly, what the hell chance do you have of doing it for someone else?"

"We are under construction." The words were squeezed through Callum's teeth.

Tessa's eyes sparkled. "Tell you what. I'll keep it to myself —for a price."

"What do you want this time?"

"Dinner in a venue of my choice." She practically oozed glee. "I hear Gordon Ramsay's restaurant is very nice."

Callum mumbled something about evil women being the bane of his life. Tessa just laughed.

# CHAPTER 28

When Dimitri snuck back into their room, Megan was asleep, sprawled face down across the middle of the bed. Even in her sleep, she took up all the space around her. He was beginning to think there was no way to contain Megan Donaldson. And he wasn't entirely sure he'd want her contained even if there were.

Knowing nothing would wake Megan when she was out cold, he showered before he slipped into bed beside her.

"G'way." Mostly asleep, Megan shoved him out of her space.

With a chuckle, Dimitri wedged himself under her and hauled her up against him.

"Joe?" Eyes closed, she tucked her head against his chest.

A feral sound escaped him. "Dimitri. Damn it woman. Why is Joe always your first guess?"

He frowned down at her, but she was oblivious. Snuggling against him, like a kitten trying to find the perfect spot to curl up.

"Screwed up today," she mumbled against his skin.

"I know. Go to sleep." The reminder he might have lost her made him fight to relax.

"Won't do it again." It was barely a whisper, but it still made his heart clench.

"Sh, go back to sleep." He wrapped his arm around her, cupping the curve of her ass.

Megan wriggled until one of her legs was over his body and her hand was tangled in his hair.

"Bossy," she said. It was barely a whisper. "You're stealing my heart."

He stilled at her words, but she was already asleep. Breathing deeply, he took the scent that was uniquely Megan into his lungs. "You've already stolen mine, Buffy."

Dimitri kissed the top of her head as he gently stroked her arm. Smooth perfect skin under his touch. A fragile shell that betrayed a heart of steel. Although Megan would balk at the thought of not being able to fight her own battles, he still couldn't stop his imagination from thinking of ways to get her out of danger. His family owned a small house in the south of Russia. No one would think to look for her there. He nuzzled her forehead, fully aware that the only way he'd get her out of London now would be if she was unconscious. Even then, as soon as she realised where she'd been stashed, she'd rip apart everything in her path to get back to the action.

His Megan was a warrior. The fact she was untrained, fearless and rash didn't diminish that fact. Training could be fixed, and experience would help her to rein in her more impulsive tendencies. Then she would be glorious. A truly amazing field operative. A formidable opponent. A perfect partner.

If he could just keep her alive long enough to get her there.

He understood Megan's need to protect her sister. The

need that had driven her to take matters into her own hands earlier that day when she didn't think the team were going to do it for her. In a lot of ways, they were exactly alike. When it came to safeguarding family they were feral in their determination not to fail. He couldn't even fault her for putting her own life on the line for her sister—he would have done exactly the same thing. He chuckled. Well, maybe not exactly the same thing. The urge to cover his groin hit him hard at the memory of Megan's warning to Rudi.

He pulled her tighter to him, making her hum in her sleep as she snuggled against him. Her warmth seeped into him, reassuring him that she was really there and she was fine. And he would do everything in his power to keep her that way. First thing in the morning, he'd talk to Callum about upping her training schedule—after he convinced the man not to carry through with his threat to fire her, that is.

Closing his eyes he took a few deep, settling breaths and let himself drown in her scent. How this woman had gotten under his skin so fast he didn't know. But now that he had her, he had no intention of ever letting go. Holding her tight, Dimitri let sleep take him, confident in his ability to put himself between Megan and danger, if it should come for her in the night.

MEGAN WOKE to the feeling of lips on her spine. *Dimitri.* The man practically made her purr. Although letting him know that wouldn't be good for his already humungous ego. A wicked smile tugged at her lips before she mumbled, "Joe?"

Her tease earned a sharp bite to the curve of her hip.

"Dimitri." She felt the bed shift. Hands landed either side of her.

A hot and heavy body pressed against her back. Sharp

teeth nipped at her earlobe. "Call me by another man's name again and you'll regret it."

"Mm? What will you do?" She wriggled her backside against his hard length.

The hair on his legs bristled against her skin. The softer hair on his chest tickled her back. It was a caress.

"I'll make sure you never forget who's touching you." It was a warning and a promise.

The words were a caress to the parts of her that were desperate for his touch.

"Show me," she challenged.

"Not now." There was a smile in his voice as he kissed his way down her neck to her shoulder. "I like you all sleepy and compliant. I want to play before you wake up and start fighting with me again."

"Devil." But it was more of a purr than an insult.

"Don't move," he whispered against her nape. "Let me do all the work."

At last, an order she actually wanted to obey. She smiled against her pillow, vaguely aware that it smelled of Dimitri, green and earthy. It made her think of walking in leaf strewn woodland. Bliss.

He pressed open mouthed kisses down the length of her spine until he was kneeling between her legs. Warm hands trailed from her shoulders, over the curve of her behind to her thighs. She shivered as he caressed the sensitive inside of her thighs, before sliding over her backside to the flare of her hips.

"So soft." The wonder in his voice warmed her soul.

She felt him lean forward to twirl his tongue lazily in the small of her back.

"Mmm." Her brain was officially closed for the duration. All she could do was revel in the sensations Dimitri produced. Delicious, delicious sensations.

"You like that?"

He didn't seem to need an answer, so she didn't give him one. She was floating in that blissful place between sleep and awareness, where sensation was everything, and she never wanted it to end.

Strong hands turned her slowly, until she was lying on her back. She opened one eye a crack, to see him in the early morning light. He knelt between her legs, his hands smoothing over her body sensitising her skin to his barest touch. A gentle brush on the backs of her knees made her purr. A tingle on her thigh made her yearn for more. A whisper of a touch on the inside of her wrist. Soft circles around the fullness of her breasts made them swollen and desperate for a stronger touch. His hand, flat and gentle, curved around her throat. His thumb stroked along her jaw and then his hand slid down the centre of her body, over her stomach to brush through her curls. Then the fleeting touch was gone again.

She moaned, deep and low. "You're making me crazy."

The answer was a knowing chuckle before the wetness of his tongue hit her sensitive nipple. With a gasp, she bowed her body up into his touch.

"Nuh, uh." Firm on her hips. "Stay."

"Do I look like a dog to you?" The complaint was weak.

"You look like perfection to me." His mouth covered her nipple and he sucked deep.

The sound he yanked from her throat was nothing she'd recognise if she heard it later. Her hands shot to his head, threading her fingers through his hair to hold on tight.

Relentlessly, he sucked and nibbled and teased, until she was panting, desperate for more. Fingers tightened on the tip of her neglected breast, squeezing hard. Electric jolts through her body.

"Yes." Widening her legs, she cradled him closer to her body.

She was slick with need, every inch of her body oversensitive as she writhed beneath him. More. She needed more. "I need you inside me."

"Not yet." He trailed his tongue down her stomach, teasing her belly button with the tip of it, while his hands stayed on her breasts, massaging, caressing, teasing.

"Please." The word was a gasp, her mind no longer cognizant of language. Sounds merged—her gasps and breaths, Dimitri's words and cooing encouragement. She heard her own blood pulsing through her body. Need was loud in every breath and moan.

There was only Dimitri's touch. Actions became purely instinctual, born of need, driven by sensation. Her hips lifted as he blew cool air over the wet trail he'd left on her skin.

Lips covered her wet core and he gave her the most intimate of kisses. Words burst from her mouth. She didn't recognise them. All she knew was the ferocious pressure building inside of her, making her primal in her need for release.

"Sh." He gentled her, before launching another assault to make her lose her mind.

Fingers slid inside her, stroking, teasing. She clamped down on him, wanting all of it, but needing more.

"Please, please, please, please..." Her neck arched, eyes pressed shut as lights blazed behind them. A kaleidoscope of colour. "Please." It was a sob. Desperate need filled with raw brutal longing. He kept her on edge, ready to snap at any moment. Hovering on the brink of losing control completely.

Suddenly his touch was gone.

"No!" It was a wail.

His body pressed over hers. His lips demanding her kiss. Demanding her surrender. Taking it anyway.

"Now." An order, pressed against her lips.

He surged into her and she shattered. Back bowed, neck taut, nails digging into his sides. There was no thought. No ability to reason. Just wonderful, overwhelming feeling. Tingles in her body. Shudders as she came down from her peak. She blinked her eyes open to find him staring at her and that's when he started to move.

"Mine." He nipped her bottom lip as he rocked into her.

She wrapped her legs around him. Lazy, drunk on him. Yet, already the pressure was starting to build anew.

"Again." It was an order.

Her tongue flicked out to wet dry lips as she let him take her where he wanted to go.

"Again." A demand.

He shifted back onto his knees, taking her with him. Holding her backside, he lifted her up to meet his thrusts. His hard length hit every sensitive spot inside her, while predatory eyes filled with ownership watched her. Cheeks flushed, lips swollen, his muscles flexing as he moved inside her, holding her tight—exactly where she needed to be.

"Again. Now."

There was no argument. She had no will against this man. No defences left. With one last moan, she exploded. Taking him with her.

# CHAPTER 29

Joe laughed at Megan when she eventually staggered into the living room. She scowled at him and headed for the coffee.

"She isn't a morning person," Dimitri said as he beat her to the buffet staff had set up at the side of the room. It held an array of continental breakfast foods, from Danish pastries, to muffins and bagels. He poured a mug of coffee and handed it to her. "Sit down. I'll get you a plate." He tucked her hair behind her ear before turning to the food.

Megan narrowed her eyes at him. Something was bothering her, but she couldn't put her finger on what it was. There was fog in her head. What brain cells might have been functioning were too damn sated with endorphins to work. The man had scrambled her brain. And she couldn't think clearly enough to figure out if that was a good thing or a bad thing. She took her coffee and curled up in the corner of one of the sofas, only to notice everyone was staring at her.

"What?" Okay, so it came out a little grumpier than she'd intended.

"Nothing." Elle's innocent grin made Megan's skin prickle.

She looked down at her clothes. Nope, she hadn't forgotten to get dressed. She was wearing the jeans and white sweater Rachel had bought for her. When she looked back up, everyone was still staring at her, as though there was a joke she just wasn't in on.

"Okay, what is it? Do I have something on my face?" She hadn't eaten yet, so not food. Maybe toothpaste? Surely, Dimitri would have told her if that was the case.

"Nothing on your face." Rachel sipped her coffee before pointing a talon at Megan. "But there is a hickey the size of a tennis ball on your neck."

"No!" Her hand flew to her throat. Now that she knew it was there, she could swear she felt the thing.

Dimitri, the beast, smothered a smile as he piled his plate high. Megan moved to climb out of the sofa, find a mirror and check for herself. A hand stopped her as Julia handed her a compact mirror. Megan aimed it at her throat and felt the blood drain from her face.

"What the hell? Dimitri? This isn't a love bite. I don't know what the hell this is. What are you? Part vampire?"

While everyone else laughed, he sauntered over to her, looking smug. He handed her a plate with a bagel slathered in cream cheese—her favourite breakfast.

"I thought you liked vampires, Buffy."

"We're going to talk about this later." It was a promise. One filled with thoughts of retribution.

"With our words, right? Because, I swear, if this talk of yours involves you kneeing me again, I won't be responsible for my response. You've experienced the Dimitriator in action now. You damage it, you're only going to hurt yourself."

That caused hysterical laughter from the peanut gallery, which made Dimitri waggle his eyebrows at her. This wasn't funny. Not even a little.

"Nobody wants to talk about your dick, Dimitri," Callum said as he helped himself to coffee.

"I do," Elle said. "When you say Dimitriator, is that a reference to the terminator? Because the terminator was out to maim, kill and annihilate. If that's what you're doing with your penis, I'm not surprised Megan is pissed."

"No more," Callum ordered. "I can't believe I got into this business voluntarily. I used to be a professional. Now I get to sit around in a hotel, paid for by my project manager, while talking about one of my team's junk."

"I'm not your project manager. You fired me," Rachel pointed out.

Callum cocked an eyebrow at her. "Since when am I allowed to fire you?"

"Since I agreed to it. I've decided to stay fired."

There was bewildered silence until Ryan spoke up. "That seems really out of character for you, Rach."

"Did I ask the cheap seats for their opinion?" Her look was pure ice.

"That's more like you." Ryan cheerfully polished off another Danish pastry.

"Fired or not, we have things to deal with. Ryan, you're first up. Status of Rachel's apartment block?" Callum sipped his coffee.

"Well, the concierge is seriously pissed with us." Ryan put his empty plate on the coffee table in front of him. "He called in extra security and informed the cops of the problem, so they're fine. Totally covered. Oh, yeah, and he also politely declined our offer to train the staff."

"He doesn't have authority to do that," Rachel said. "He's only the concierge."

"Yeah, well, he's a concierge with a grudge against Benson Security." Ryan looked around for more food.

Megan caught him eyeing her plate and moved it out of

reach.

"Dimitri," Callum said. "The office."

Dimitri took a deep breath. "The office is a tip. Sorry, Julia." Megan saw Julia's shoulders firm in response, ready to jump into action and sort out the mess. "There's broken furniture and equipment everywhere. The walls have holes. The windows are smashed and the reception area is toast after the bomb went off in there."

"Bomb?" Julia squeaked.

"Only a little one." Dimitri smiled at her. "Barely big enough to make a noise. Your office is a goner though."

Megan gave her friend a sympathetic smile. She knew how attached Julia was to her whiteboards.

"I have everything backed up on my iPad," Julia said softly. "I'll get right onto arranging a clean-up and further construction once this meeting is over."

"Check with the cops first, make sure it's okay to get back into the building," Dimitri said. "Work with Ryan to get a full security system in there. We want the place air tight." He looked at Ryan. "You know the specs, right?"

"No prob." Ryan had managed to find another bagel from somewhere. He waved it at Callum. "You want a panic room? I keep getting voicemails from the gramps asking me about it."

"Aye," was all Callum said.

"Do we know if the attack was Abramovich or Durand?" Joe waved a coffee pot to see if anyone else wanted a refill. Unsurprisingly, Ryan raised his mug.

"Durand, definitely," Elle said, with an apologetic smile at Megan.

Megan stiffened in her seat then fought to look relaxed. The last thing she wanted was for people to know how much this was getting to her. It was her fault. She needed to be strong.

Dimitri relaxed back into the sofa beside her. His arm stretched along the back of it. He wasn't looking at her, or touching her, but then she felt his thumb caress the nape of her neck. Strangely, she relaxed at his touch, reassured by it.

"Megan got another text from Durand last night," Elle said.

Callum sat up straight. "Why wasn't I informed immediately?"

"You were busy with the office aftermath," Rachel said. "I didn't think it was a priority, so I told Elle to continue her efforts to trace him."

Callum's expression would have turned a lesser person to dust. Rachel was unaffected. "I thought you didn't work for me anymore?"

"I never did." Rachel gave him her own version of the death glare.

"The text said," Elle interrupted their stare off, "*You can run, but you can't hide.*"

"No originality." Megan was disgusted at the lack of imagination. If she'd sent the text she would have put way more effort into it.

Dimitri squeezed her neck.

"What?" she demanded when she looked at him.

"You can give him lessons on creative threatening messages when we get him."

She blinked at him. How the hell did he know what she was thinking?

"There was a photo as well," Elle said. "It was your bedroom."

Megan's stomach revolted. "He's been in my room? That's gross." She looked at Dimitri. "My room has Durand cooties."

"You need to move." He was playing with her. The thought gave her tingles that weren't appropriate in the middle of a meeting.

"Rachel needs a roommate," Megan said.

"No," Rachel said.

"Joe?" Callum said. "What's the word on Abramovich?"

Joe sat forward on the edge of the other sofa. Megan noticed that Julia was positioned as far away from the man as possible without actually leaving the room. Interesting.

"I've spoken to everyone I can get a hold of." Joe ran a hand through his hair. "Rudi is still in London. In a private clinic. He was in surgery. No word as to whether they were able to save his dick or not."

The men in the room turned green as Megan reached over and fist bumped Elle.

"What about the organisation?" Callum said.

"Business as usual. Rudi is still in control, just out of action for a bit. Nobody seems that worried. The word is this was a personal vendetta and the matter is now closed."

"The bully ran," Rachel said to Megan with a gleam in her eye.

"Yeah," Megan said with a touch of wonder and a whole lot of gratefulness.

Joe gave a reassuring nod. "All rumour and chatter involving Claire has died down. I'd say she's safe. Rudi has other things on his mind right now."

Megan felt lightheaded. She'd done it. She'd scared him off Claire. Only, "Are we sure he won't go after her?"

"There's a chance he'll pick up his vendetta when he's healed. *If* he heals." Joe winced. "But by then, he'll be in custody. So yeah, Claire is definitely safe." His smile was dazzling. "That doesn't mean Grunt won't carry on watching her twenty-four seven, though."

Megan couldn't help but blast Dimitri with a megawatt smile. Ignoring the people in the room, he wrapped an arm around her shoulder and tugged her to his side. He kissed her temple. "That's good," was all he said, but Megan heard the depth behind it and knew he understood. Instead of pushing him away she relaxed into his hold. So what if it wasn't professional? Right now, she needed his touch. Later, she'd remind him that hugging in a meeting wasn't a good look for them.

Callum shook his head at Dimitri's behaviour but didn't say anything. Instead he turned his attention to Elle. "How's it going decrypting Rudi's files? You've been forwarding the information to the authorities right?"

She nodded. "Every word as I get it. We're making steady progress."

Dimitri cleared his throat. "Katrina," was all he said, but Megan felt his muscles tense.

"I'm sure the information is in the files that are still decrypting. We've already come across details on other women that were sold as slaves." Elle's face was soft with compassion in her voice. "As soon as Katrina's information pops up I'll let you know. Promise."

Dimitri gave a terse nod and Megan patted his chest.

"You two need to get a room," Ryan said.

"We have a room. We were happy in there, until you lot decided you needed yet another meeting," Megan pointed out. She angled her face up to Dimitri. "I think we need to head back there. You know, to debrief." She waggled her eyebrows at him.

A second later, he was on his feet and dragging her towards their room.

"Guess the meeting is over then," Callum said behind them. "This sort of thing never happened in the army. What the hell have I got myself into?"

Megan grinned at Callum's grumpy complaint. She didn't care if they were being unprofessional. Claire was safe and Dimitri was hot. Everything else could wait.

# CHAPTER 30

"You can't avoid me forever."

Julia jerked at the voice, but kept her focus firmly on the iPad in her lap. Joe might think she couldn't avoid him forever, but she was happy to prove him wrong.

They were in the sitting room of the suite. Julia wasn't dumb enough to wander off to work on her own, taking the chance Joe would corner her again. She honestly didn't know what she would do if he did. The temptation to touch the man was so strong it actually made her fingertips ache. But there was no way she could do it, not when he was the embodiment of everything that terrified her.

He crouched down beside her chair, but thankfully he didn't touch her. She'd spent most of the night awake thinking about his last touch. Her system couldn't handle anymore.

"I know I came on a little strong." Joe kept his voice low, just for the two of them. The intimacy of it sent shivers up her spine. "I didn't want to scare you. I just wanted to make my intentions clear."

He'd terrified her, but not for the reasons he thought. "We

can't…date." Was that even the right word for the things she thought when it came to Joe?

A heavy pause. "Why not?" There was no censure in the question. No anger.

Julia fought not to panic. She glanced around the room. Elle was sitting at her computers, tapping away. Ryan was poring over security plans for the office. Rachel was on her phone, but no doubt aware of everything going on around her. The rest of the team were off doing who knew what, but at least she wasn't alone with Joe. She didn't think she could handle that at all.

"I deserve to know why, Jules, don't you think?" It was a soft question. Gentle, the way only Joe could be.

She nodded, but the words wouldn't come. Not yet. Her cheeks heated. She hated this about herself. Hated that her shyness paralysed her sometimes. Hated that she was so easily intimidated when it came to personal things.

"Who are you contracting for a panic room?" Joe's question surprised her. Her eyes flicked to his beautiful face. She saw his movie star smile before her eyes flew back to her iPad. "Please tell me you aren't letting the Granger brothers build a secure shed in the basement."

Her lips quirked at the thought. It was almost a smile. "No," she said softly. "I have a number of companies who specialise in panic rooms shortlisted." This she could talk about. Work was a safe topic. It wasn't personal. It was outside of herself and based in facts and figures. It wasn't emotional and it didn't reveal the gaping holes in her personality.

"The boys are going to be disappointed," Joe said. "Although, I hear tell that they want a room like the one Jodie Foster had in the movie."

Julia nodded. "They watched the film on a date night with their wives." She smiled at the reminder of that conversation.

"Ryan pointed out that by the time the panic room is up and running the boys won't be working in the office anymore. They were insulted." She could hear the grin in Joe's voice. "I think they're planning to hang around indefinitely."

Yeah, she'd gotten that impression too. "They think Benson Security is more fun than retirement." She thought about it. "Or hanging out with their wives."

Joe's chuckle was deep and sensual. The sound translated into a taste sensation on her tongue. He was melted chocolate. Delicious, dark, sensual. A temptation for every woman.

"You trust me, don't you Julia?" His tone changed. Intimate. Earnest.

She nodded. She did trust him. Who wouldn't? The man was a born protector with a core of honour so bright it was almost a beacon. When it came to work, to safety, she trusted him with her life.

"Could you trust me with you?"

She gasped at the low question, astonished he'd know there was a difference for her. A huge difference between trusting him professionally and trusting him personally. He waited, a font of endless patience beside her. It was soothing, the lack of judgment she picked up from his quiet presence.

"I don't know." Honesty was the least she could give him.

He shifted slightly before she felt his fingers brush a loose strand of her hair behind her ear. She stiffened, alert, focused, waiting. To her relief, and dismay, he backed off. Confused, he confused her so much. Just being around him filled her to overflowing with longing and fear. The constant pull in two directions was exhausting.

"Here's the thing," Joe said. "I think you're special, Jules. You think no one can see you, that you slip in under the radar, but you're wrong. I see you. I see your strength, the way you take care of the people around you, the genius ability you have to organise even the most complicated scenario. I see the wicked sense of humour that bursts out every so often. I see the core of strength inside of you."

His fingertip caressed the back of her hand. A touch so soft and fleeting most people wouldn't even have felt it. Julia did. She felt it reverberate throughout her body. The touch made her lightheaded. Because it wasn't just a touch. It was Joe. His hand retreated and she caught herself before she swayed towards him.

"I know," he said, "that whoever gets inside that wall you've built will be a lucky man. That guy will get to experience the whole package that is you, without you holding back from fear or worry."

She stilled, his words piercing her defences.

"I want to be that man. I want to be the only man in the world who knows the real Julia. The only man who gets to experience all of you. The only man you trust with everything. I want to be that man so badly, I can taste it."

She heard it, the conviction. The need, but she couldn't prevent the question that slipped from her lips. "Why?" She was under no delusions—she was no prize. Most men would be put off with how much work getting to know her took. Yanking her courage firmly around her, she looked into his beautiful eyes. "Why, Joe?" she whispered.

His jaw firmed, his determination clear. "Because, I see you and I know the prize you hide. The you underneath all of this is worth possessing."

She was mesmerised by him. No one ever said the things Joe said to her. It didn't make sense, that someone so wonderful would want her. Yet, there he was, whispering earnestly. His eyes heated and she looked away, blushing.

"I don't know if I can." She'd been hurt before, decimated. She didn't know if she could be vulnerable like that again, if she could trust someone with herself that way again.

"Can you think about it?" His words were a caress that filled her with longing. "Please?"

The words were more precious than rubies to her. The answer wasn't one she planned to give. "Yes," she breathed.

His slow, and oh so sexy smile, made her heart race. It was the smile of a man who never gave up on a challenge. It was the smile of a man who knew he would win. It was a smile that should have made her run. Instead, it made her lips feel dry and her fingers tingle to touch.

That's when Julia knew she was already in out of her depth. To go any further would be to drown. And yet, in that moment, she wasn't sure that drowning in Joe wouldn't be a wonderful way to go.

# CHAPTER 31

The call came at eight that evening.

Dimitri was at the office building, helping Ryan to fit a new security system, while a cleaning crew sorted out the mess. He pulled his phone out of his back pocket, saw it was Elle and his heart stopped dead.

"Go," he said when he answered.

"She's in Morocco."

The world around Dimitri became magnified. He was painfully aware of the sound of his own breathing, of the rough surface of the wall under his hand, of the fly that buzzed around his face.

"You have an address?" His voice was sandpaper.

"Yep. We have an address. Along with the name of the guy who bought her." There was a pause. "Callum has a contact locally. We have him seeking confirmation that she's still in the house."

*And hasn't been sold on.* He heard the words Elle didn't say and his hand tightened on his phone.

Ryan stepped back into the room, took one look at Dimitri and his face closed up. He put the gear he was carrying on the table beside him, folded his arms and waited for instruction.

"How long until we head over there?" Dimitri kept his eyes on Ryan.

"Couple of hours. Callum wants you back here to go over strategy."

"I'm on my way." He flicked the phone off and stared at it.

For long minutes Ryan said nothing, then he took a step towards Dimitri. "What do you need?"

The question was simple, but in it Dimitri knew Ryan was offering his complete support for whatever Dimitri decided to do.

"We need to head back to the hotel." He didn't need to explain further. It was clear what this was about.

Ryan nodded once. "Let me tell the gramps." He jogged off to inform the old men that they were in charge.

Dimitri was sitting behind the driver's wheel of the SUV when Ryan climbed in. His usual easy-going façade was gone —in its place was a trained soldier ready for duty. In that moment, Dimitri could clearly see why Lake Benson had hired the guy.

"We need more guys. I feel like an amateur leaving my grandad to watch the office." There was disgust in Ryan's voice.

"There's a cop there too." Tessa had stationed one of her constables in the building in case of a return visit from Durand.

"Not the point."

No, it wasn't. "Lake and Callum are on it." The office wasn't even supposed to be up and running yet. The mission to find Katrina and eliminate the threat of Rudi Abramovich was a private one. An in-house undertaking that had nothing to do with business and everything to do with family.

"I hope they speed up. We're seriously undermanned. If

this is what it's like when we aren't even open for business, what will it be like a month from now?" Ryan angled himself to look at Dimitri. "You'll be here a month from now, right? You're staying on after we find Katrina, aren't you?"

"Yeah." If there was one thing Dimitri was certain of, it was that he'd found a professional home with Benson Security—and a personal one with Megan. Although, he suspected telling Megan he'd decided they were long-term would be a whole lot harder than telling Callum.

"Good," was all Ryan said.

The streets of London zoomed past them in a kaleidoscope of neon lights. They drove through Westminster past the many generic office blocks that housed the worker bees of the British government. The office streets were quiet, but that changed as soon as they hit Westminster Abbey. The streets around the Abbey, Parliament Building and Big Ben were crowded with tourists. Dimitri's eyes skirted the black depths of the Thames to focus on the clock tower that watched over the city. Each minute that ticked on the ornate dial was one more minute his sister was trapped.

They swung a left along the river, watching the large wheel of the London Eye move slowly through the night. So many people, going about their business, getting home from work, or off to dinner. Visiting with friends or sight-seeing. None of them aware of the evil lurking at the edges of their lives. It all seemed so ordinary, so pedestrian, when all Dimitri could think of was his sister. All he could see when he looked out at the picture postcard views was Katrina's face. All he could hear was her cry for help. For his help.

"We're nearly there." Ryan's voice cut through his thoughts and Dimitri realised he had a death grip on the steering wheel. They'd driven under Jubilee Bridge and were coming up on the Savoy, but he didn't think that was what

Ryan meant. Ryan confirmed it when he said, "She'll be home soon."

Yeah, she'd be home soon. Dimitri wouldn't allow for anything else. He pulled into the hotel, yet another building with a clock atop it that mocked him with how long he'd taken to find his sister. He threw his car keys at the valet and entered the hotel. The glitz and glamour of the building, with its Art Deco details and marble columns, hit him as painfully out of place. He wasn't there to enjoy his time in London. He was there to plan a rescue mission for his sister. Somehow, knowing that made the chandeliers feel like an insult.

They rode the elevator in silence and when they entered the suite, they were greeted by the rest of the team, plus two welcome additions.

"Lake." Dimitri shook the ex-SAS specialist's hand. "Thanks for coming."

"No need for thanks. You're a member of the team."

Dimitri had been a member of a team all of his adult life. This was different. This was more. It was family. He nodded his thanks before turning to the giant American flanking Lake.

"Grunt." He held out his hand and it was instantly swallowed by the man mountain's.

With this one act, coming down from Scotland to help him find his sister, the men had earned his loyalty. Any thought of leaving Lake Benson's team after he'd retrieved his sister was gone. He was now a Benson Security guy for life.

"Claire?" he asked the giant.

"She's covered." Grunt folded his meaty arms, obviously having decided that was all he had to say on the matter.

"With the threat of Abramovich removed, it was safe to leave her with a couple of my guys," Lake added. "Anyway, seemed like you lot needed a hand down here."

Dimitri nodded as he felt Megan sidle up to him. He normally would have laughed at her effort to appear unconcerned and casual—instead he wrapped an arm around her shoulder and pulled her tight against him.

"Freaking caveman," she muttered as she thumped a fist on his chest. But there was no force behind it and she didn't try to pull away.

Grunt looked between Dimitri and Megan, his brow furrowed in thought. When he'd come to a conclusion, he looked Dimitri straight in the eye.

"Hurt her, you pay."

There was no need to say anything else—the Hulk would be able to take him with one well-placed punch.

"Grunt!" Megan tried to step away from him, presumably to give her brother-in-law grief. Dimitri didn't let her go. He needed the comfort of having her in his arms. Just for a moment. This moment. It didn't deter Megan. She shouted at Grunt anyway. "You can't go all King Kong on me. I'm not your wife. Butt out of my life, ape face, or you'll regret it."

Grunt stared at Megan, his face unreadable, then he looked back at Dimitri. There was no need for words, it was clear the threat still stood.

"Oh, that's it." Megan struggled to get free. "I've had enough of bossy men. I'm going to teach you a lesson, Grunt Dayton."

The woman obviously had a death wish.

"See what I mean?" Joe said to Dimitri. "No fear." He shook his head in wonder as he stared at Megan.

Lake's lips twitched in his approximation of a smile. "We ready to get this show on the road?"

"Definitely." Dimitri felt Megan still beside him.

She looked up at him, fire in her blue eyes. "I've got your back."

He kissed her forehead. Crazy woman.

His crazy woman.

Once everyone was settled into their seats in the living room, all eyes turned to Elle. She stood beside her computer monitors, dressed in blue jeans and a Star Trek original series T-shirt. Dimitri was geek enough to recognise the shirt as the yellow Captain Kirk wore. Her hair was in two bunches, each tied with bands that had plastic strawberries attached to them. The red made her blue hair seem even more luminous.

"Who's the Smurf?" Grunt surprised everyone when he volunteered to talk instead of someone having to pry words from him.

"The *Smurf*," Elle said, "is the woman who's going to wipe out your credit rating for the next ten years if you don't learn some manners."

Grunt chuckled and took up a spot beside the window. He stood feet apart, arms folded and tense, as though ready to spring into action. Joe shook his head in amusement then grabbed a chair beside his best friend and fellow ex-Marine.

A screen had been rigged up above the fireplace, a data projector pointing at it. The Savoy really could provide anything you needed. Elle tapped on her iPad and an aerial image of a house appeared. Not a house, Dimitri corrected himself, an estate.

"This is the Moroccan home of Henri Boudin. It's where Katrina is being held."

After almost a year, he had the name of the man who held his sister. Pure, ice-cold fury surged through his veins at the thought. Dimitri felt something on his chest and ripped his eyes away from the image to find Megan petting him as they sat side by side on the sofa. It was an attempt to soothe him. Wrapping an arm around her shoulders, he pressed a kiss to her temple to let her know he was okay. He was holding it together. He couldn't lose it now. Not when he was this close.

"We're sure she's there?" For once Rachel's tone wasn't mocking.

Elle nodded. "Callum's contact in the area confirmed she was in the house as of seven o'clock this morning."

"Is that seven our time, or seven Moroccan time?" Megan asked.

"We're on the same time zone as Morocco," Callum answered. "Seven there, is seven here."

"So, she was there almost fourteen hours ago," Megan said. "For certain?"

"For certain." There was no doubt in Callum's tone or demeanour.

Dimitri realised his fingertips were digging into Megan's shoulder and relaxed his grip. She patted his chest again to tell him she understood.

"What do we know about this Henri Boudin?" Lake said.

Elle tapped her iPad and data appeared on the screen. "Basically, he's rich, he's ruthless and he's connected. His family have been involved in French politics for over a century. His parents squandered the family money living the high life. Henri here built his own empire from scratch. Although, he didn't exactly start poor, just not as uber-rich as he is now. He runs several successful corporations. He has a toe in everything from new tech to real estate, but his main business is import/export. He isn't afraid to play nasty and there's plenty of evidence to suggest that not everything he's dealing in is legal. If I had more time I could give you details."

"Makes sense. You don't run in the same circles as Rudi Abramovich if your business is above board." Joe looked at Grunt who grunted in agreement.

"Security?" Lake said.

The image flicked back to the house. The house that held his sister. A short three hour flight from London.

"We have surveillance information from various cameras, databases near the estate. We also have the information Callum's contact sent us." Elle pursed her lips. "I'm in the process of hacking his home network. That will give us more detailed information on security rotations. It shouldn't take long." The woman had serious skills hidden under her Manga persona.

"Then we plan." Callum glanced at Lake before looking to Dimitri for agreement.

"I don't want to wait for Elle to hack the house before we move." Dimitri wanted his sister out now.

"I'll have the information within the hour." Elle sounded more than confident. "It isn't exactly the Pentagon."

"More informed we are, less likely we screw up," Callum said.

Reluctantly Dimitri inclined his head in agreement. "Then we plan."

"Was the armoury at the office hit?" Lake's light blue eyes were full of cold calculation.

"It wasn't touched." Ryan wasn't eating for once. "No sign of tampering with the access panel. It's secure, and still loaded with toys."

"I have a jet on standby at City airport," Rachel said. "It's ready to go when you are."

Megan perked up. "You have your own plane?"

"No. I don't need my own plane. I borrow my father's when the occasion arises."

"Why don't you have your own plane? You can afford it." Megan was undeterred. "You could call up a plane dealer and order a Cessna in pink."

People started to chuckle as Rachel stared at Megan. "It really doesn't take much to amuse you, does it?"

"Nope." Megan grinned at the woman.

"Okay." Callum stood. "Dimitri, this is your op. We're here for you. But Lake has a lot of experience in extractions like this. I'd take his advice. Ryan, Joe, you two head to the office and pick up the gear we'll need. Grunt, Lake, Dimitri and myself will get started on the planning. Any questions?"

"Yeah, what about me?" Megan said. "Don't I get to come too?"

"No!" Every man in the room shouted at the same time.

Megan sat back down in a huff. She folded her arms and glared at Dimitri. "The only reason you aren't getting an argument right now is because I know how important this is."

"And because you don't work for me any more," Callum pointed out.

"Oh," Megan pouted. "I forgot about that."

Dimitri leaned over, clasped the back of Megan's neck and kissed her hard. "I appreciate you want to come, Buffy, but I need you safe too. I can only handle worrying about one woman I care about at a time."

Megan seemed a little stunned as Dimitri turned back to Callum. "What about protection for Megan while we're gone?"

"Ryan and I will stay here. Durand is still a problem. We don't want to take risks."

"I'd like to point out, again," Megan said loudly, "that I don't need a keeper. I can actually look after myself. I have self-defence skills and I'm good at thinking on my feet."

"Nobody questions that, Buff." Dimitri tucked her hair behind her ear. "It's *what* you think that scares the life out of us."

"Idiot," she grumbled, but stayed in place.

# CHAPTER 32

They arrived in the outskirts of Morocco's capital, Rabat, just after two in the morning. They drove through the city from the airport, watching the mix of French colonial and Islamic architecture slide past. Modern white apartment blocks were dwarfed by the red stone walls of the Roman-built Kasbah fort, small blue mosaicked houses peeked out amongst modern office buildings and green oasis gardens were interspersed throughout the city landscape. The large tiled domes of the mosques were lit up in warm colours that glowed against the black night. Palm trees lined their route along the coast, with the blank void of the Atlantic their constant companion.

They were a four man team: Lake Benson, Grunt, Joe and Dimitri. One ex-SAS specialist, two ex-Marines and one ex-Ranger. They were kitted out in black tactical vests over black T-shirts and cargo pants. They all wore kneepads, boots and fingerless gloves. Each of them carried an M4, with a Berretta and knife strapped to their thighs.

Warmth spread through him as he remembered Megan's goodbye before he'd left. Other women would have kissed him and told him to be careful. Megan had taken one look at his tactical vest and demanded he buy her one for Christmas. Crazy woman.

"We ready?" Lake was driving, as he knew the capital city of Morocco well. Dimitri didn't ask how he'd gained his familiarity with the city. They all had their secrets.

"Yeah." Dimitri was more than ready. He was desperate to get to his sister. A desperation he was trying to keep a lid on, because impatience would cause mistakes. Ones he couldn't afford to make.

Grunt grunted and Joe nodded as he checked his gear one more time. It felt like a ritual. Like they'd been a team for a very long time. And even though Dimitri was the only member of their team who had never set foot in Morocco before then, he still felt an overwhelming sense of familiarity about everything they saw and did.

"Lake's on point," Dimitri said, although they knew this. "I'm second. Comms check."

They each activated their comm units which ran up from their vests to sit flush against their throats.

Without being prompted, Lake cut the lights on their SUV as they swung into the suburb where Henri Boudin's estate was located. They'd gone over the security information in detail. They knew exactly what to expect. They were ready.

Once they parked the car along the road from the house, they headed for the side wall. What felt like a minute later, they had disabled the cameras and were over the wall. Crouching low, M4s in hand, they approached the house in tight formation, scanning for the enemy, moving in silence towards the rear of the property.

Lights were on in the three-storeyed mansion. The vast windows left nothing to the imagination. From this angle the house had amazing views of the ocean, but was completely open to observation. And there was something wrong. There were no people. The estate was silent in a way that only ever occurred when a place was empty.

Dimitri made hand signals indicating they should spread out. They automatically split up into two pairs. Joe with Grunt. Lake with Dimitri. They kept to the shadows, scanning constantly. Nothing.

Dimitri tapped Lake's shoulder and pointed to the corner of the terrace where he knew a guard was usually posted. Lake nodded and they moved together, covering each other as they did so. Lake saw it first. He held up a fist to stop Dimitri, then signalled for him to cover him. Dimitri tapped his shoulder to acknowledge his order. A minute later Lake broke radio silence.

"One down. Throat slit."

Everything within Dimitri shut down. It was a trained reaction.

"Two down." Grunt said. "Throat slit."

A litany of curses erupted in Dimitri's head. He tapped Lake's shoulder and pointed to the doors, knowing that Joe and Grunt would be doing the same thing. They found blood on the carpet in the sitting room. Bullet holes in the wall. Another guard fallen behind the French sofas. Dimitri's heart began to race. On the surface he was contained, efficient and silent, inside there was terror.

They moved quickly through the rooms, checking each in turn. Keeping their guns, and their guards, up ready for attack. None came. Instead they found an ever-increasing body count.

In the upstairs bedroom—the master bedroom—they found Henri Boudin.

There were at least three bullet holes in his body. His grey Savile Row suit was drenched in blood. It pooled out onto the Persian rug, staining its beauty the same way Henri had stained everything in his life. Dimitri looked into the face of the man who'd imprisoned his sister and felt only violent, cold hatred.

"Over here." It was Lake. There was no longer any need to keep radio silence, or any other kind of silence. Everyone on the estate was dead and there was no sign of Katrina.

Dimitri strode to the walk in closet, where Lake was standing in the doorway. His usually stoic face was grim. He stepped back to let Dimitri pass. A cold dread washed over Dimitri's skin as he caught the hard fury in Lake's eyes. At the back of the closet was another door. One that blended a little too well with the décor. At first glance you wouldn't have seen it amongst the clothes.

"What we got?" Joe said as he came up behind them.

Lake just gave him a look.

"Hell." Joe looked at Grunt.

They stopped at the entrance to the closet. Waiting for Dimitri. The message was clear: they had his back, but this was for him to do alone.

With muscles so taut they felt like they would snap, Dimitri pushed open the door to the concealed room behind it.

It was empty.

Relief that he hadn't found the body of his sister almost took him to his knees.

He looked back at Lake, saw the grim line of his mouth and turned back to study the room. A single mattress on the floor, bare except for one blanket. A toilet in the corner of the room. A tiny sink with a bar of soap, toothpaste and brush. There were no windows. No decoration. Nothing. Bare wooden floorboards under foot, marred by the marks made from the chains. Chains that were attached to the wall near the bed and ended in ankle cuffs that lay open on the floor. There were no clothes in the room.

Shaking, Dimitri stepped deeper inside the room. It was barely bigger than the closet behind him. He knew, just from looking, that the chains would stretch as far as the toilet, but not as far as the door. Henri could have left the door unlocked and his captive still would never have gotten free.

He'd seen enough. He turned to leave and his knees gave way. He hit the floor with a loud thump. The wall, where the door sat, had been papered with Polaroid photos. Thousands of Polaroid photos.

All of Katrina.

"Get him out of there," Lake ordered.

Joe was already in the room when the order came. He glanced at the wall. Saw the horror and cursed. "Let's go. You don't need to see that." A hand clasped Dimitri's shoulder.

Rage surged and Dimitri roared, throwing off Joe's hand. He clawed at the photos, ripping them off the wall, tearing them to nothing, letting them fall until the floor was littered with them. It was what he imagined his sister would have done if she'd been able to reach them. If she hadn't been chained in place to stare at them, to be reminded every minute of every day of why she was there and what her captor could do to her. With his bare hands, he destroyed the evidence of her torture at the hands of Henri Boudin. The same way he wanted to rip apart the man who'd done this to her.

Lake and Joe stood sentry while he worked out his rage. They didn't try to stop him. They didn't comment. When every image was gone, he stood gasping at the horror around his feet. It wasn't enough. It would never be enough. He wanted to rip the place apart until he bled. Until everyone bled. All of them.

"I want this gone." He didn't give Lake a choice. "I want it all gone. I want to raze this place to the ground. Nothing left. Nothing."

There was agreement in Lake's icy eyes.

"We need to find out where she's gone first." Joe ran a hand over his face. "Someone took her."

He was too late. Again. He saw red. Literally. Everything else was obliterated.

"Got security footage," Grunt called from the bedroom.

Joe and Lake waited for Dimitri to walk out first before they followed him. Grunt was leaning over the desk that sat in front of one of the huge windows overlooking the ocean.

"He had the security feeds come through here." Grunt pointed to the desktop computer. "That's from two hours ago." Grunt stepped back so they could see the screen.

As soon as the image registered, Dimitri snapped. One second he was looking at Durand's smug smile as he dragged Katrina from the building, the next he was throwing the machine through the window and out onto the grass beyond.

"Get the security footage and any other records you can find," Lake told Grunt.

Without a word Grunt jogged off in search of the security room.

"See what you can do about bringing the house down," Lake said to Joe.

Dimitri stood, hands on hips, staring at the man who lay dead on the carpet. Wishing he was still alive so he could make the bastard suffer.

"I don't know about bringing the house down," Joe said. "I'll see what's in their arsenal, but we can definitely wipe that room." He pointed to the closet. "I'll let you know." And then he was gone.

Dimitri couldn't take his eyes off Henri Boudin. He felt a hand on his shoulder. It took effort to drag his gaze up to Lake's.

"She's still alive," Lake said.

Dimitri couldn't think. Couldn't talk. All he could see

were the images in Katrina's prison cell. All he could hear were her screams. Had she begged for her brother to rescue her? Had she wept when he didn't come? He'd taken too long. He was too late.

"She's still alive." Lake squeezed his shoulder.

"She won't be the same." The words were wrenched from him. They left a gaping wound inside his heart. One he knew would never heal.

"No. We'll help her. We'll make her stronger." His voice was a deadly growl. "She's still alive. This isn't over."

No. Dimitri looked back at Henri Boudin. This wasn't over. He turned his back on the bastard. Lake slapped him on the shoulder and without another word they went in search of clues as to where Durand had taken his sister. Because this wasn't over. Not until Durand had breathed his last.

# CHAPTER 33

The men were on their way back from Morocco and the team were back to square one. It wasn't a good place to be.

Megan left her sombre friends and retreated to the room she shared with Dimitri. As she lay on their bed, watching shadows play on the ceiling, her mind was on the man who'd wormed his way into her heart. She couldn't even begin to imagine how he would deal with this latest setback. It was beyond cruel to get so close to rescuing his sister just to have her snatched away at the last minute. She wished she was with him, even though she knew there was nothing she could do to help. At some point, when she hadn't been looking, Dimitri had made a home for himself deep inside her heart. It beat for him now. The arrogant, annoying, sexy, caring man was hers. And she wished she was with him.

"You still up?" Callum called as he knocked at her door.

"Yeah." She swung her legs over the side of the bed to sit facing the window as Callum came into the room. His footsteps were silent on the plush carpet.

Still dressed in the white cashmere sweater and jeans Rachel had provided for her, Megan was ready to hear what

Callum had to say. He sat beside her on the edge of the bed, keeping a respectable distance between them, skin illuminated by the dim glow coming from golden street lights. He rested his elbows on his knees and looked at her.

"What happened?" It was a struggle to get the words out through her rapidly closing throat. "Dimitri?"

"No." He ran a hand through his military short hair. "Sorry, no, he's fine. On his way back. They're due in London about six thirty. This is something else."

"Is it about Julia?" The woman was inconsolable. Blaming herself for Durand's actions, knowing he had seen the files on Katrina when he'd broken into her office.

"No. It wasn't her fault. Nobody could predict this."

"It's because of me, isn't it? That's why he took her."

To his credit, Callum didn't lie and tell her she was wrong. They all knew there was only one reason Durand would go after what the team wanted—to get to Megan.

"There's been another text." Callum faced her, solemn, worried.

"What did it say?" Her voice was steady. That was good.

"He wants to trade."

*Of course.* "Me for Katrina." Megan felt a strange calm come over her. It made perfect sense. The only possible outcome from Durand's actions.

"Aye."

"I'll do it." There was no hesitation. No second thoughts. She would do this and more for the man she loved. And she did love him. It was a calm knowing. Dimitri was in her heart and she would sacrifice the rest of herself for him. Just as she knew he would for her.

"You sure?" There was no judgement in the question.

"Yes."

Dimitri's sister had been through hell, she had to come home. And Megan knew this was her fault. All of it. There was no getting around it. If she hadn't shot Durand in Scotland, he wouldn't be obsessed with getting to her. He wouldn't have taken Katrina and Dimitri would have rescued his sister in Rabat.

"Durand wants to trade at six." Callum's voice was soft, but even.

Megan picked up on the significance of the time instantly. "Half an hour before the rest of the guys get back."

"Aye." His gentle Scottish accent was soothing to her.

"What do you need me to do?" Her stomach spasmed. She placed a hand flat on it and hoped Callum didn't notice.

"I need you to do what you're told."

She nodded once. It was a promise. "Point me at them, boss." Then a stab of loss as she remembered he was no longer her boss. "I mean…"

His hand covered hers. "You got it right the first time. When this is over, you're going to be Benson Security's first official trainee. Think you can hack it?"

Her answer was a weak smile.

"Okay." Callum stood. "Let's get to work."

DIMITRI WATCHED Lake's unreadable face as he spoke with Callum. The roar of the plane's engines drowned out what Lake was saying, making Dimitri's imagination run riot. The only clue he had that things were bad was the way Lake's knuckles whitened as he clutched the arm of his chair.

He glanced across the aisle to where Grunt and Joe were seated. They faced each other, each man looking equally out of place in the plush cream interior. A small table between them held forgotten bottles of water. Their eyes were also on Lake's face. Dimitri focused on breathing evenly while he waited for Lake to finish.

Lake didn't make them wait to find out what he'd been

told. "Durand contacted Megan. He wants to exchange her for Katrina at six this morning."

Dimitri's hearing was momentarily blocked out by a ferocious rushing sound, followed closely by the rapid thud of his heart.

"No." The word shot from his mouth. "No."

Grim faces stared at him, each one as angry and frustrated as he was.

"No." He didn't realise until that moment that he wasn't vetoing the exchange, he was saying no to the horror of it. No, he couldn't exchange one woman he loved for another. No. This wasn't a choice. It wasn't. He loved them both. He loved his sister. He loved Megan. His vision blurred. He loved Megan. He tested the words with his tongue and knew them to be true. He loved the crazy, fearless woman. Damn it to hell. No. No exchange. No choosing. Just no.

"Other options?" His voice was dark and rusty.

"The meet's in forty minutes," Lake said. "We're an hour and ten minutes from London. There are no other options."

"No!" He surged to his feet, followed quickly by Joe. His hand clamped on Dimitri's shoulder.

"Callum and Ryan are there." It was unsaid that both men would stand in front of a bullet to save the women.

Dimitri put his hands on his hips and stared at the roof of the cabin. White plastic, it was all that was between him and death. White plastic. What was between Megan and death? Katrina and death? He wanted to punch a hole through the white plastic. A hole to symbolise his endless frustrated need to protect them. A hole where his heart would be if they didn't make it. If Megan didn't make it.

"You okay?" Joe squeezed his shoulder.

Dimitri nodded. He wasn't okay, but he was contained. For now. Joe relaxed slightly, but he didn't sit until Dimitri took his seat again.

"What's the plan?" Dimitri asked Lake.

"We can't call in the cops." The way Lake said it revealed he was expecting an argument.

He didn't get one. Dimitri nodded, once. He knew how Durand worked. Any hint of a police presence and he'd put a bullet in Katrina's brain. Then he'd dedicate himself to finding another way to get his hands on Megan.

Lake opened a bottle of water and handed it to Dimitri. He took it and gulped the ice cold liquid down fast. It helped. A small thing to focus on while he fought to think clearly.

"What did Durand specify?"

"He told Megan to wait outside Norwood Junction train station. She's to be there in half an hour. Once there she'll be told where the final meeting place will be."

"This guy has watched way too many spy movies," Joe said.

Grunt grunted in agreement.

"Smart though," Lake said. "It means Callum can't scope out the location ahead of him."

"Will they make it to the location on time?" Dimitri hated that he even asked that question. The thought of this happening in any way, shape or form repulsed him on a cellular level.

"Yeah, they'll make it. Ryan knows London as well as I do, he'll get them there."

Joe leaned forward, resting his elbows on his knees. "It's early. The roads won't be clogged with rush hour traffic yet. It also means Durand will have a quick getaway."

Dimitri clenched his fists, fighting back the urge to lash out. "What's the earliest we can get to Norwood Junction?"

Lake stared at him. "From London City airport it's a forty minute drive. We arrive just after six, earlier if we're lucky."

Forty minutes was too long. Durand would be long gone by the time they got there, Megan along with him.

Lake tapped his phone's screen. "There's an airport that's closer. Biggin Hill. It's south of the Norwood meeting point. It would cut twenty minutes off our arrival time." He nodded to Joe who was already on his feet, heading for the pilot.

"Twenty minutes." Still too late. Dimitri stared at Lake as the man dialled and arranged for a car to be at the field waiting for them, engine running.

"It's doable." Grunt surprised him by speaking.

"Callum will text us the final meeting point when he gets it," Lake said. "At least we'll be in the area and not that far behind them."

"Yeah," was all Dimitri could say.

Once the car was sorted, Lake called Callum back to tell him about the change of plans and ask him to stall until they got there.

Joe returned and perched on the edge of his seat. "It's done. Arriving at Biggin Hill will take a few minutes off our flight time. We should touch down a couple of minutes before six."

"Good," Lake said. "Now all we need is that final location, the meeting point for the exchange, and we're good to go."

There was nothing they could do but wait. They were helpless. Stuck high above continental Europe while Megan walked into danger. For Katrina. No. For him. She was doing it for him. On the outside, Dimitri knew all his teammates would see was a trained soldier who was calm and ready for action. Inside, his mind was stuck on repeat. A continual desperate prayer. One sentence over and over. One fear consuming him. One action he hoped never to make. His prayer was simple.

"Don't make me choose."

# CHAPTER 34

They had to leave in seven minutes, otherwise they wouldn't make it to the meeting point Durand had chosen. Seven minutes. There was time enough to change her mind. Time enough to call the whole thing off. She could run back to Scotland. She could hide until someone else found Reynard Durand and dealt with him.

She could leave Katrina Raast to die.

Megan leaned her forehead on the cool glass of the mirror. Her hands clasped tightly on the porcelain sink. One breath. Two. A glance at her wristwatch. Six minutes to change her mind. Only a fool would run into a situation she probably wouldn't come out of. What made Katrina's life worth more than hers?

She rolled her forehead on the glass, letting the solidity of it press against the bone. It was a stupid question. One that only made her feel ill with the implications of it. The truth was that there was no choice here. She couldn't let Durand take Katrina's life when it was really hers he wanted. There was no running away. No hiding. No hoping someone else would step in in her stead. This was her mess and she was going to sort it out.

A thump at the door jerked her out of her thoughts. Her eyes shot open and she stared at her reflection. Dark circles under blue eyes. Pale skin, made more so by stress.

"Yeah?" she called, proud her voice betrayed none of her inner turmoil.

"We're heading down. One minute." She heard Ryan's boots shuffle on the spot outside the door. "No one will blame you if you back out, Megan. No one will think badly of you."

"I would," she whispered to her image.

Right now, she could look herself in the eye. If she left Katrina with Durand, she wouldn't be able to do that. Not ever again. She took a shaky breath and opened the door.

"You okay?" Ryan ran his knuckles over her cheek.

"Yeah." She pushed her shoulders back. "I'm ready."

His eyes softened. "Callum and I won't let you out of our sight. We'll have you covered constantly."

"I know." She also knew he couldn't make any promises. They had no control over this situation. Durand had made sure they had no time to prepare. They were going in blind.

He gave her an admiring nod before turning. They headed through her bedroom and out into the sitting room. The mood was sombre. Megan looked at each of the faces in turn.

"It's going to be fine," she said. "Do I need to remind everyone that I can take care of myself?"

No one smiled at her joke.

"I wish you were going in armed." Elle shuffled nervously on the spot. Her usual bright blue hair looked dull and sad. "Or at least wired for sound and GPS."

They both knew the first thing Durand would do would

be to check her for any sort of tech or weapon. She had to go in bare, with only herself to rely on.

And her team. She had to trust they'd get her out of whatever happened.

Rachel stepped forward. Her lips were pinched, her eyes dark. Arms folded over a beige Chanel pantsuit, she looked dressed for the boardroom—at five thirty in the morning. Megan shook her head at the sight.

"Say the word," Rachel said. "I'll get you on another plane and out of here. You don't have to do this. We *will* come up with something else." There was no doubting she was completely and utterly serious.

"I appreciate it, Rach, really, I do." But she couldn't accept.

Rachel nodded. "Think about it. You have a thirty minute drive. You can abort at any time."

"You keep talking like that and I'll think you care," Megan told her. "It may even make me want to hug you."

Rachel hurriedly took a step back.

Julia rushed up to Megan's side and put her arms around her. She squeezed hard.

"This is all my fault," her friend said. "I should have locked away the files on Dimitri's sister, then Durand would never have known we were looking for her."

Megan hugged Julia back, more for herself than her friend. In that moment, she really wished her twin was there. She always felt more confident when there were two of them. She'd wanted to send a text message to Claire, but thought better of it. The only thing she could think of to write were the words Captain Lawrence Oates said before he went for a suicidal walk in the Antarctic, in an attempt to save the rest of his expedition team: "I am just going outside, I may be some time." She didn't think Claire would appreciate the joke.

"It's not your fault," she told Julia again. "You couldn't have known Durand would break into the office. If it wasn't Katrina, he would have found something else to use against us. At least this way we know where Katrina is and we know how to get her back. That's good, right?" She tried to give Julia a reassuring smile, but didn't quite pull it off.

Julia's eyes were filled with unshed tears, but she forced a smile. "We'll be here when you get back."

"Good. We're seriously going to need a girls' night after this is over." Megan saw Callum shift in place and knew he was straining to leave.

No one said a word when Megan shrugged into Dimitri's denim jacket instead of the coat Rachel had bought for her. She rolled up the too long sleeves, inhaling deeply to pull the scent into her lungs. She wished he was there with her. Dumb. If he was he'd just drive her crazy trying to keep her safe, when they both knew that wasn't possible. Not in this situation.

"Ready?" Callum said.

"Yeah. Let's go." She gave one last smile to her teammates. No, her friends. As they headed out of the suite, she looked up at Callum. "I don't think it's fair that I don't get to wear a tactical vest. The guys got to wear them when they went on their mission."

"We'll get you one when this is over," Callum promised as they stepped into the elevator.

She stood between Ryan and her boss, letting them protect her by their presence when it really wasn't needed. Letting them do it now, because she knew it would be unlikely they'd be able to do it later.

"Can mine be pink?" she asked her boss.

"It can have glitter and bows if you get your backside out of this in one piece." His words were a growl.

"You're on." Megan tugged Dimitri's jacket tight around her and followed the men out into the early morning darkness.

# CHAPTER 35

The final destination was texted to them when they hit Norwood Junction in South London. It was an abandoned school, slated for demolition. At only five minutes' drive from their location, the building was wedged between a recreation reserve and an empty industrial estate. It was an isolated area, away from residential streets and with plenty of access points. A warren of buildings was interspersed with wide open spaces that were easy to monitor. The perfect meeting ground.

The one storey, square 1970s construct was cordoned off with tall wire barriers emblazoned with large red letters: DANGER. Behind the barriers the school was lit up with floodlights.

Ryan scowled at the lights. "They'll see us coming a mile off."

"I don't see any other cars." Callum stared at the building. "Those lights are blinding us. I can't see if there's anyone on the roof."

"I'd put someone on the roof." Ryan pulled the car up at an angle to the front of the building.

"Aye. So would I."

It wasn't reassuring to hear Callum's agreement. She looked at the men in their armour plated vests. "I really wish I had a tactical vest."

"Babe," Ryan said. "If there's a sniper up there, he'll aim for your head. A vest wouldn't be much use."

Megan's eyes shot to his and saw his grin. She burst out laughing. So what if it was a touch hysterical. It helped. She gave his arm a quick squeeze in thanks and he winked at her.

Callum's phone buzzed. "It's Elle. She's got a floor plan of the school." He stared at the screen. "There's a main corridor from that door. It goes to a central atrium then shoots off into two other corridors that circle the school. There are fourteen exits." His jaw clenched. "He could be stationed at any one of them."

His phone buzzed again. "Durand." He spat the word. "He knows we're here. He wants you to walk in the front door. He'll have Katrina walk out."

Megan concentrated on her manicure to stop from passing out. The pink polish was chipped. Spa day. That's what she needed. A spa day with her sister and the rest of her gang. Claire already got on well with Julia and she'd love Elle. Hell, she'd even invite Rachel along, so long as she promised not to fight with Harry's wife Magenta. Yeah, she needed a spa day.

A hand on her shoulder. "You ready?"

"Yep." This was it. As ready as she would ever get.

"We'll get you out." The firm line of Callum's jaw betrayed the depth of his resolve.

"I know." She took a deep breath. "Let's go."

They climbed out of the car. The men drew their sidearms. Together they headed towards the double doors at the front of the building. Megan kept her eyes glued to the doors as Callum and Ryan scanned their surroundings, ready to react to the slightest threat.

They made it to the entrance without incident. Megan clutched the metal handle that was worn and scratched from years of use. Through the glass panes she could see that the lights from outside had bled into the building. A figure stepped out at the other end of the corridor. Then two. Three.

In the dim light Megan could make out a woman between two men, but nothing else.

This was it. No going back—even if she wanted to. She thought she'd be more nervous, maybe even physically sick. Instead all she felt was a strange sense of calm. Of rightness.

"Tell Claire to name the baby Megan. And tell Dimitri…" She shook her head as her throat tightened. "Tell him, I kept my promise. He doesn't have to choose."

The men were silent. She looked up into Callum's dark eyes. There was nothing else to say. Nothing that his body language and eyes weren't already shouting at her. She knew any of the men would run into this situation in her place. She knew they hated letting her go. She knew they would do everything possible to stop Durand from taking her from this building. She also knew that if he did manage to take her, they'd raise hell to find her and get her home.

Megan went up on tiptoe and kissed Callum's cheek. "It's okay. I can do this."

With that, she pulled open the door and stepped into the corridor. Torn linoleum underfoot. Faded green walls covered in graffiti tags. Broken glass from smashed windows that crunched with each step.

"Send Katrina." Callum's order came from behind her.

Without looking, she knew they were standing in the doorway, Ryan guarding Callum's back while he kept his gun trained on the men at the other end of the corridor. The woman between them was shoved forward. She stumbled, then hurried forward down the corridor. Megan heard a sob and anger flared inside her, a white hot flame that wouldn't be snuffed until Durand paid.

Shadows. Torn pictures painted by kids long gone. Rat droppings. Light fittings hanging from the ceiling. Tiles torn out from above her, now on the floor. She took it all in with every step that brought her closer to the man who hunted her.

When she came level with Dimitri's sister she paused. The woman was wrapped in a thin white robe, nothing more. Her long dark hair was matted. She was thin, frail. Her face was gaunt, her eyes wide and haunted. Megan reached for her. Katrina jerked back as though expecting a blow and Megan's rage blazed brighter. Slowly, she placed her hand on Katrina's fragile arm.

"You'll be safe now. I promise," Megan said to her. "Tell your brother, I love him."

She saw the flare of hope in Katrina's eyes at the realisation she'd see her brother. Hope and determination. Strength. With that one look, Megan knew it wasn't too late for the woman. She had the same spine of steel as her brother.

"Don't let them break you." Katrina's voice was a rasp. It was advice borne of bitter experience and of victory.

"I do the breaking, honey," Megan whispered back.

She gave Katrina's arm one more squeeze as Durand's voice echoed down the corridor. "I have a gun pointed at both of your heads. Walk to me now, Megan, or you both die."

"You are such an asshole," Megan shouted back and felt Katrina stiffen under her touch.

Megan glanced down at the smaller woman and noticed she was barefoot.

"Ryan?" she shouted as she continued her walk to Durand. "She's barefoot and there's glass."

"Don't shoot," Callum shouted. "We're going to pick her up."

She heard running and knew Ryan would help Katrina the rest of the way.

"I won't shoot," Durand called. "Not if I get what I want."

Megan came to a stop a couple of feet in front of Durand. He was decked out the way Hollywood thought mercenaries should look. Camouflage pants and jacket, sidearm harness and leather half gloves. Oh yeah, and a checked scarf around his neck to keep out the sand. Sand. In South London. She almost rolled her eyes.

"Hi Renny," she said. "How's your backside? Still sore?"

The smack came out of nowhere. A backhand across her cheekbone that sent her to the floor. There was a roar from the other end of the corridor. Callum. Someone grabbed her arm and pulled her to her feet. If they thought she was going easy, they were wrong. She elbowed the guy in the gut. Another bloody armour-plated vest. Pain spasmed through her body from her elbow.

"Move, move," Durand shouted, and then she was being dragged away from the corridor.

Away from Callum and Ryan.

Away from freedom.

# CHAPTER 36

"Move it. Move it." Dimitri bellowed the order, even though he knew logically that the car was going as fast as it could.

Gold from the street lamps lit their way to the destination Elle had sent them. The streets were a blur of Victorian terraced houses and multi-levelled office buildings. They swerved past cars, causing horns to blast. Not caring.

"Comms on." Lake barked out a frequency. "Callum, you hearing me?"

Nothing.

Dimitri gripped the panic handle as the car swerved around a corner.

"Callum, come in."

Silence.

"There's about four hundred exits in this place," Joe complained as he studied the map Elle had sent. "The guys have the front. We spread out. A side each."

There was no argument.

"Callum?" Lake shot round another corner taking the SUV to two wheels.

It still wasn't fast enough. What if he didn't make it? What if he was too late? Dimitri clenched his fist so hard he thought he felt bone snap.

"Callum, come in."

"Callum here," came the voice, and relief swept through the car.

"Report." Lake shot through a red light.

"We've got her. We've got Katrina."

Dimitri's head fell back as he stared at the roof of the car. *Thank you, God.*

"Status?" Thankfully Lake asked because Dimitri couldn't speak yet.

"She's in one piece. Ryan's taking her to hospital."

*She's okay. She's okay. She's okay...*

"Megan?" Lake cast a glance over to him before focusing on the road again.

"They have her."

It was like a punch to the gut.

"I'm covering the front," Callum's voice was lethal. "I can't see the other exits. No sound of a vehicle. They're still on site."

Good. That was good.

"Coming up on your location now. We're heading to the rear of the school."

"Roger that."

There was silence. The car screeched to a halt beside a metal barrier. The men were out of the SUV and over the fence before the engine died. Lake signalled to them and they spread out, keeping low, using construction equipment and overgrown bushes to avoid the lights.

A shot kicked up the dirt beside Dimitri. He pressed flat against rusted playground equipment. "Shooter on the roof. My side."

"Take out the lights," Lake replied.

There were a series of shots and the place fell into darkness. Silence. Stillness. No one moved.

"Move in," Lake ordered.

Easier now there was darkness, the men crept to the building. Another shot hit the metal climbing frame beside Dimitri.

"Can you see him?" Callum's voice.

"No. He's got me pinned." Dimitri could hear seconds ticking loudly in his head. Each one took Megan further from him. He kept his ears peeled for the sound of a car. None. She was still here.

"I'm on the roof." Joe's voice. "I see the bastard." There was a grunt. "Threat disabled."

Dimitri came out of hiding and ran low to the building. No more shots from the roof.

"There are skylights up here." Joe again. "I'm going to scout, see if I can spot her."

Dimitri pressed his back to the stucco wall. The cold was barely noticeable. He held his gun up as he spun and checked his line of sight through the smashed window. Empty. A minute later he was up and inside the old classroom. The walls were covered in graffiti, the furniture was long gone. Torn paper and leaves littered the floor.

"I'm in." He made his way silently to the door.

"I'm in." It was Grunt.

"Northwest sector," came Joe's voice. "I count four men. Running."

There was gunfire. "Two men. Northeast sector." Lake's voice.

"I see her," Joe again. "Northwest."

"Lake?" Grunt asked.

"I've got this," Lake barked. "Get Megan."

Dimitri kept low, back to the wall, gun high as he headed in the direction of his woman.

.   .   .

*GUNFIRE?* Gunfire! The noise cut through Megan's bruised brain, her thoughts dulled from where she'd hit her head on the floor after being struck. She was being dragged along the corridor, her hands secured behind her back. Durand wasn't taking any chances—the man walked behind her. She smirked at that. Ahead of her were two other men. Four huge men, all carrying massive guns. Yeah. It didn't look good escape-wise.

On the other hand, it sounded like she didn't have to escape. It sounded like she was being rescued. Yay for her.

Durand muttered something behind her and she realised he was talking into a comms unit. She caught the words, two down, and grinned. Her team were here and they were cleaning house.

"Change direction," Durand snapped. "West exit. They're heading to the north. Fritz," he shouted at a man in front of Megan. "Get the vehicle. Keep it running outside the west exit."

The guy jogged off. Megan looked up at the monster holding her. His fingers dug into her arm hard enough to bruise. "Is his name really Fritz?" The guy's eyes were dead. As in, nobody home. He just stared at her. "Really," she said. "It's no wonder he's taken to a life of crime. There can't be that many career options open to you when you're called Fritz."

A hand grabbed her ponytail and yanked until her neck felt like it was going to break. Tears leaked from her eyes at the pain. It felt like her hair was being ripped from her head. Why did guys always go for the hair?

"No talking, bitch." Durand's face was just as ugly upside down.

"Or what?" Megan asked. "You're going to kill me? Not much of a threat if you plan to do it anyway."

Shark eyes gleamed. "Kill you? You'll wish you were dead. But no, I don't plan to kill. Not at first."

That wasn't reassuring. "Seriously though, how's your backside? Healing well?"

A knife tip pressed against her throat. "You keep talking and I'll slice out your tongue." Blood ran down her throat as the point broke skin. "Or," he whispered against her ear in a dark parody of intimacy. "Maybe, I'll leave your tongue and slice off your nipples. That way I can hear you scream my name when they're removed."

Megan swallowed back the bile that shot up her throat. There was no doubt he meant every word. His eyes were a flat pond. There was no emotion there, no sense of moral judgement, only a determination to get what he wanted.

A shot rang out ahead of them. Durand swore and the men jerked left into a classroom. She fell to the floor behind the door.

"Status?" Durand barked.

The guy who'd been holding her, crouched in front of her as she struggled to sit. His head was shaved bald and tattooed with Nazi symbols. Very attractive—not. His smile was a leer that oozed toxic waste. One hand curled around her throat and held tight, keeping her in place. His other hand covered her breast and squeezed hard, laughing when she winced. Big fingers grabbed her nipple and pinched until tears ran down her cheeks.

"I'll make sure I get to play with these before the boss removes them." He twisted his grip.

Megan gasped in pain as he tightened his hold on her throat and her breast. She struggled to breathe. White lights flickered in front of her eyes and she prayed she wouldn't pass out. Being unconscious around these guys was not a good idea.

"You have…" She forced the words out. "A really…tiny… dick…don't you?"

The hold on her throat tightened before Durand pulled him off her. Megan gasped, each breath painful. Her breast throbbed and she wanted to cry, but she wouldn't. Not here. Not for them.

"Leave her." Durand glanced down at her. "You can play later."

The bald guy gave her a grin that made her stomach turn.

"Copy that," Durand said into his comm unit, before speaking to the lanky guy who was covering the window. "Our exit is blocked. We've lost contact with Ray and Fritz. Stew is bringing the car around. We're going out that window." He pointed to the window, because his team were too damn dumb to figure it out for themselves. "Clear it."

Lanky guy did that by hitting the glass with the butt of his gun.

"Why are you doing this?" Against her better judgement, Megan felt the need to engage the madman.

Durand looked down at her. "You owe me."

"For what? Freeing myself from your kidnapping attempt? For blowing your career prospects with Rudi's organisation? For shooting you in the bum? What exactly did I do that makes me so special?"

He crouched down beside her and gently tucked a stray strand of hair behind her ear. "You were lucky in Scotland. I can see that now. I'd thought it was skill, but it was luck. Still, you got the better of me and *no one* gets the better of me. You will act as a reminder to anyone who dares try in the future. After I'm finished with you, no one will make the same mistake."

All Megan saw when she looked in his eyes was a calculated and calm determination. No emotion. No reaction. For Durand this was about settling a score and sending a message. It was about protecting his reputation as a ruthless lunatic. He was the most terrifyingly dangerous kind of man, one who treated violence purely as business.

"Done." The lanky guy motioned to the window, again in case they didn't know what he was talking about.

Durand stood. "Take her out of here. I'll follow," he said to the bald guy and then pointed to the lanky one. "You bring up the rear. No one follows. You hear me."

The lanky guy nodded and pointed his gun at the door.

The bald guy threw Megan over his shoulder, fireman style, and held her in place by wedging his hand into her crotch. He laughed when Megan yelped and struggled to get away from him.

"Keep fighting me." He climbed through the window. "I like it."

More laughter when Megan went still.

"Stop screwing around," Durand snapped.

A shot rang out behind them. Shouting. Running. There weren't many street lights behind the school and it was dark. Megan was upside down. She arched her back to see anything, something. Nothing. All she saw was the ground swinging beneath her. More screaming. A car screeched to a halt, tyres on gravel. There were sirens in the distance. The police were coming.

"Get her in the car." Another order from Durand.

A car door slammed.

"No!" They were not taking her in the car. Megan knew if they could get her away from the building her chance of survival was next to zero.

She bucked and thrashed in the bald guy's hold. He grasped her tighter, his nails digging in to sensitive flesh. She wished her hands were free. Wished they weren't tied up behind her back. Tensing her muscles, she kicked out with all her might in an attempt to unbalance him, to force him to release her. The move made him stumble. His grip loosened. And then she was falling.

"I dropped her," the bald guy yelled.

Megan hit the ground with a thud, catching most of the impact on her shoulder. She screamed as something snapped. Dislocated? She wasn't sure. Blinking hard, she fought not to pass out. She was on her back, her head towards the car which was about six feet away. The driver was on the other side of the car, using it for cover as he fired at the school. Durand grabbed her hair and started pulling her towards the car. Dragging her along the dirt. Megan roared as she lifted her body onto her shoulders. The pain almost made her black out, but she managed to kick his arm. He lost his hold on her hair.

"Bitch." He pointed the gun at her.

She rolled, but not before she felt the bullet hit her leg.

"No!" A voice bellowed in the darkness.

Dimitri.

Bullets hit the car, making Durand take cover behind the open passenger door. The bald guy backed up towards her, aiming his gun at the school. Megan lifted her legs and used all of her strength to kick the back of his knees. He crumpled with a shout. She pulled her legs up until she was in a ball, then brought them through her bound hands so that they were now in front of her instead of behind her. Pain sliced through her, making her vision blur. Her breathing was choppy and she knew she didn't have long before unconsciousness took her. She kept one eye on the bald guy. He didn't move. He must have taken a bullet.

It was a chance. If she could get to his gun, she could end this. She threw herself beside his body, scrambling for his gun. Cold metal under her fingertips. She grasped it. With no time to think, she rolled and pointed the gun at Durand. There was no hesitation. She pulled the trigger. Nothing happened. Bloody automatic weapon. Too many freaking bells and whistles.

"This ends here." Durand aimed his weapon at her. "I would have liked to have done so much more, but a bullet to the head is a message in itself."

Megan closed her eyes as pain washed over her. What little strength she had left seeped away. There was nothing else she could do. It was over. A shot rang out. Her body jerked. And then there was nothing.

# CHAPTER 37

"No!" Dimitri was running as soon as he saw Durand point the gun at Megan's leg. "Cover me," he snapped into the comm unit.

He didn't even bother to duck and cover. He just ran. Straight for her. He saw her kick the big bald guy. Saw Grunt shoot, taking the guy out when he went to his knees. He saw Megan get her bound hands in front of her. Saw her reach for the gun and aim at Durand. He saw it all. Each movement in terrifyingly painful slow motion.

He roared when her gun didn't fire.

He roared as Durand stepped out from cover to shoot Megan.

And he roared as he emptied his weapon into the man.

Dimitri didn't spare a glance for Durand's body.

Falling to his knees beside Megan, he dropped his empty gun, knowing the guys would cover them, and pulled her unconscious body into his arms. Frantic fingers felt her throat for a pulse. There. A beat. Another. Alive. She was alive. Relief made his hands shake. He fought to still them as he checked her body for wounds. Blood on his fingers. Her blood. Panic threatened and he swallowed it down. Wounds. He needed to deal with the wounds.

Vaguely aware of sirens getting closer, he checked her face. Neck. Chest. No bullet wounds. Stomach clear. Thigh. He found the bullet wound in her thigh. Straight through muscle, when it could so easily have hit her femoral artery.

Car doors slammed. He needed something to pad the wound and stem the blood flow. Someone knelt beside him. Words were said. Dimitri couldn't understand them. He needed a tourniquet, that's what he needed. Elevate the leg. Put pressure on the wound. His mind went over the steps for first aid, as though locked in a loop.

A strong hand on his shoulder. He jerked, grabbed his empty gun and aimed it at the intruder.

"It's me. Lower your weapon." He blinked until a face came into focus. Callum.

Dimitri let the gun drop to the ground beside him. Callum bent and retrieved it.

"Let them do their job," he ordered, but his words were soft.

Dimitri looked in the direction Callum nodded. Paramedics. An ambulance.

"What have we got here?" said the female paramedic who crouched beside him. Her eyes were kind. Calm. Professional. "Will you let me examine her?"

He looked down and realised he was clutching Megan to his chest. Shielding her from view with his body.

"Gunshot wound to her right leg. Cuts, bruises. Her shoulder feels wrong. Broken, or dislocated." His words came as if from far away.

"Let me look at her." The woman gently pried Megan from his grasp.

Dimitri fought back a growl of warning. It took all of his self-control to surrender her to the woman.

"They've got her," Callum said. "Let them do their job. She's going to be fine."

Dimitri curled his hands into fists as the paramedics placed Megan on a stretcher and examined her. There were more injuries on her body than he'd realised. Everywhere he looked there was another wound, another mark, another reason Reynard Durand should be killed all over again.

Callum kept a firm hand on his shoulder as they watched Megan being loaded into the ambulance.

"Katrina?" Dimitri asked as he kept his eyes glued to Megan.

"Ryan took her to the hospital. Same one Megan will be taken to."

"He's watching her?"

"Hasn't left her side."

He felt his heartbeat slow to almost normal. "Team injuries?"

"Grunt has a flesh wound. Lake cut his hand. Nothing major."

"The other team?"

"Two dead." Durand and the bald guy. "The rest are incapacitated."

Dimitri never took his eyes off the ambulance. Megan's frame was so small, so delicate. She should never have been in the midst of a situation like this.

"This is going to be a helluva mess to sort out," Callum said.

Dimitri glanced around—there were police everywhere. "Yeah," he said.

The paramedic caught his eye and signalled it was time to go. Callum patted him on the back. "I'll let Tessa know where you are. You'll need to make a statement."

"Thanks." Dimitri climbed into the back of the ambulance

and intertwined his fingers with the unconscious woman's in front of him.

"She's going to be fine," the paramedic said.

"There's no other option," Dimitri vowed in reply.

When they reached the emergency department, Megan was whisked away and Dimitri was told to stay in the waiting room. Even though he knew the risk to her was over, it was hard to watch her go. It would be a very long time before he could believe she was fine, without actually having his hands on her to prove it. With strict instructions to call him at the slightest change in her condition, and especially when she woke, he left them to do their jobs. And he went in search of his sister.

He found Katrina in a private room on the third floor. For a moment, he stood in the corridor and stared at her through the glass. The sight hit him square in the gut. She was really here. Alive. He'd found her.

Then the Polaroid images from the house in Rabat assaulted him. He crumpled. Sliding down the wall to crouch at the bottom of it. He hung his head, rubbing his fists on his forehead.

Shoes appeared in front of him. "You going in there?" Ryan said.

Dimitri rubbed his eyes. "I just need a minute."

A minute to make sure his face didn't betray him, and his sister never guessed that he'd seen the evidence of what had been done to her.

"She's strong." Ryan crouched in front of him.

"You didn't see what we found in Rabat." Dimitri shook his head. "What she suffered."

"Not suffered, *survived.*"

He lifted his head and looked at the man. Something shifted inside him. "Yeah. Survived."

With a nod, Ryan stood and held out a hand to help

Dimitri up. One he gratefully accepted. Together they strode to Katrina's room. Ryan stopped outside the room, ready to stand sentry again. His arms folded and his jaw set as he stared at Katrina. Dimitri recognised the look in his eye. It was the one a man had when he wanted revenge for the damage that had been done. Dimitri nodded his thanks to Ryan, but then hesitated in the doorway.

His sister was so small. She lay in the middle of the bed, wearing a generic white hospital gown. There was an IV line in her arm and a bag of fluids on the stand beside it. Dehydrated, they'd said. Her white skin, too pale by far, was bruised. The purple marks peeked out from the neckline of her gown, a brutal reminder of everything she'd survived. Dark circles under her lashes. Cheekbones that were far too pronounced. Fragile. She looked fragile.

As if sensing he was there, her eyes fluttered open and she looked straight at him. A second of shock, followed by pure joy, and then her eyes welled up. By the time the first tear fell Dimitri had his sister wrapped in his arms. He sat on the edge of the bed beside her and rocked her while she sobbed, cooing nonsense to reassure her that he was really there. That she was really free. Telling her she would be okay and he would be there for her no matter how long it took. They were family. And she was home.

# CHAPTER 38

Every single inch of Megan's body hurt. Her eyelashes hurt. Seriously. How was that even possible?

"I know you're awake," said the deep voice that made her insides melt like sugar over a flame.

She cracked open her eyes. "I told you I needed to learn how to use a machine gun."

"Those are your first words to me?"

He sounded affronted so she shut her eyes again. "Go away. Come back when I feel better."

"Nuh, uh." She felt him gently squeeze her fingers and realised he was holding her hand. "You and I have things to talk about."

"I need a drink." She meant vodka. Instead the bed rose with a mechanical hum until she was sitting up and a glass of water hit her lips.

"There's no point keeping your eyes shut now, is there?"

She opened them and found Dimitri's chocolate gaze right in front of her. "I was kind of hoping that if I kept them shut, this would all be a dream."

"Which part? The part where you traded yourself for

Katrina? The part where you were injured? Or the part where you told me you loved me for the first time via a message to my sister?"

"Are you annoyed about that?" He looked annoyed, but then he had grumpy resting face so it was sometimes hard to tell. "Guy's really don't give a crap about that whole 'I love you' stuff. It's like anniversaries. They only put up with them to humour the women in their lives."

A small smile tugged at his lips. "It's a strange and mysterious place, your brain."

Megan took another sip of water when he held the glass back to her lips. The overly bright lights had told her she was in a hospital even before she'd opened her eyes. The smell confirmed it. That antiseptic smell, with undertones of rot, couldn't be found anywhere else. Neither could that baby poop green colour they insisted on painting the walls.

"I have two questions for you." She rubbed her thumb over the back of Dimitri's hand. Warm. He always felt so warm. "Is he dead? And, how bad do I look?"

His eyes turned to stone. "He's dead."

"Good." There was nothing else to say. Reynard Durand had been a predator without a conscience. If he hadn't decided to hunt and hurt her, it would have been someone else. Men like that didn't stop and they didn't change. It was a relief he was gone.

Dimitri brought her out of her heavy thoughts with a kiss to the tip of her nose. "To answer your second question. You're beautiful."

She rolled her eyes, then winced. Damn it, her eyeballs were sore too. "What's the damage?"

"Dislocated shoulder. Gunshot wound to your thigh. Knife wound to your neck. Bruises and scrapes. Including a black eye and severe bruising on your breast." His voice turned dangerously low. "Finger marks."

Yeah, she doubted she would ever forget getting those finger marks. "The bald guy with the swastika on his head?"

"Dead."

She added him to the list of people she would never mourn.

Megan let him fluff the pillows behind her until he was satisfied she was comfortable. The nurse bustled in, far too loudly in Megan's opinion. She checked Megan's blood pressure, temperature and IV line. Then she forced some pain meds and antibiotics down her throat.

"I want to go home," Megan complained when the woman was gone.

Dimitri froze. "To Scotland?"

"No." Had he taken a hit to the head? "To the flat above the office." He relaxed, then he looked guilty. "What?" Megan demanded.

"Katrina is going to stay in your flat at the office."

"There are only two bedrooms." The rest of the floor was still under construction. Give it a few weeks and there would be more rooms—right now it was just her tatty flat that was liveable.

"Yeah." He ran the fingers of his free hand through his hair, while the other one tightened its hold on her hand. "She's going to take your room."

And just like that her blood pressure shot up. "Where am I going to stay?" Panic hit her. "Wait, am I still fired? I thought I'd been rehired. Am I being sent back to Scotland?"

The guilt was still there, plain as day in his beautiful brown eyes. The grey sweater rippled when he shrugged his broad shoulders. "You're still hired. You have trainee status."

"Does that mean I get to learn how to use an automatic weapon?" Because that knowledge would have come in damn handy when she'd had one pointed at Durand.

"I'll train you myself."

"Great. So where am I living? I liked that flat. It was close to work." And it was free.

A pause set off warning bells. "I've moved you in with me."

Megan stilled. "How long have I been in hospital?"

"You came in this morning. About fourteen hours ago."

"And in that time, you moved me in with you?"

"Yeah."

"Into your hotel room?"

He squirmed. It wasn't a big squirm. But she spotted it. "No, I found an apartment for us, near the office."

"Pinch me," she said, because she was pretty sure she was still unconscious.

"I'm not going to pinch you, you're bruised enough."

"Fine, then tell me how you managed to find an apartment and move me into it in fourteen hours? Without my consent, I might add, due to extreme unconsciousness." Seriously, if it didn't hurt so much to glare, she would have glared his head to a burning ember.

"It didn't take long. Rachel owns it. We're renting from her."

A ray of sunshine peeked through her ire. "Does it have a pool?"

"No."

*Typical.* Megan tugged at her hand, but he wouldn't let go. "I'm not moving in with you. You can't just arrange my life while I'm unconscious." She frowned at him. That hurt too, damn it. "Did I mention the unconsciousness?"

"Get over it," the idiot said. "It's a done deal, Buffy."

And to think she'd accused her sister of falling in love with a caveman. At least Grunt had *asked* Claire to move in with him. He didn't sneak her in while she was unconscious!

"I don't want to live with you."

"Of course you want to live with me. You love me."

It must have been the drugs, because her heart melted a little at his words and her irritation faded. "Your ego knows no bounds."

"So I've been told." His smile was dazzling.

And a touch too smug. "As soon as I get out of here, I'm moving back to the office."

The smile faded. "And kick my sister out? My poor recovering sister, who needs the security the building affords while she copes with the aftermath of her ordeal?" It was a miracle he didn't try to flutter his eyelashes at her too.

Megan's eyes narrowed before she remembered it hurt to move. "Do you really think you can manipulate me into getting what you want?"

In reply, the damn man leaned over and kissed her. It was slow, delicate tease of a kiss. His lips pressed softly against hers and she felt everything within her sigh. His forehead rested against hers when the kiss ended. His eyes were closed.

"I nearly lost you. I need you beside me. I need to know I can protect you." His eyes flickered open. "Please," her warrior said.

It wasn't needed, he'd already broken her down with his tender kiss. "You realise none of that makes any logical sense, right?"

"Humour me." Another gentle kiss that robbed her senses.

"Only if you admit that I'm only doing this to humour you and I know how to take care of myself."

"Never going to happen."

She opened her mouth to argue, but he kissed the words away. A possessive, demanding kiss that left her panting for more, only her body wasn't in any fit state to follow up on her need.

Dimitri enfolded her in his arms and pulled her into his chest. Breathing deeply, she filled herself with the scent of summer woodland. The scent of home. Megan closed her eyes and let him take her weight. He kissed the top of her head before nuzzling her temple.

"I love you too, Buffy," he whispered against her ear.

Sleep began to steal her senses. Safe. She was safe.

"Buffy was a superhero," she mumbled.

"So are you, baby, so are you."

With a contented smile on her face, Megan slipped into a healing sleep, safe in the arms of the man she loved.

It was a week after the showdown at the abandoned school—something Dimitri knew would take years for him to get over. The team were gathered around the conference room table, pastries and coffee in abundance. Dimitri sat back in his chair, his legs stretched out in front of him and a smile on his face. Callum and Rachel were arguing at the head of the table, like a pair of dysfunctional parents. Julia was hiding behind the plant that shouldn't even be in the building. Joe stared at the plant with a curious look on his face, as though he was trying to figure something out. Elle's hair colour had changed to bubble gum pink. Dimitri missed the blue. She currently had her head together with Megan, plotting. In the past week, the two of them had done a lot of plotting. Megan thought the team would be more successful if they were equipped with spy gear from the sixties and their computer tech agreed. Thankfully, so far Callum had managed to keep their crazy ideas to a minimum.

Ryan was over at the buffet table, as usual. He piled a plate high with pastries, then made up a second one with a single chocolate croissant on it. As he passed Katrina, he placed the plate in front of her without saying a word. Katrina recoiled from him, but once he was far enough away from her, she pulled the plate towards her and nibbled on the pastry. Her eyes firmly avoided Ryan, and every other man at the table. Except for her brother. When she looked at Dimitri, he gave her a reassuring smile.

Sharing the flat upstairs with Julia seemed to be helping his sister to cope. The security of the building helped and the partners had promised him his sister could stay there as long as she needed. Another reason he was a Benson Security guy for life. Katrina showed no signs of wanting to leave the office, but it was early days yet. She was putting on weight, her skin wasn't so pale and the only scars remaining were the ones on the inside. Rachel, for reasons known only to herself, was paying for a counsellor for Katrina. With the support of the team, and time, his sister would make it. He just knew she would.

"Okay." Callum stood and folded his arms over his grey Henley. "Rachel has an announcement before we begin the debrief on the Abramovich case."

Katrina stiffened, but Megan leaned into her and whispered something that made his sister smile. He caught Megan's eye and used telepathy to tell her she had a reward in her very near future. She must have got the message because her cheeks flushed.

Rachel stood, flipped her long brown hair behind her shoulder and scanned the group. She still looked dismayed to find them all there.

"As you know, after the Abramovich incident, where Megan went off the reservation, I decided I didn't want to work for Benson Security any longer."

Ryan held up a hand to stop her. "You mean, when you were fired because you followed Megan off the reservation?"

Rachel carried on talking as though he was invisible. "I've

since had a change of heart and approached the partners about an idea I have. After some negotiation, they agreed to my proposal." Her smile was pure evil delight that had everyone in the room worried. "I wanted to start a business that specialises in putting together holistic security packages for discerning women, so I bought into the Benson Security partnership."

There was silence. Which Megan broke. "Does this mean you're starting a women-only part of the operation? Like *Charlie's Angels*? Will you be Bosley?"

There was laughter. Rachel narrowed her eyes at Megan. "You've been assigned to my team."

That took the smile off Megan's face. She blustered, at a loss for words for the first time since Dimitri met her in Scotland. That's when it hit him. When he knew what he wanted. The idea appeared in his mind fully formed and he knew absolutely that it was the right thing to do. Suddenly, his future was crystal clear before him. And Megan was at the heart of it. He already knew he loved her. Now he knew he wanted it to last forever.

"I have an announcement too," Dimitri said, making Megan's eyes shoot to his. He smiled at her which made her look worried. "Megan and I are getting married."

There were whoops of delight, followed by a shout of "What the heck?" from Megan.

She shuffled forward in her chair and slapped her hands on the table between them. "You can't announce that. You haven't even asked me. Shouldn't I have a choice in the matter? And, seriously, Dim Boy, I've known you less than two months."

Dimitri grinned at the nickname. It was a new one she was trying out in her never-ending attempt to drive him insane. But he was strong enough to handle her. Standing, he strode round the table, put his hand on the nape of her neck and kissed her hard. Which merited a cheer. He sat back down feeling pretty damn smug at the rosy cheeks and swollen lips he'd left behind. He also felt pretty smug about the fact she was currently using a cane to get around, which would make running away from him a whole lot harder for her. Talk about perfect timing.

"We're going to talk about this later." She pointed at him. "At home. In private." She sat back with an air of dignity. "While you wait for that chat, you can think about the fact that if you marry me, you get Grunt for a brother-in-law."

That wiped the smile off Dimitri's face. It was Megan's turn to look smug.

"We done?" Callum said. "You think we could stop kissing during team meetings or at any other point during work hours? Bloody hell, how about you pretend to make an effort to behave professionally? You would never have gotten away with this soppy crap in the armed forces."

"Good job we're not in the armed forces then," Megan said.

"As I was saying." Callum glared at Megan, who grinned. "Rachel is now one of four partners. We'll be discussing the new side of the business at future meetings."

"What about other vacancies?" Ryan asked, once it had quietened down. "We need more men."

"Team members," Julia gently corrected from behind her plant.

Ryan grinned at the foliage. "I don't care what gender they are as long as they know how to work as a team and they can handle their Chinese food."

Megan groaned. "Never going to live that down," she mumbled.

"We're on it," Callum told Ryan. "We're interviewing. We'll get the team members we need." That seemed to appease Ryan. "Now, to the Abramovich case. Joe, an update." Callum sat back down.

Joe leaned forward, elbows on the table. "We got word this morning that an operation is tabled for this weekend. Authorities in eleven countries will close in on all of the Abramovich-owned brothels."

"So soon." Megan sat up straight. "The Met police said it would be months."

Joe cocked his head at her. "Apparently Rudi is in no condition to warn off his empire. He's currently undergoing extensive plastic surgery. The joint teams think that striking sooner rather than later is a better scenario."

Megan's whole face lit up. The sight made Dimitri's heart swell. "I helped," she said with awe.

"Yes, you did." Dimitri wished he was sitting beside her. He'd pull her into his lap and damn the business meeting.

"The names and addresses of every woman Rudi sold are in the hands of the authorities. Raids will be happening over the next few days. Those women will be going home."

Katrina let out a gentle sob. Ryan moved towards her, but a swift shake of the head from Dimitri made him sit down again. The younger man's jaw was clenched tight. Julia quietly sneaked out from behind her plant to sit beside Katrina, with a box of tissues in her hand. Katrina's smile when she saw them lit up Dimitri's heart. His sister was healing. He knew it would be a slow process and a painful one, but she was home and it would happen.

"There are still a lot of threads to unravel," Joe said. "But the core of the operation will be gone by the end of next week. Rudi's money has already been confiscated and the Met expect arrests to number in the hundreds." He smiled at Elle. "The data storage unit in Switzerland was corrupted, so no one can access it. The only comprehensive records of the Abramovich empire are in the hands of the police and Rudi will be locked up for the rest of his life." He sat back in his chair. "It's over, people."

Katrina hiccupped and Julia rubbed her back.

Megan leaned forwards, mischief in her eyes. "I think we should have a party to celebrate. A 'so long you bastard' party. And Rachel should pay, because she's totally minted and needs the goodwill she'll earn from the gesture." She grinned widely as laughter broke out.

As everyone started to shout out suggestions for a party, Megan sat back and smiled at Dimitri. It was a smile that went straight to that secret place inside of him. The place she owned.

He cocked an eyebrow and mouthed the word, "So?" A challenge. His woman couldn't resist a challenge.

Eyes gleaming, she mouthed one word back to him.

"Yes."

Julia's phone rang as the meeting degenerated into gleeful chaos. She heard Megan demand that someone go fetch champagne and watched as Dimitri grinned at her with pride. Megan was coping remarkably well with her injuries. The bullet wound in her leg was healing nicely, her dislocated shoulder was still a little sensitive and her bruises had almost faded. It would take a whole lot more than a psycho on her tail to keep that woman down.

Slipping out of the room, Julia answered her phone as she walked to her office. She didn't recognise the number, but expected it to be one of the companies she'd contracted to finish the building. She was wrong.

"Julia darling?" her grandmother bellowed down the line, making Julia smile.

"Hey Gran, what's up? Are you home?" The last email Julia received had informed her that her grandmother was off sightseeing in Peru.

"Not quite." The hesitation in her tone made Julia stop dead in the corridor.

"What do you mean 'not quite'?" Oh, she had a bad feeling about this call. She placed a hand on the wall beside her, steadying herself for whatever her grandmother was about to tell her.

"I'm still in Peru, darling," her gran said. "I need you to come and get me." There was a pause. "And you can't tell your mother."

Yep. It was bad. Julia leaned her shoulder against the cool wall. "Why do I need to come and get you? And why can't I tell Mum?"

"I've been arrested, darling."

"Arrested?" It came out as a high pitched squeak.

"Yes. I'm in Lima. You'll need to bring someone you can trust who's fluent in Spanish. I need you to find a decent lawyer to represent me once you're here."

Julia's head was spinning so fast it was hard to think straight. "Start at the beginning. What have you been arrested for? And where's your friend Alice?"

"Alice has gone missing." There was panic in her grandmother's voice now.

"They don't think you have something to do with that, do they?" Julia could actually feel her blood pressure spike. "Is that what you've been arrested for? And what do you mean gone missing?"

"I don't know what happened to Alice, we were separated and she disappeared. I was looking for her when I was arrested."

"Gran, spit it out. What did they arrest you for?"

"They think I stole a mummified body."

Julia blinked as time stood still. "A mummified body?"

There was silence.

"Did you?"

"Well, I'm not going to answer that over the phone! For

goodness sake, Julia, use your brain. You're supposed to be the sensible one in the family. Now are you coming to get me out or not?"

There was only one answer. "I'll be there as soon as I can."

"Thank you, darling." Her grandmother sounded relieved. "I'll get them to send you the details of where they're holding me. Please hurry."

The line went dead. Julia let her hand drop to her side, still holding the phone. Peru. A stolen mummy. A missing woman. And her grandmother in jail. She automatically thought of calling her mum then remembered her gran's order not to.

Placing a hand on her roiling stomach, Julia began to make a mental checklist of everything she needed to do. Right at the top was informing Callum that she'd need some time off immediately. She bit her lip and wondered if she could do it by email. Probably not.

Gathering her courage, she turned back towards the conference room. The party mood had gained momentum in the short time she'd been gone. Megan was sitting in Dimitri's lap while calling for pizza. Ryan was on his way out to pick up drinks and trying to gently convince Katrina to go along for the ride. Although Katrina was keeping her distance physically from Ryan, she had no problem telling him that she didn't want to go. Elle was demanding cake. Rachel was sitting off to the side studying everyone as though they were aliens and Callum looked like he was getting ready to run. She didn't know what Joe was doing, because she was still trying to stay as far away from him as possible until she figured out how to deal with the effect he had on her.

Julia skirted the room and sidled up to Callum.

"Um, Callum." She spoke in the direction of his shoulder.

"Is this about work? Please, let it be about work." He stood, ready to run as she'd suspected.

Julia swallowed hard. "I, um, got a call. There's a family emergency."

She found herself in the uncomfortable position of being the sole focus of Callum's laser-like attention.

"Whose family?" he said.

"Oh." She folded her arms around her stomach. "Mine. Sorry. Should have said. My grandmother has been arrested." Daring a peek up at his face, all she saw was concern. Okay, so it was grumpy concern, but it was still there.

"Your grandmother's been arrested?"

There was incredulous disbelief in his voice. Most people, when they thought of grandmothers, would imagine a tiny, grey haired woman who sat around knitting all day long. That wasn't Julia's grandmother.

"Yes. I wondered if it would be okay to have some time off, to go…" She wasn't sure what the right term was. "Bail her out?" She looked up at him and he nodded. Okay, that was good, she was making sense. "I might need quite a bit of time—she's in Peru."

"Peru?" Callum's voice rose and attracted unwanted attention.

Julia shuffled around slightly, to make sure her back was to the room.

Callum ran a hand down his face. "Okay, Peru. Who's going with you?"

She startled. "No one. My gran told me not to tell the family."

He cocked an eyebrow at her. "You're going to deal with the Peruvian authorities alone?"

She nodded, even though his scepticism was clear. Callum let out a sigh.

"Julia, you know you can't go alone, right?" he said softly.

"You have trouble dealing with authority figures. Do you even speak Spanish?"

"I'm going to hire someone to help with that." Fingers crossed. It was on her list.

His sigh was heavy. "Things are slow right now. The office doesn't officially open for another month. You can hand your oversight of the renovations to Ryan. It will keep him out of trouble."

Julia nodded as relief surged through her. She could also tick off the first item on her to-do list—she'd managed to successfully talk to Callum. Her joy was short-lived as he kept on talking.

"I don't like the idea of you dealing with this alone. And I definitely don't like you relying on a stranger to translate for you." He raised his head and shouted. "Joe, come here."

*Panic! Alert! Abort mission! Retreat! Run, woman, run!*

Unfortunately, her feet stayed stuck to the spot. She felt, rather than saw, Joe approach. He stood a little too close to her, his hands in the pockets of his faded jeans.

"What's up?" He glanced at her, but spoke to Callum.

"Julia here has to go to Peru to get her grandmother out of jail. You speak Spanish, right?"

"Fluently." It was a low, amused rumble.

*Run! Run now!* Still Julia remained frozen.

"Great," Callum said. "You mind going with Julia? Helping her out?"

"It would be my pleasure." Joe's lazy drawl momentarily robbed her of thought.

"Fantastic," Callum said. "Keep in touch and let me know if you need anything." He looked behind Julia. "Crap, it's turning into a party. I need to go." And then he shot for the door.

It took time, but Julia eventually looked up at Joe. Dark eyes considered her, making her want to hide behind her plant. Those eyes started to sparkle and a slow, sexy grin appeared.

"Gonna be hard to avoid me now, Jules," the infuriating man said.

And as usual, Julia couldn't get any appropriate words out of her mouth.

Julia Collins had issues. She'd even made a list of them—in order of priority, of course. Her OCD tendencies sat in joint first place with her pathological shyness. This was closely followed by the paralysis she felt when dealing with the opposite sex, then came the way she crumpled in the face of authority and, finally, the raging panic that overcame her anytime she was out of her comfort zone. In other words, she was *absolutely* the best person to ask for help when you were languishing in a foreign jail.

"Have you found me a decent lawyer yet?" her grandmother said from the other side of the bars.

Yes.

Bars.

"Not yet. I only had time to check into the hotel, leave my bags and clean up before I came straight here." All of which had taken longer than she'd anticipated, because she couldn't speak Spanish and hadn't realised the hotel she'd booked was about a two-hour taxi trip from the prison—although she suspected her driver had taken the circuitous route.

Of course, if she'd brought Joe along with her, as her boss

had insisted she do, then she would have known where to book a hotel. The ex-marine had spent time in Peru and, unlike Julia, could speak the language.

A flash of guilt speared through Julia at the thought of Joe Barone. She'd deliberately emailed Joe flight details that were false. In fact, she hadn't even booked him on a flight at all. Mainly because the thought of spending fourteen hours sitting on a plane next to a man who attracted and terrified her in equal parts was just too much to handle. She very much feared he was still sitting in Heathrow waiting for her to turn up.

"Julia? Are you awake?" Her gran's ludicrous question brought her back to her present situation.

"Of course I'm awake. I'm standing here, talking to you."

"Mmm, for a minute there, I wasn't sure. You do realise that this is a time-sensitive issue you're dealing with? I'd like to get out of prison before some woman called Bertha makes me her bitch."

"Gran!" Julia gave her a disapproving glare. "You are joking, right? I mean, you aren't being threatened or anything, are you?"

"Only by poor hygiene and terrible food. There's a good chance I'll die of the bubonic plague before I'm released." She raised her stubborn chin. "To hell with a lawyer. Just break me out of here. I mean, look at the place." She waved a hand. "How hard could it be?"

"You can't talk like that," Julia hissed as she looked around to see if anyone had overheard. All she saw was the industrial grey concrete that made up the short-term holding area of Lima's notorious female prison. It wasn't much, but after the chaos Julia had witnessed in the general area of the prison, she was glad her gran was being held separately.

She looked down at the stamps running up her forearms and shuddered. Once she'd queued outside the prison, with all the other visitors, she'd had her personal space invaded by a leering man who'd patted her body looking for weapons. Julia suspected she'd have nightmares about that for years to come. After that, her paperwork had been scrutinised and she'd been questioned in rapid-fire Spanish that she didn't understand. A lifetime later, her arms had been stamped—to prove she wasn't an inmate—and she'd been allowed inside. Julia didn't go clubbing, so she'd never had a club stamp on her arm, but she imagined it was a very similar experience to the one she'd just endured.

"Oh, darling." Patricia Matthews sighed heavily. "This is too much for you. I should have bitten the bullet and called your mother instead."

"No. I'm fine. I can do this. It's just jetlag and culture shock rolled into one. Don't worry about me; you're the one who needs help. You did the right thing. Who knows what Mum would have done if she was here?" Libby Collins wasn't exactly known for her restrained reaction in a crisis. Julia well remembered the dramas she'd endured growing up, especially seeing as, in her family, almost everything constituted a crisis.

Her gran folded her arms over her pale blue peasant blouse. There were no prison uniforms for these inmates. As far as Julia could see, there was nothing at all for the inmates. The glimpses she'd had of overcrowded cells, with pallets made of rags for beds, made her cringe.

Julia suddenly thought of something horrific. "You do have a toilet in your cell, don't you?" She put a hand over her heart as it raced at her next thought. "You have to share it, don't you? Please tell me you at least have privacy when you use it?"

Her gran pinched the bridge of her nose and closed her eyes. When she looked back at Julia, she seemed more resigned than hopeful to see her there.

"I don't want to talk about the toilet. I want to talk about your plan to get me out of here. What are you doing about finding a decent lawyer? The ones that have approached me only want money. They're promising to get the charges dropped and get me out of here in seconds—if I fork over all my cash." She rolled her eyes. "Like I'd fall for that. That's why I sent Alice off to find someone honest, or at least someone with a solid reputation." She bit her lip and suddenly looked closer to her age than usual. "Then Alice didn't come back."

Gran's best friend had been missing for four days, a fact that didn't seem to bother the Peruvian authorities any. After she got her gran out of jail, Julia planned to hire an interpreter and grill the police on exactly what they were doing to find Alice. She felt nauseated at the thought. Okay, maybe not grill. Maybe ask politely and quietly…or send a firmly worded email…or maybe a text…

"Julia, are you listening to me? What are you doing about a lawyer?"

"Sorry, I was thinking. You don't have to worry about a lawyer. I have a plan all written out. I'm going to look in the yellow pages, or do a Google search, and then I'm going to get someone at the hotel to call around for me—"

"Or," came the deep American voice behind her, "you could have trusted that I knew a guy, like I told you before you dumped me at the airport."

Julia froze.

Joe Barone.

Here.

In Lima.

Every instinct within her was screaming that if she didn't move, maybe he wouldn't see her—and eat her alive. She was pretty sure she'd react exactly the same way if she was ever confronted with a hungry T-Rex.

Julia watched her gran's eyes go wide at the sight of Joe, then she smiled with appreciation. "You must be a friend of my granddaughter."

"You must be her incarcerated grandmother." Two hands landed on Julia's shoulders and Joe was standing at her back. *Right against her back.* "I'm Joe. I work with Julia."

Her grandmother's eyes sparkled. "Is that *all* you do with my granddaughter, Joe?"

*Danger! Abort! Hide!* Julia's inner voice, which was remarkably similar to the robot in *Lost in Space,* was no help at all.

"With all due respect"—Joe's soft American accent vibrated through Julia as he spoke to her gran—"that's between Julia and me."

He leaned into Julia, and she felt his breath whisper against her ear. "Later, we're going to talk about the stunt you pulled at the airport."

With a gentle squeeze of her shoulders, he stepped back. Julia couldn't speak or move. She just stood useless and frozen in the middle of the room—painfully aware that her attempt to blend in with her environment and disappear entirely had failed miserably.

"This is Eduardo Sanchez," Joe said to her grandmother. "He's taking your case."

Julia kept her head down, but peeked up to see a handsome middle-aged man in an expensive navy suit. He seemed to jerk backwards when he looked at her, which made Julia step closer to Joe—for some reason. The lawyer gave a little shake of his head before turning to her gran with a smile.

"Call me Ed," he said. "When Joe here said we were running to the rescue of a grandmother, you weren't what I had in mind."

Julia almost snorted. She imagined they'd envisioned a short, round elderly woman with a cap of curly grey hair, who dressed in shapeless beige clothes and sensible shoes.

Julia looked down at her clothes, dismayed to realise she'd described her own dress sense. Yep, she wasn't going to think about that. Patricia Matthews was the exact opposite of a typical granny. She might have been in her late sixties, but she was gorgeous in the same way Helen Mirren or Susan Sarandon were gorgeous. She was tall, willowy and stylish. Even behind bars, her shoulder-length blonde hair was perfectly styled and her face was tastefully made up. Dressed in figure-hugging jeans, an embroidered peasant blouse and beige leather high-heeled boots, she was stunning. The few lines on her face did nothing but enhance her beauty. The wicked look in her eyes made her seem far more vital than her age would usually suggest.

She waved a dismissive hand at Ed's comment. "Age is just a number, darling."

His eyes sparkled; he was obviously enamoured with Julia's gran. It was no surprise—all of her female relatives stopped men in their tracks. Julia was used to being the exception.

"You're charged with stealing a mummified body." Ed consulted his notes. "Is that correct?"

"That's the charge." Patricia gave him a haughty look. "Are you going to ask me if I did it?"

"I wouldn't dare." Ed grinned as though she was delightful. "I haven't had a lot of time to go over the paperwork, but it looks to me like there are some gaping holes in the case against you. I'm pretty sure we can get you out of here in no time at all."

Patricia's eyes narrowed. "What's it going to cost me?"

"Ah, I see you've dealt with some of my esteemed colleagues." Ed seemed unfazed by the implied insult. "Don't worry—I charge a horrendous hourly fee, but there's nothing on top of that, unless you want to buy me a drink sometime as a thank you for a job well done."

Patricia beamed widely. "I think I can manage that."

Julia stared at the two of them. Were they *flirting? In a jail?*

"That didn't take long," Joe muttered with a shake of his head, which reminded Julia that they were all speaking English.

And if that was the case, there was no need for Joe to stay and interpret. Suddenly giddy with the thought of getting rid of the man who unnerved her so, she tugged on Joe's sleeve. When he looked down at her, she addressed her comments to the vicinity of his chin. "He speaks English better than I do. There's no need for you to stay. You can go back to England."

"Not going to happen, babe."

Julia frowned, her eyes still on his chin. "I wouldn't want to inconvenience you, Joe, or take you away from your other obligations. Mr. Sanchez can easily translate for us."

"I'm not only here to translate. I'm here to watch your back."

"But…"

"I'm staying." His tone told her he was immovable

Julia knew there was no point in arguing. Arguing with Joe never got her anywhere. It was better just to do what she had to and deal with the consequences later. Or, hopefully, never. That was why she'd been so underhanded at London airport. It was either that or do everything the man wanted her to do.

"Can you get me out today?" Patricia asked Ed.

He shook his head. "Tomorrow at the earliest. You okay in here for another night?"

"I'll manage." She looked at Julia. "Can you give me some cash, darling? The food they provide is abominable, but there's a delightful woman from Thailand who's here on a drug charge, and she's selling the most amazing green curry."

Julia couldn't even begin to get her head around the fact

that the Peruvian prison system seemed to involve its inmates setting up businesses to survive. She dug around in her oversized messenger bag, came out with her wallet and handed over a couple of hundred dollars.

"Is that enough?"

"More than enough, especially if Ed here can get me out tomorrow." The light in Patricia's eyes faded as she turned sombre. "I need to get out of here. I need to find Alice."

Ed consulted his notes. "That's your friend who's gone missing?"

"We've been best friends since childhood. And now I don't know where she is or what's happened to her."

"Don't worry." Joe's confidence rang out through his words. "We'll find her. But first we need to get you out of here."

"And that's where I come in." Ed motioned to the laconic guard and had a tense discussion with him in Spanish. When he was finished, he turned back to them. "Patricia and I are going to have a private meeting. We'll get this sorted. You two need to leave. I'll call with updates."

Joe nodded. Julia hesitated. It felt wrong to go back to her luxury hotel when her gran was behind bars.

Patricia seemed to read her mind, and her face softened. "It's okay, darling. You go have a good night's sleep and we'll catch up properly tomorrow."

A hand pressed against the small of her back. "I'll take care of her," Joe told her gran.

"See that you do," Patricia ordered.

"Love you, Gran," Julia whispered as Joe led her from the room.

"Love you too, sweetie." The words followed them out.

Julia looked over her shoulder at her gran and actually wished she was in the cell with her, rather than going to her doom with Joe. Okay, maybe not doom, but she was sure she was better equipped to deal with prison than she was to deal with the sexy American beside her.

The oppressive heat of Lima, which always seemed to press down on the city like a heavy blanket, hit them as soon as they walked out of the prison gates. Joe looked down at Julia and wondered when she'd last had something to drink. The dry heat of the desert city meant that dehydration could sneak up on a person. As they looked out at the dust-covered highway, crowded with cars and trucks, Joe reached into his day pack for a bottle of water. He unscrewed the cap and handed it to Julia.

As usual, she didn't look him in the eye when she spoke. "I'm not thirsty."

"Take it." He pressed it into her hand. "This type of heat can fool you into thinking you aren't thirsty, but you need to keep your fluids up. Drink regularly, even if you don't feel like it."

She eyed the bottle with suspicion, and Joe knew exactly what the problem was; he'd seen her do this with everything she'd consumed over the past few months. "I bought it at the airport and only just opened it. It was sealed properly and I haven't drunk out of the bottle. It's safe."

Her cheeks turned the same shade of pink as those luscious lips of hers, which made Joe's chest tighten. For some reason, Julia thought her quirks were a sign she was deficient in some way—a belief he hoped to divest her of before the trip was over. There was nothing wrong with Julia Collins. Nothing at all.

A fact Ed seemed to have noticed when he'd looked at her. Ed's reaction to Julia had made him bristle. He'd warned his old friend about Julia being painfully shy and not to force her to interact. He hadn't warned him about the impact Julia could have on a man.

Joe knew exactly how Ed felt. Seeing Julia for the first time was like a sucker punch. She was one of those rare treasures, a beautiful woman who had absolutely no idea that was what she was. Ed's gaze had taken in the shapeless beige dress, flat sports sandals and the large messenger bag Julia wore across her body like a shield, before resting on her makeup-free face. Her features were perfection. Creamy, smooth skin, a tiny upturned nose, wide amber eyes with lashes so thick it was hard to believe they were real. Pronounced cheekbones made her look even more exotic, but it was her full, peach-coloured lips that made a man's thoughts turn darker. Julia Collins had the mouth of a temptress.

"What hotel are we in?" Joe dragged his mind out of the dark, sensual places it always seemed to find when he was around Julia.

"*I'm* in the Sheraton in the city centre."

He smiled at the emphasis and the subtle rebuke it was intended to be. "I'll have someone pick up your bags and bring them to our new hotel."

"What?" Her eyes snapped up to his, and for a second Joe lost his train of thought.

"You can't stay there, babe. It's at least an hour in crap traffic to get here from there. Longer sometimes. You need to be closer to your grandmother, so you can get to the prison fast if needed."

Her eyes moved back down to focus on her feet, and Joe felt bereft at the loss. "I know, but…"

She pulled her bottom lip between her teeth and nodded as though she was having a silent conversation with herself and had come to a conclusion. She rummaged around in her bag and pulled out her iPad. "I'll see what's near here." Her slim fingers flitted across the screen before they stilled. "I forgot. I need Wi-Fi access first."

"I know a hotel." Joe held her elbow as he led them along the crowded street.

"But, I-I…"

"It's okay. I know a perfect place. Trust me." He wanted her to see that he knew her and what she needed to be comfortable in her environment. He'd made a study of Julia these past few months, and wherever possible he'd move mountains to give her what she needed.

"Okay." She sounded so resigned that Joe had to remind himself trust came with time.

He had to be patient. At least now they were together. For the past couple of weeks—since he'd kissed her—she'd taken great pains to hide from him.

He slid his hand down her arm to hold her hand, feeling her tense, and led her across the busy road, where seven lanes of traffic randomly crowded into four official lanes. Cars blasted their horns at them, but Joe ignored it. When they got to the other side of the wide street, he caught sight of something out of the corner of his eye that made the hairs on the back of his neck stand to attention.

Two men.

And they seemed to be following them.

"Maybe we should go get my bags first?" Julia said softly.

He heard her, but his attention was focused on the men. They were out of place and stood out like Trump at a feminist rally. First, they were taller than most of the people rushing around them. They were also fitter, with the kind of muscles serious working out would develop. Both men were dressed in black, when most people around them were dressed in faded clothes that had seen better days. But it was the way they moved that had Joe on alert. They moved like men who were trained. Ex-military or private army, Joe guessed. Neither option reassured him.

As he hauled Julia around the corner of the concrete

prison compound, she tugged at his hand. "My legs are shorter than yours."

"Sorry." He shortened his stride, at the same time noticing that she'd almost tripped over the uneven sidewalk. He needed to be more careful. He eyed the guys behind them. But more importantly, he needed to get her to safety.

"Well, what do you think?" Julia asked.

Joe cast a glance down at her. She was looking at him nervously, but hopefully.

"About what?"

She frowned, at the same time Joe spotted the guys turn into the road behind them. They hugged the shadows, keeping their distance, clearly thinking they hadn't been spotted.

"You weren't listening," Julia gently admonished. "I said, wouldn't it be best if we stayed at the Sheraton tonight and moved closer to the prison tomorrow? That way, I could use the hotel Wi-Fi to research hotels and make a booking for us. Plus"—she cast a pointed glance around at the half-finished brick buildings surrounding them—"I don't think there are many hotels in this area."

She was right. This part of Lima was a step up from a shantytown. People here could afford to build houses, but only a bit at a time—hence all the half-finished buildings with rebar sticking out, waiting for a second floor to be added.

"Joe, what do you think?"

What he thought was that they had to get off the street. And fast. Until he knew who wanted to keep tabs on them, and what they wanted, he could better protect Julia inside a hotel.

"No." It came out more firmly than he'd intended. "We need to be close to your grandmother in case Ed needs us for something. He might even get her released tonight."

Plus, he wasn't sure if Julia had been followed from the airport, or what kind of surveillance had already been set up at her hotel. It was best if they started again—in an environment he could control.

Joe stuck his hand out and waved at passing cars. One of them had to be a cab. Seeing as most taxis didn't come with signage, it wasn't always easy to tell. He tugged Julia closer to him. He needed to get her off the street before nightfall. A small Volkswagen, which had seen better days, swerved through the traffic and screeched to a halt at the curb beside them. Joe pulled open the door to the back seat and urged Julia to get in.

"Is this a cab?" Julia was clearly horrified. No doubt she was examining the interior for the driver's official registration. She wasn't going to find any.

Joe pushed in beside her, his knees around his ears, slammed the door and ordered the driver to head for Miraflores. It was the closest suburb with decent hotels. And by decent, he meant big chain hotels. To Joe, those places were seriously lacking in atmosphere, but he knew Julia would appreciate the generic feel and familiarity.

As the car zoomed into the flow of traffic, horn blasting as it did so, Joe spotted one of the men dig into his pocket and come out with his phone. Checking in. Joe tried to keep an eye on the men, but there was too much chaos on the road behind them to see if they got into a vehicle to follow them.

"It's so dusty here," Julia whispered beside him, her eyes on the hills around Lima that housed the sandy-coloured shantytowns. The thousands of small houses, made out of reed matting and plywood sheets, were barely visible against the barren hills.

"When we get things sorted out with your gran, I'll take you to Cusco and the jungle. Lots of green there for you to look at."

She stiffened beside him, and Joe wondered if he would ever break through her defences to the point where she was relaxed and comfortable around him. He had to believe he would, because Julia Collins had become as essential to him as breathing.

"Is she going to be okay?" Julia's soft question broke into Joe's musings. "Is your lawyer friend good?"

"Yeah." Joe placed a hand on Julia's arm and watched her freeze in place. When he didn't move it, she relaxed slightly. Baby steps, Joe reminded himself, baby steps. "He's more than capable. If anyone can sort out this mess and get your gran out of there, Ed can. And she's definitely going to be okay. Patricia is in the safest part of the prison."

"But if Ed can't get her out, she'll be moved to the other part, right?"

"That's not going to happen. I promise you that."

Julia seemed to relax further at his vow, and Joe prayed he would be able to keep it. To hell with that—he would *definitely* keep it. He'd move heaven and earth to make sure he did. First, he needed to get her into their new hotel room, then he was going to make some calls to find out what the police were doing about the missing Alice. Then he planned to talk to his boss, Callum. He didn't know what was going on here, but one thing was clear—things were a whole lot more complicated than Julia's grandmother had led them to believe.

Get Relentless now and keep reading!

## ABOUT THE AUTHOR

I'm a Scot, living in New Zealand and married to a Dutch man. I write contemporary romance with a humorous bent – this is mainly due to the fact I have an odd sense of humour and can't keep it out of anything I do! If I wasn't a writer, I'd like to be Buffy the Vampire Slayer, or Indiana Jones. Unfortunately, both these roles have already been filled. Which may be a good thing as I have no fighting skills, wouldn't know a precious relic if it hit me in the face and have an aversion to blood. When I'm not living in my head, I'm a mother to two kids, several pet sheep, one dog, four cats, three alpacas, two miniature horses, eight guinea pigs and an escape artist chicken.

www.ingramcontent.com/pod-product-compliance
Lightning Source LLC
Chambersburg PA
CBHW020922110726
47900CB00001B/254